THE WRITE HOOK

MY SO-CALLED MYSTICAL MIDLIFE BOOK ONE

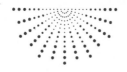

ROBYN PETERMAN

VISIT MY WEBSITE!

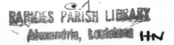

ACKNOWLEDGMENTS

Writing Paranormal Women's Fiction rocks. Bring heroines my age to life is fabulous. LOL I loved writing the **Good to the Last Death** series so much, I'm diving into a new one! **The Write Hook: My So-Called Mystical Midlife book 1** flew from my fingertips and was a blast to write. It's action packed, snarky and my mom says it's hilarious!

As always, while writing is a solitary experience getting a book into the world is a group project.

The PWF Fab 13 Gals — Thank you for a wild ride. You rock.

Renee — Thank you for all your support, your friendship, your formatting expertise and for being the best Cookie ever. You saved my butt on this one. Forever in your debt. TMB. AND the freaking cover rocks. You are brilliant.

Wanda — Thank you for knowing what I mean even when I don't. LOL You are the best and this writing business wouldn't be any fun without you.

Kelli — Thank you for saving me from scary grammar and timeline mistakes. You rock. And thank you for letting me be late... again. LOL

Nancy, Jessica, Susan, Heather and Wanda — Thank you for being kickass betas. You are all wonderful.

Mom — Thank you for listening to me hash out the plot and for giving me brilliant ideas. You really need to write a book!

Steve, Henry and Audrey — Thank you. The three of you are my world. Without you, none of this would make sense. I love you.

DEDICATION

This one is for Jessica. Long time friend. Long time partner in crime.

MORE IN MY SO-CALLED MYSTICAL MIDLIFE SERIES

BOOK DESCRIPTION

THE WRITE HOOK

Midlife is full of surprises. Not all of them are working for me.

At forty-two I've had my share of ups and downs. Relatively normal, except when the definition of normal changes... drastically.

NYT Bestselling Romance Author: Check
Amazing besties: Check
Lovely home: Check
Pet cat named Thick Stella who wants to kill me: Check
Wacky Tabacky Dealing Aunt: Check
Cheating husband banging the weather girl on our kitchen table: Check
Nasty Divorce: Oh yes
Characters from my novels coming to life: Umm... yes
Crazy: Possibly

Four months of wallowing in embarrassed depression should be enough. I'm beginning to realize that no one is who they seem to be, and my life story might be spinning out of my control. It's time to take a shower, put on a bra, and wear something other than sweatpants. Difficult, but doable.

With my friends—real and imaginary—by my side, I need to edit my life before the elusive darkness comes for all of us.

The plot is no longer fiction. It's my reality, and I'm writing a happy ever after no matter what. I just have to find the *write hook.*

"Mother humper," I grunted as I pushed my monstrosity of a bed from one side of the bedroom to the other. "This weighs a damn ton."

I'd burned all the bedding seven weeks ago. The bonfire had been cathartic. I'd taken pictures as the five hundred thread count sheets had gone up in flame. I'd kept the comforter. I'd paid a fortune for it. It had been thoroughly saged and washed five times. Even though there was no trace of Darren left in the bedroom, I'd been sleeping in my office.

The house was huge, beautiful... and mine—a gorgeously restored Victorian where I'd spent tons of time as a child. It had an enchanted feel to it that I adored. I didn't need such an enormous abode, but I loved the location—the middle of nowhere. The internet was iffy, but I solved that by going into town to the local coffee shop if I had something important to download or send.

Darren, with the wandering pecker, thought he would get a piece of the house. He was wrong. I'd inherited it from my whackadoo grandmother and great-aunt Flip. My parents hadn't always been too keen on me spending so much time with Granny and Aunt Flip growing up, but I adored the two old gals so much they'd relented. Since I spent a lot of time in an imaginary dream world, my mom and dad were delighted when I related to actual people— even if they were left of center.

Granny and Flip made sure the house was in my name only—nontransferable and non-sellable. It was stipulated that I had to pass it to a family member or the Historical Society when I died. Basically, I had life rights. It was as if

Granny and Aunt Flip had known I would waste two decades of my life married to a jackhole who couldn't keep his salami in his pants and would need someplace to live. God rest Granny's insane soul. Aunt Flip was still kicking, although I hadn't seen her in a few years.

Aunt Flip put the K in kooky. She'd bought a cottage in the hills about an hour away and grew medicinal marijuana —before it was legal. The old gal was the black sheep of the family and preferred her solitude and her pot to company. She hadn't liked Darren a bit. She and Granny both had worn black to my wedding. Everyone had been appalled— even me—but in the end, it made perfect sense. I had to hand it to the old broads. They'd been smarter than me by a long shot. And the house? It had always been my charmed haven in the storm.

Even though there were four spare bedrooms plus the master suite, I chose my office. It felt safe to me.

Thick Stella preferred my office, and I needed to be around something that had a heartbeat. It didn't matter that Thick Stella was bitchy and swiped at me with her deadly kitty claws every time I passed her. I loved her. The feeling didn't seem mutual, but she hadn't left me for a twenty-three-year-old with silicone breast implants and huge, bright white teeth.

"Thick Stella, do you think Sasha should wear red to her stepmother's funeral?" I asked as I plopped down on my newly Feng Shuied couch and narrowly missed getting gouged by my cat. "Yes or no? Hiss at me if it's a yes. Growl at me if it's a no."

Thick Stella had a go at her privates. She was useless.

"That wasn't an answer." I grabbed my laptop from my desk. Deciding it was too dangerous to sit near my cat, I settled for the love seat. The irony of the piece of furniture I'd chosen didn't escape me.

"I think she should wear red," I told Thick Stella, who didn't give a crap what Sasha wore. "Her stepmother was an asshat, and it would show fabu disrespect."

Typing felt good. Getting lost in a story felt great. I dressed Sasha in a red Prada sheath, then had her behead her ex-husband with a dull butter knife when he and his bimbo showed up unexpectedly to pay their respects at the funeral home. It was a bloodbath. Putting Sasha in red was an excellent move. The blood matched her frock to a T.

Quickly rethinking the necessary murder, I moved the scene of the decapitation to the empty lobby of the funeral home. It would suck if I had to send Sasha to prison. She hadn't banged Damien yet, and everyone was eagerly awaiting the sexy buildup—including me. It was the fourth book in the series, and it was about time they got together. The sexual tension was palpable.

"What in the freaking hell?" I snapped my laptop shut and groaned. "Sasha doesn't have an ex-husband. I can't do this. I've got nothing." Where was my muse hiding? I needed the elusive imaginary idiot if I was going to get any writing done. "Chauncey, dammit, where are you?"

"My God, you're loud, Clementine," a busty, beautiful woman dressed in a deep purple Regency gown said with an eye roll.

She was seated on the couch next to Thick Stella, who barely acknowledged her. My cat attacked strangers and friends. Not today. My fat feline simply glanced over at the intruder and yawned. The cat was a traitor.

Forget the furry betrayer. How in the heck did the woman get into my house—not to mention my office— without me seeing her enter? For a brief moment, I wondered if she'd banged my husband too but pushed the sordid thought out of my head. She looked to be close to thirty—too old for the asshole.

"Who are you?" I demanded, holding my laptop over my head as a weapon.

If I threw it and it shattered, I would be screwed. I couldn't remember the last time I'd backed it up. If I lost the measly, somewhat disjointed fifty thousand words I'd written so far, I'd have to start over. That wouldn't fly with my agent or my publisher.

"Don't be daft," the woman replied. "It's rather unbecoming. May I ask a question?"

"No, you may not," I shot back, trying to place her.

She was clearly a nutjob. The woman was rolling up on thirty but had the vernacular of a seventy-year-old British society matron. She was dressed like she'd walked off the set of a film starring Emma Thompson. Her blonde hair shone to the point of absurdity and was twisted into an elaborate up-do. Wispy tendrils framed her perfectly heart-shaped face. Her sparkling eyes were lavender, enhanced by the over-the-top gown she wore.

Strangely, she was vaguely familiar. I just couldn't remember how I knew her.

"How long has it been since you attended to your hygiene?" she inquired.

Putting my laptop down and picking up a lamp, I eyed her. I didn't care much for the lamp or her question. I had been thinking about Marie Condo-ing my life, and the lamp didn't bring me all that much joy. If it met its demise by use of self-defense, so be it. "I don't see how that's any of your business, lady. What I'd suggest is that you leave. Now. Or else I'll call the police. Breaking and entering is a crime."

She laughed. It sounded like freaking bells. Even though she was either a criminal or certifiable, she was incredibly charming.

"Oh dear," she said, placing her hand delicately on her still heaving, milky-white bosom. "You are so silly. The constable knows quite well that I'm here. He advised me to come."

"The constable?" I asked, wondering how far off her rocker she was.

She nodded coyly. "Most certainly. We're all terribly concerned."

I squinted at her. "About my hygiene?"

"That, amongst other things," she confirmed. "Darling girl, you are not an ace of spades or, heaven forbid, an adventuress. Unless you want to be an ape leader, I'd recommend bathing."

"Are you right in the head?" I asked, wondering where I'd left my damn cell phone. It was probably in the laundry room. I was going to be murdered by a nutjob, and I'd lost my chance to save myself because I'd been playing Candy Jelly Crush. The headline would be horrifying—*Homeless-looking, Hygiene-free Paranormal Romance Author Beheaded by Victorian Psycho.*

11

If I lived through the next hour, I was deleting the game for good.

"I think it would do wonders for your spirit if you donned a nice tight corset and a clean chemise," she suggested, skillfully ignoring my question. "You must pull yourself together. Your behavior is dicked in the nob."

I sat down and studied her. My about-to-be-murdered radar relaxed a tiny bit, but I kept the lamp clutched tightly in my hand. My gut told me she wasn't going to strangle me. Of course, I could be mistaken, but Purple Gal didn't seem violent—just bizarre. Plus, the lamp was heavy. I could knock her ladylike ass out with one good swing.

How in the heck did I know her? College? Grad School? The grocery store? At forty-two, I'd met a lot of people in my life. Was she with the local community theater troop? I was eighty-six percent sure she wasn't here to off me. However, I'd been wrong about life-altering events before— like not knowing my husband was boffing someone young enough to have been our daughter.

"What language are you speaking?" I spotted a pair of scissors on my desk. If I needed them, it was a quick move to grab them. I'd never actually killed anyone except in ficti-tious situations, but there was a first time for everything.

Pulling an embroidered lavender hankey from her cleav-age, she clutched it and twisted it in her slim fingers. "Clementine, *you* should know."

"I'm at a little disadvantage here," I said, fascinated by the batshit crazy woman who'd broken into my home. "You seem to know my name, but I don't know yours."

And that was when the tears started. Hers. Not mine.

"Such claptrap. How very unkind of you, Clementine," she burst out through her stupidly attractive sobs.

It was ridiculous how good the woman looked while crying. I got all blotchy and red, but not the mystery gal in purple. She grew even more lovely. It wasn't fair. I still had no clue what the hell she was talking about, but on the off chance she might throw a tantrum if I asked more questions, I kept my mouth shut.

And yes, she had a point, but my *hygiene* was none of her damn business. I couldn't quite put my finger on the last time I'd showered. If I had to guess, it was probably in the last five to twelve days. I was on a deadline for a book. To be more precise, I was late for my deadline on a book. I didn't exactly have time for personal sanitation right now.

And speaking of deadlines...

"How about this?" My tone was excessively polite. I almost laughed. The woman had illegally entered my house, and I was behaving like she was a guest. "I'll take a shower later today after I get through a few pivotal chapters. Right now, you should leave so I can work."

"Yes, of course," she replied, absently stroking Fat Stella, who purred. If I'd done that, I would be minus a finger. "It would be dreadfully sad if you were under the hatches."

I nodded. "Right. That would, umm... suck."

The woman in purple smiled. It was radiant, and I would have sworn I heard birds happily chirping. I was losing it.

"Excellent," she said, pulling a small periwinkle velvet bag from her cleavage. I wondered what else she had stored in there and hoped there wasn't a weapon. "I shall leave you with two gold coins. While the Grape Nuts were tasty, I

13

would prefer that you purchase some Lucky Charms. I understand they are magically delicious."

"It was you?" I asked, wildly relieved that I hadn't been sleep eating. I had enough problems at the moment. Gaining weight from midnight dates with cereal wasn't on the to-do list.

"It was," she confirmed, getting to her feet and dropping the coins into my hand. "The consistency was quite different from porridge, but I found it tasty—very crunchy."

"Right… well… thank you for putting the bowl in the sink." Wait. Why the hell was I thanking her? She'd wandered in and eaten my Grape Nuts.

"You are most welcome, Clementine," she said with a disarming smile that lit up her unusual eyes. "It was lovely finally meeting you even if your disheveled outward show is entirely astonishing."

I was reasonably sure I had just been insulted by the cereal lover, but it was presented with excellent manners. However, she did answer a question. We hadn't met. I wasn't sure why she seemed familiar. The fact that she knew my name was alarming.

"Are you a stalker?" I asked before I could stop myself.

I'd had a few over the years. Being a *New York Times* bestselling author was something I was proud of, but it had come with a little baggage here and there. Some people seemed to have difficulty discerning fiction from reality. If I had to guess, I'd say Purple Gal might be one of those people.

I'd only written one Regency novel, and that had been at the beginning of my career, before I'd found my groove in paranormal romance. I was way more comfortable writing about demons and vampires than people dressed in top hats and hoopskirts. Maybe the crazy woman had read my first book. It hadn't done well, and for good reason. It was over-the-top bad. I'd blocked the entire novel out of my mind. Live and learn. It had been my homage to Elizabeth Hoyt well over a decade ago. It had been clear to all that I should leave Regency romance to the masters.

"Don't be a Merry Andrew," the woman chided me. "Your bone box is addled. We must see to it at once. I shall pay a visit again soon."

The only part of her gibberish I understood was that she thought she was coming back. Note to self—change all the locks on the doors. Since it wasn't clear if she was packing heat in her cleavage, I just smiled and nodded.

"Alrighty then…" I was unsure if I should walk her to the door or if she would let herself out. Deciding it would be better to make sure she actually left instead of letting her hide in my pantry to finish off my cereal, I gestured to the door. "Follow me."

Thick Stella growled at me. I was so tempted to flip her off but thought it might earn another lecture from Purple Gal. It was more than enough to be lambasted for my appearance. I didn't need my manners picked apart by someone with a tenuous grip on reality.

My own grip was dubious as it was.

"You might want to reconsider breaking into homes," I said, holding the front door open. "It could end badly—for you."

Part of me couldn't believe that I was trying to help the

nutty woman out, but I couldn't seem to stop myself. I kind of liked her.

"I'll keep that in mind," she replied as she sauntered out of my house into the warm spring afternoon. "Remember, Clementine, there is always sunshine after the rain."

As she made her way down the long sunlit, tree-lined drive, she didn't look back. It was disturbingly like watching the end of a period movie where the heroine left her old life behind and walked proudly toward her new and promising future.

Glancing around for a car, I didn't spot one. Had she left it parked on the road so she could make a clean getaway after she'd bludgeoned me? Had I just politely escorted a murderer out of my house?

Had I lost it for real?

Probably.

As she disappeared from sight, I felt the weight of the gold coins still clutched in my hand. Today couldn't get any stranger.

At least, I hoped not.

Opening my fist to examine the coins, I gasped. "What in the heck?"

There was nothing in my hand.

Had I dropped them? Getting down on all fours, I searched. Thick Stella joined me, kind of—more like watched me as I crawled around and wondered if anything that had just happened had actually happened.

"Purple Gal gave me coins to buy Lucky Charms," I told my cat, my search now growing frantic. "You saw her do it. Right? She sat next to you. And you didn't attack her. *Right?*"

Thick Stella simply stared at me. What did I expect? If my cat answered me, I'd have to commit myself. That option might still be on the table. Had I just imagined the entire exchange with the strange woman? Should I call the cops?

"And tell them what?" I asked, standing back up and locking the front door securely. "That a woman in a purple gown broke in and ate my cereal while politely insulting my hygiene? Oh, and she left me two gold coins that disappeared in my hand as soon as she was out of sight? That's not going to work."

I'd call the police if she came back, since I wasn't sure she'd been here at all. She hadn't threatened to harm me. Purple Gal had been charming and well-mannered the entire time she'd badmouthed my cleanliness habits. And to be quite honest, real or not, she'd made a solid point. I could use a shower.

Maybe four months of wallowing in self-pity and only living inside the fictional worlds I created on paper had taken more of a toll than I was aware of. Getting lost in my stories was one of my favorite things to do. It had saved me more than once over the years. It was possible that I'd let it go too far. Hence, the Purple Gal hallucination.

Shit.

First things first. Delete Candy Jelly Crush. Getting rid of the white noise in my life was the first step to... well, the first step to something.

I'd figure it out later.

CHAPTER TWO

"THANK YOU," I SAID, SITTING AT THE BREAKFAST BAR IN MY
bright, sunny kitchen watching my best friend Jessica
unload the groceries she'd brought over. "Did you happen to
buy Lucky Charms by any chance?"

My five-foot-nothing, dark-haired, curvy-in-all-the-
right-places buddy pushed her glasses up her nose and
squinted at me. She'd missed the Purple Stalker's visit by an
hour. That was a good thing, since I didn't want to explain
it... or even know *how* to explain it.

"Since when do you eat Lucky Charms?"

"I don't," I admitted.

"Okay," she said. "I'll ignore the question."

"Good thinking." I grabbed a banana and peeled it. "And
thank you."

Jess smiled and began to restock my mostly empty
fridge. "You already said that, but you're welcome. You did
it for me. I'm doing it for you. That's what besties are for."

The banana felt like lead in my mouth. She was right, and she was wrong. I'd stocked her pantry when she'd broken her leg in five places after a wicked wipeout on the ice four years ago. She'd been loading me up for the past few months because I was a hot mess of depression—too embarrassed to leave the house because I didn't want to run into people who felt sorry for me or were secretly gloating at my painfully public crash and burn.

Living in the smallish Kentucky town that I'd grown up in could suck. Like now.

"How's the creative black hole?" Jess asked, pouring both of us full-sugared sodas and sitting down across from me.

"Fathomless," I said with an attempt at a smile, thinking about Purple Gal. "I might be going insane."

"Normal," she said with a nod. "The whole world seems a little wonky lately. As long as you keep the general craziness on paper, you'll be fine. Speaking of… how is the book going?"

"Chauncey disappeared."

"You need a new invisible muse," she suggested, getting up and washing the bowl and spoon that Purple Gal had used—or more likely that I had used and forgotten. "Try a woman. Men are shits."

The fact that my bestie had never blinked an eye that I had an imaginary writing muse made me love her even more. Plus, Jess made a fine point. Men could be shits. Darren was a colossal shit. I'd spent my twenties, thirties, and part of my forties married to the ass. Technically, I was *still* married to the loser. Thank God we'd never had kids. Darren's low sperm count had put a kibosh on that dream. I'd brought up adoption repeatedly over the years, but he wasn't into it. It had broken a small piece of my heart, but now I was grateful there wasn't a little human who would have to live through the shitshow that had become my life.

I'd wasted my good years on a bastard who'd cast me aside for the local weather girl who had more filler in her face than all of my forty-something friends combined.

"Would I make a good lesbian?"

Jess stared at me for a long beat. "Do vaginas turn you on?"

"Sadly, no," I admitted. Life would be a lot easier if they did.

"Then, no. You would not make a good lesbian."

"Do you think I should get Botox?" I asked.

"How about a lobotomy?" she shot back with a raised brow. "Do not go there. You're stupidly gorgeous. Well, not today. You're a little ripe, but normally speaking, you're a damn knockout, Clementine. I don't want to hear any bullshit about putting botulism in your head."

"Filler?" I asked with a tiny smirk. I loved my people. They called it like it was. "I'd look great with fish lips. Don't you think?"

"Fabulous," Jess replied dryly, over-puckering her lips to make her point. "Trust me, I will let you know when it's time to go under the knife."

I rolled my eyes. I was terrified of needles. Going under the knife wasn't my idea of a good time. I'd just drink more water...

"Anyhoo," Jess continued. "As much as I love your

21

natural state, I'm thinking you could use a seriously long shower."

"Et tu, Bruté?" I asked, wondering how bad I looked. First Purple Gal, now Jess. Maybe I should look in the mirror.

She grinned. "Someone else suggested you might have crossed into the Land of Funky?"

"Umm... well, Thick Stella doesn't seem too thrilled with me," I said, avoiding telling her about the possible break-in.

Jess would be worried sick, and she'd have the cops over here in a hot second. That would be a bad plan. Darren used to work on the force. It was a long time ago, but he still knew most of the cops. I certainly didn't need it getting back to the son of a bitch that I was stinky and had a Victorian stalker who may or may not exist.

As long as Purple Gal didn't stop by for another snack, I'd put her out of my mind. She didn't seem like a murderer —just bizarre.

And maybe I *should* shower.

I'd put it on the list.

"Thick Stella hates everyone. Her opinion about your bathing habits or lack thereof is moot," Jess pointed out correctly.

"True," I agreed with a small laugh. "She is rather opinionated."

Jess shrugged and began wiping down the counters. "Opinions are like assholes. Everybody's got one. I'd just prefer not to look at anyone's asshole—especially Thick Stella's. However, I think you might feel good if you removed the reek. And your hair kind of looks like you got electrocuted."

I winced. "It's that bad?"

"Gettin' there," she replied. "I don't want to see him win. He's not worth it."

I sighed. Feeling torn between crying and laughing, I nodded. "Look, I know... I umm... I'm aware that I'm behaving like a pathetic loser. None of my characters would wallow in self-pity for months on end, but..."

"You are *not* fiction. What happened to you was unimaginable." Jess wrapped her arms around me and hugged me tightly. "You're real. You were blindsided by a shitbag in the worst way ever. Screw him. Goodbye to bad rubbish with a bushy-looking pornstache. You can wallow as long as you want, and I'll support you every second. I just think a shower might help you clear your head to write."

Leaning into her warm body, I let the tears flow... again. I didn't know what I'd done right in my past to have Jess in my life, but I was so very grateful.

"The mustache is gross," I mumbled through my tears.

"And he was packing a cocktail weenie," she reminded me.

"Oh my God," I choked out with a horrified laugh. "Did I say that?"

Jess grinned and tucked my messy hair behind my ears. "Six times. Two weeks ago, when Mandy and I brought over sushi. Granted, you'd downed a few hot sakes, but I clearly recall The One Who Shall Not Be Named's privates being referred to as a Vienna sausage, a schnauzer tail, a schmeckle, a dinky winky, a baby carrot, a baby's thumb and a wee nug."

"I should write erotica," I said with a giggle, swiping at my tears. "I seem to have a knack with descriptive ways to describe a penis."

"It will all be over soon," Jess said. "Has the asshat agreed to settle out of court?"

I shuddered. "He wants a percentage of my backlist and all my future earnings."

"Shut the front door!" Jess shouted, throwing the dishrag in the sink. "All he ever did was spend your money and play golf. That jackoff doesn't get a damn penny more."

"There was no prenup," I reminded her. "We got married long before I hit paydirt."

Jess paced the kitchen like a caged tiger. Twice she picked up a steak knife off of the counter. Twice she put it back down. While the murderous thought was appreciated, the reality of my BFF offing my ex would suck.

"I call so much bullshit," she snapped. "The minute you made a dime, he quit his job and lived the life of leisure."

Why was hindsight 20/20? I'd never seen it... or maybe I hadn't wanted to. For the first ten years of our marriage, Darren had worked on the police force. I'd taught creative writing at the community college while hammering away at my dream of writing novels and getting my graduate degree in English. Those were the good old days. We'd saved for vacations and dreamed about buying a house with a yard. We used to laugh a lot. And then we didn't.

While I loved Jess's slanted memory, to be fair, the douchecanoe hadn't quit work immediately. He'd waited until I inherited the house with the yard and started making more in a year than he could make in ten. That was fifteen years ago. The lazy asswipe hadn't had a job in fifteen years.

Why was I mourning a jerk? Where in the hell was my self-worth? The bastard had ruined my life in a humiliatingly public way.

Shaking my head and catching an unpleasant whiff of myself, I downed the soda like it was a shot of sake and regretted it immediately.

"Brain freeze," I hissed, hopping around the kitchen and pressing my forehead with the heel of my palm. "That asshole just gave me a brain freeze. On top of banging the weather girl for the world to see and trying to live off of me for the rest of his tiny-peckered life, he gave me a brain freeze."

"Unacceptable," Jess grunted, her small fists clenched at her sides.

"Damn right," I said, feeling more like my old self than I had in months. Anger was so much better than self-pity. "You know what? I'm better than he is, and I am no one's damn meal ticket."

"Yesssss," Jess yelled, retrieving the rag from the sink and scrubbing my counters like she was trying to wipe the finish off the granite. "That defective penis lost the best damned woman he'll ever have. You don't need a cheating, mooching assbag with a teeny weenie."

"I'm going to take a shower," I shouted, still hopping off the brain freeze. "I'm going to use the blow dryer on my hair if I can find it."

"Go guuurl," Jess grunted as she continued her cardio

workout on my countertops. "And I'm calling Mandy. She'll have a plan. She always has a plan. Not all of them are good…"

"Or legal," I pointed out.

"True," Jess agreed. "But she was a lawyer for a gazillion years before she blew out the triplets."

I nodded and glanced at my reflection in the window. I screamed. "I'm heinous."

"Correct," Jess confirmed. "You shower. I'm going over to Mandy's. Call Mr. Ted and make an appointment."

"On it," I said, searching for my cell phone and avoiding anything that might show my reflection. The phone was AWOL. "You know, it's incredibly weird that I call my lawyer Mr. Ted."

"Habits," Jess said, shoving her cell phone into my hands. "Old habits die hard. We've known Mr. Ted since we were kids. Feels disrespectful to call him Ted. Kind of like calling one of your high school teachers by their first name. I can't do it."

"Exactly," I replied. "Do you have Mr. Ted's number in your phone?"

She nodded. "Yep. It's under Mr. Ted. He helped my parents do their will."

"Got it." I quickly scrolled her contacts. It was actually under Mr. Ted Walters, right above Seth Walters.

Seth Walters—I hadn't seen Smexy Seth Walters since high school a million years ago. He was Jess's older brother Jack's best friend. Jess thought her brother and all of his buddies were *icky*. I did not. Seth had been two years ahead of me and was the object of my teenage girl dreams. Hell, I'd modeled half of my fictional heroes on my silly memories of Seth Walters. He was probably married to a stunningly perfect gal and living out his happily ever after. Good for him. "It's ringing," I whispered.

"Walters and Walters," a friendly female answered. "How can I help you?"

"Hi, it's Clementine Roberts. I was wondering if I could schedule an appointment with Mr. Ted... I mean, Ted. Ted Walters... my lawyer. Umm... about my divorce."

"Hi, Clementine! It's Nancy. I just loved *Exotic* and *Exquisite* and *Extravagant*," she gushed. "Aaaaaand, I preordered *Exclusive*! Sasha and Damien are killing me. I can't get enough. Pretty sure I've read them all cover to cover at least six times!"

"Wow... thanks," I said. I'd known Nancy since grade school. She'd taken my writing success as her own personal accomplishment since I'd cheated off her spelling test in the third grade. It had been the first and last time I'd ever cheated. One, Nancy couldn't spell any better than I could, and the disappointment on my beloved teacher's face occasionally still popped up in my nightmares—I'd used the gut-sinking feeling in my books repeatedly. Of course, no spelling tests were involved, just the feeling of severe humiliation. I was the kid who loved all her teachers in elementary school to a distraction. I was a pleaser. If Nancy felt responsible for my writing career, so be it.

"Sasha's stepmother is just horrid. I hate her. I couldn't believe all the lies and deception. However, I do envy her wardrobe. Let me tell you something, I was tense for days. I yelled at my husband repeatedly for talking to me while I was reading—almost killed him. Good thing I work for a law firm. Free representation. No one gets between Damien and me—except Sasha," Nancy said with a giggle. "I just *adore* Sasha."

"Well, umm… that's awesome," I replied, wondering if Nancy knew the difference between fantasy and reality. Not to mention, Sasha and Damien were fictional demons— albeit *good demons*. "So, does Mr. Ted have any openings to chat?"

"Let me see," Nancy said. "And by the way, I think Darren is the scum of the earth."

"Join the club," I muttered.

I could hear her porcelain nails clicking on a keyboard. My God, she typed fast. I kept my nails short and polish-free. The sound of fingernails on a keyboard made me want to tear my own head off. Biting down on my lips, I kept my mouth shut. I needed an appointment. Explaining to Nancy that I would love to pull her nails off with pliers wouldn't help me reach my end goal.

"Looks like you missed a couple of appointments," Nancy said, clicking her tongue—another habit that made me want to headbutt her.

"Right," I said, racking my brain for an excuse that had nothing to do with lack of hygiene or the inability to leave my house. "I… I'm on a deadline for *Exclusive,* and I keep getting lost in the story."

It was kind of true. I was definitely lost.

Nancy squealed with delight. I might have lost a fraction of hearing in my right ear. "That's an acceptable excuse," she assured me. "Would you like to share what might be happening in the book?"

"I can't," I told her. "It's… you know, in my contract. Top secret."

Hell, I wasn't even sure what was happening in the book.

"Darn it," she said with another giggle. "I just had to try. And if I may put in my two cents, I would love to see Sasha's stepmother get decapitated. Something really bloody would be very satisfying."

I was at a loss for words. It was an exceptionally violent suggestion. Nancy was a little cray-cray. Although, I'd fantasized about beheading Darren not even an hour ago. Maybe Nancy made a good point. Or more likely, I was as loony as she was. "I'll take that under consideration," I told her, trying to stay diplomatic. I still needed an appointment. "So, is there an opening?"

"Tomorrow," she replied. "Ten AM."

"I'll take it," I said quickly. "And thank you."

"You're most welcome! If I bring in my hardbacks, would you autograph them for me? It would make my crappy year."

"Yep. I'd be delighted to."

Again, Nancy squealed. Again, I might have lost some hearing ability.

"See you tomorrow," she said.

"Tomorrow," I replied, hanging up the phone and handing it back to Jess. "Nancy is a little much."

"Understatement," Jess said with a laugh. "But tomorrow is perfect. I'm going to go get Mandy, and we're going to make a plan."

"Here?" I asked with a wince.

"Here," Jess confirmed. "I'll give you a few hours to defunk. We'll bring food and alcohol."

"No sake," I told her.

"Absolutely no sake," Jess agreed with a laugh. "I don't need to learn any more terms for tiny penises."

Jess was out the door before I could weasel out of the plan. That was for the best. It was time to reenter the human race. Lots of women got divorced. It wasn't as if I was the first one who had lost her husband to a younger woman who had perkier breasts and whiter teeth. Plenty of women had been humiliated in grand fashion. There had to be tons of others who had walked in on a rat bastard banging a bottled blonde on the kitchen table. A rat bastard who had spent thousands of her hard-earned dollars on golf clubs, safaris, hair transplants, Cuban cigars and vacations with weather hookers.

Of course, I was hard-pressed to think of another gal who'd happened to have a local news film crew following her for publicity on her latest romance novel release when she'd caught her husband balls-deep in the weather hooker. The footage had gone viral on the internet. The camera jerk who'd put my humiliation on Twitter had been fired, but it was too late. I wasn't exactly a household name as a romance author, but it was an incredibly juicy, awful story. It had made the national tabloids with an unfortunate vengeance.

The Queen of Paranormal Romance got Cuckqueaned. I'd had to look that one up.

Others were *explicitly* creative.

Famed Author of Exotic Catches Husband in X-RATED Extracurriculars

Exasperated Romance Queen Exploited by Explosive Soon-To-Be Ex

Will Clementine Roberts—the Author of Exotic—Expunge the Excrement Who Exchanged Her for an Exhibitionist?

The headlines were bad enough. The footage that hit the trashy entertainment shows was almost debilitating. Although, I did enjoy the part where I grabbed the bucket of dirty mop water that just so happened to be handy and doused Darren's naked ass. His girly scream of horror was beautiful. I'd received more fan mail that week than I had in my entire career. My agent was ecstatic. My books were flying off the shelves. While the sales were thrilling, the way I got them was anything but. Thankfully a butcher knife hadn't been handy because I would have used it. There would have been no way to get away with giving him an extra ass crack if there had been filmed proof. I wouldn't do well in the big house.

That had been exactly four months and five days ago.

One would think I could get out of my sham of a marriage easily. Nope. The adulterer wanted to be paid. A lot. Thankfully, Mr. Ted was a shark. The new wrinkle of Darren the Wandering Dick wanting his cut of my future earnings and backlist was worrisome, but maybe Jess had a point in bringing in Mandy. Mandy was crafty and she hated Darren. She was also smart and she loved *me*.

Thick Stella hissed as I passed her in the hallway on my way to the shower.

"You're rude," I told her, swerving to the left to avoid her sharp claws. "However, you have no hidden agenda. You're an asshole and you own it. I like that."

We had a silent standoff for about a minute and twenty seconds. I refused to back down. My cat might want to gouge my eyes out, but part of her loved me. I could feel it. Of course, it might be because I fed her daily, but right now I would take what I could get.

The fat fur ball was the first to break. She plopped onto her bulbous ass, extended her back leg like a ballerina and had a go at her hoo-hoo.

I laughed. "Good thinking, Thick Stella. I'm going to clean up too. Not exactly like that because that would send me into traction. But you do you. I'll do me."

It was time to get out of my own way.

It was time to take back my life.

And it was definitely time to take a shower.

CHAPTER THREE

"REMEMBER, CLEMENTINE, THERE'S ALWAYS SUNSHINE AFTER the rain," I whispered to my reflection in the bathroom mirror, repeating Purple Gal's cryptic parting words.

Whether she was real or not, she'd laid out some interesting points.

Wiping away the floating steam for the third time, I continued to study my face. The small lines at the corners of my eyes didn't bother me a bit. I'd earned them from smiling. Remembering how to smile was a constant challenge lately, but one I was up for. The shower was my metaphorical rain. Hopefully, my new attitude would be the sunshine.

My body and mind still felt weighed down by the recent catastrophic events, but it was what it was. There was no rewriting the truth, as much as I wanted to do so. Accepting the ugly situation and moving on was the goal. While it felt semi-impossible, I embraced it. It was either that or keep hiding.

I was tired of hiding. I had nothing to be ashamed of. I hadn't broken my marriage vows on national television by fornicating with a weather hooker on a kitchen table. Nope. I'd simply stayed in a situation that had deteriorated years ago.

"Maybe I'm partially to blame for pretending nothing was wrong," I told my sad face.

Thick Stella yowled her disagreement and circled my wet legs. The violent feline did love me. Smiling at my moody cat, I nodded my head. "Thank you, Thick Stella. Your support is noted and will earn you extra treats. Not that you need any."

She meowed, crawled into the dirty laundry basket and began to groom herself. My cat was done with me for now. I agreed. I was done with me too—the old me. Hopefully, I'd washed her down the drain. The shower had been like a long overdue orgasm. My hair was a nest of tangles. I'd washed it three times and left the conditioner in while I'd attacked my hairy legs and armpits with a razor.

Hot mess didn't begin to describe the state of decay I'd fallen into.

"That wore me out," I said with a laugh, walking out of the bathroom and to my closet.

Eyeing my clothes, I sighed dramatically. While it felt invigorating to be clean, I couldn't get it up to coordinate an outfit. Pulling on a clean pair of black yoga pants and a Bob Marley t-shirt, I slipped my feet into my favorite sparkly pink flip-flops. The ensemble wasn't anything special, but it was a far cry better than the sweats and t-shirt I'd been sporting for over a week… or two.

For thirty seconds, I debated whether or not to blow dry and straighten my massive amount of dark curly hair. I was leaning towards a no when the ringing of the doorbell made the decision for me. Wet curly hair for the win.

"Coming," I called out, wondering why Jess hadn't used her key.

There was a good reason Jess hadn't used her key. It wasn't Jess or Mandy. It was a man. And if I had to guess, I'd say he was a cop... or even worse, a reporter.

My sordid life story had stayed in the headlines of the rag magazines for a week and then was eclipsed by a celebrity orgy. Thank God for heinous behavior. I was old news, or so I'd thought.

Peering through the peephole, I examined the unwelcome man, from his balding head down to his unattractive orthopedic shoes. He looked to be around sixtyish. His navy suit was wrinkled, and I spotted what looked like a faint mustard stain on his lapel. Everything about him was a mess except his eyes. They were shrewd, heavily lashed and bright blue—bizarrely attractive. I could have sworn I knew those eyes.

First, I thought I knew Purple Gal and now Mustard Man. My hygiene might have improved, but my memory had not.

Pretty eyes or no, I wasn't in the mood for dealing with anyone other than my friends.

"Who is it?" I yelled through the closed door.

"Police, ma'am. Here about a break-in," he replied.

I squinted at him through the peephole. He was lying. I didn't report the break-in. I wasn't even sure a break-in had occurred. I was being set up. Maybe that was why he looked familiar. He'd probably been on the force since Darren's days… Darren had to be behind this.

Maybe the woman *had* been real. It was doubtful but entirely possible that I'd dropped the coins and they'd rolled onto the front porch and fallen through the slats. I would have thought I'd hear something like that, but it was plausible. The coins disappearing into thin air was absurd.

Had Darren sent Purple Gal to mess with me? And now a cop? My soon-to-be ex wasn't all that creative, but he wanted money. Was he trying to make me think I'd gone nuts? I was doing well enough with that on my own, I didn't need Darren's help. Actually, I couldn't figure out how my having a nervous breakdown would get him more money, but it was all I could come up with at the moment.

Son of a bitch. If Darren had thrown the first pitch, I was going to knock it out of the damn park. Time to play hardball.

"Hang on a sec," I yelled, still looking through the peep-hole. "I'm going to get my cell phone, mace and a butcher's knife. You know, just in case you aren't who you say you are."

"Sounds like a plan," the man said, waving his hand politely.

It was astounding how polite the people who were up to no good behaved. But then again, we were in the south.

My phone was in the laundry room, the mace was in the junk drawer in the kitchen and the butcher's knife was in the wooden knife block. I winced when I realized this was the second time today I'd been prepared to off someone.

36

Since I was pretty sure I didn't have the balls to actually stab anyone, I was pleased I'd thought of the mace. Leaving the knife on the counter, I tucked the phone into my waistband and grabbed a second bottle of the spray.

I was armed and ready. For what? I had no freaking clue. The smartest thing would be to tell the pretty-eyed man to leave, but I was curious.

Thick Stella growled.

"Yep," I told her. "I'm very aware that curiosity killed the cat, but my writer mind can't resist."

My writer brain might land me six feet under, but my stupid need to know what happened next eclipsed my self-preservation gene. Plus, I could possibly use it in a book— my revenge book about a loser with a tiny package who tried to fleece the fabulous heroine he'd cheated on with a weather hooker... or something like that. I'd make all the characters shapeshifters so no one would recognize it was my life. Probably a horrid plan, but sometimes bad plans turned into brilliant books.

Cracking open the door, I showed Mustard Man the mace. "One wrong move and you're blind. You feel me?"

"Roger that, ma'am," he replied, backing away a bit.

"State your business," I said. "Be advised if it sounds even remotely hinky, you can kiss your eyesight bye-bye. You don't want to get involved in a soup sandwich with me. I've been in a seriously bad mood for a few months."

I could speak cop until the cows came home. I'd written so many werewolf cops over the years, I couldn't even recall half of them.

"Affirmative," he said with a curt nod. He pulled a ratty-looking notepad from his breast pocket, then searched his other pockets. "Darn it," he muttered.

"What?" I asked.

"Forgot my pen," he replied, reddening a little.

I rolled my eyes. The dude was inept. "Hang on." I closed the door and locked it. Running to my office, I grabbed a pen. I picked one I didn't like. He'd probably pilfer it. Cops were like that. Actually, I wasn't fond of pens at all. I loved really sharp pencils. If I got stuck on a chapter at the computer, I would handwrite myself out of the writer's block. It was as if the connection of my hand on the pencil and the lead to the paper was magical. Tucking an extra-pointy pencil behind each ear, I figured they might come in handy if I did indeed need to stab the cop.

"Here you go," I said, tossing the pen to the ground at his feet and keeping the door mostly closed.

There was no way I was inviting him in. He wasn't huge —probably about my height, five foot nine. However, size and looks could be deceiving. I might be on the edge of insanity, but I still had my street smarts.

"Thank you, ma'am," he replied with another curt nod, squatting down to pick up the pen. As he stood back up, he began to rock back and forth on his feet and nibble at the end of the pen.

I did not want that pen back. Ever.

The man pulled distractedly on his left ear for a moment, then leveled his bright blue gaze on me.

Dammit, I was sure I knew him. The rocking and nibbling were buried in my memories somewhere. Problem was, my brain was full of fiction, reality and self-pity. Sometimes, I couldn't remember the difference.

"Do I know you?" I asked, keeping the mace aimed at his head.

"I should say so," he replied, beginning to take notes.

"How?" I demanded, glad that I was correct and alarmed that I couldn't recall how.

"Ma'am, I'm here to ask the questions. Not answer them."

"Rude," I muttered.

He wrote that down too.

"So, as I understand it, an Adam Henry broke into your abode and ate your Grape Nuts?" he questioned.

Was this really happening?

"Her name was Adam Henry?" I asked, shocked. She didn't look like an Adam Henry at all. If Purple Gal was a guy in drag, he was absolutely fabulous. I would have bet my life that Purple Gal was a woman. Color me impressed.

"No ma'am," he replied. "Adam Henry is code for asshole."

Color me unimpressed. "You're an asshole," I snapped. "Purple Gal was very pleasant for the most part. Yes, she was in my home illegally, but she was *not* an asshole—she was just batshit crazy. So, if you're going to be nasty, you can leave. Name-calling people with a limited grasp on reality is ugly."

The words flying from my mouth were outrageous even to me. So surprising, I laughed. I was defending a criminal who had eaten my cereal. Whatever. I had on clean clothes and no hair on my legs. I was winning.

"My apologies, ma'am," Mustard Man said, blushing again. "Most perps who breach entryways are cloaking something nefarious."

"Fine. Apology accepted," I said, feeling kind of bad for him. "Who sent you? I didn't report the break-in."

He looked perplexed. "We received a report of a STOLO this morning and traced the vehicle here. Caught the subject red-handed with two boxes of Grape Nuts under her skirt. When we shook her down, she admitted to pilfering the evidence from this address."

"Ohhhh my GOD," I said with a laugh. "That's priceless. You're so full of shit your eyes should be brown, mister."

"Not following, ma'am," he replied, more confused than ever.

"Of course you are," I said, rolling my eyes so hard they should've gotten stuck in the back of my head. "Jig is up, copper. Darren sent you to screw with me just like he sent the purple cereal eater. You can tell the dickless jackoff that I'm onto him and he's not getting another penny out of me. Write that down."

Mustard Man did as requested but seemed bewildered by the demand. Darren had clearly hired idiots.

"Tell me your name," I insisted.

"Clark Dark, ma'am. Detective Clark Dark."

My mouth dropped open. No. Freaking. Way.

I was furious. Not only was Darren trying to make me think I was nuts, he'd told his henchman to use one of my characters' names. My God, he'd been wily enough to find someone who actually resembled my fictional cop. No wonder the man seemed so familiar.

Detective Clark Dark was a beloved character to me. He was my brilliantly sloppy werewolf detective in my Darkness series. It was a ten-book series that I'd ended about three years ago—one of my most popular. The real—albeit fictional—Clark Dark was slightly better looking than Mustard Man, but the imposter was very close to accurate. His eyes were a perfect match. And Clark Dark did love his hotdogs. The mustard on the lapel was positively inspired.

I had to hand it to Darren. It was deviously brilliant. However, I was too smart for him. I'd always been smarter than him. I'd had to dumb down my conversations and dreams for years so he wouldn't get his tighty whities in a knot.

Wait... I *had* swallowed my thoughts and dreams so Darren wouldn't get butthurt. What the hell was wrong with me?

No time for introspective thought. I had an imposter on my porch who was up to no good. I'd visit my decades of stupidity later.

"Well, Clark Dark—or whatever your real name is," I said flatly, "it's time for you to leave. If you show up again, I'll mace you blind, then call the real cops to lock your ass up for impersonating a fictional character and an officer of the law."

Mustard Man nodded jerkily and looked like he might cry. Made me feel like shit, but this was getting out of hand. I found myself tempted to apologize and invite him in.

"As you wish," he said, using one of the most memorable lines I'd written for the real/fictitious Clark Dark.

The phony spoke the words exactly like I'd imagined

them in my mind. It was perfection. And I was perfectly crazy.

"Look," I said, still holding the mace, but cracking the door open a little wider. "I'm sorry you got mixed up in this. You seem like a nice man. Darren is not a nice man. You need to disassociate yourself from him. He's no good."

Mustard Man tucked his notebook back into the breast pocket of his wrinkled suit and offered me back my pen.

"Keep it," I told him. Even though I tried to stop myself, my mouth kept moving. The words spilled from my lips. I couldn't help it. "Do you need money? If you took the shitty job for a paycheck, I can give you some money. No strings attached."

Clark Dark smiled at me. It lit up his lined face, and I felt on top of the world.

"No, ma'am, but thank you. I knew you would be kind," he replied, turning to leave.

A huge part of me wanted him to stay. My stomach tightened as he slowly walked down the drive just like Purple Gal had. He didn't look back. I wasn't sure he was walking into a better future. Maybe I should insist he take some money. He didn't even have a dang car. Had he walked?

"Detective Dark," I called out.

He turned and rocked back and forth on his feet... just the way I'd written him.

"It really isn't any trouble to give you some money. I'd like to," I told him. "Please?"

Again, he smiled. Again, my breath caught in my throat. "Money's no good where I come from," he said.

"Thought's appreciated though, Clementine. A word of advice?"

"Umm... sure," I said.

"Figure out your expenses," he suggested. "And time is of the essence."

"My expenses?" I asked, confused. "For my books?"

"Bingo," he replied with a wink. "Might get you out of a mess. We need you."

On those puzzling words, Fake Detective Clark Dark aka Mustard Man walked away without a backward glance. Watching him leave tore at my heart. Inhaling deeply, I pushed away the need to chase him down and force him to take a few hundred dollars. His final words rang in my ears. Purple Girl's cryptic message had made sense in the scheme of my life. Would Mustard Man's advice be an omen as well?

But wait. Had Darren sent him?

Was Darren that smart?

Did I have other enemies who wanted to steal my sanity?

Was Mustard Man another stalker? Had a Clementine Roberts stalker convention come to town and I was simply being barraged by people who were bananas?

Shit. The possibilities were endless and all whackadoo.

Whatever. I smelled good. Jess and Mandy would be here shortly with food and alcohol. Thick Stella hadn't drawn blood today. Granted, I hadn't gotten any words on the page, but my mind felt freer than it had in months.

Nighttime was my creative time. I'd been trying to change it up and write during the day. Bad plan. I had a good feeling that the elusive, imaginary Chauncey would show up tonight and we'd bang out a couple of brilliant chapters.

And if he didn't show? Screw him. Jess was right. Maybe I needed a female muse. If Chauncey was a no-show this evening, he was fired.

"Life is going to be okay," I announced as I shut the door and bolted it. "Enough rain. Time for some damn sunshine."

Thick Stella showed me her butt, then waddled off.

"That's the spirit," I muttered with a laugh. My cat's attitude was horrible, but very little seemed to bother her. Maybe she had it right.

It was time to look into my expenses. I wasn't sure why, but it would give me something to do till my besties arrived.

And who knew? Maybe Clark Dark was onto something.

CHAPTER FOUR

THE ATMOSPHERE IN MY KITCHEN FELT ALIVE AND HAPPY FOR the first time in a long while. My two favorite women in the world were laughing and bustling around. While Jess was short, dark and delightfully curvy, Mandy was tall like me. She was a striking blonde with piercing and intelligent hazel eyes. We'd been the Three Musketeers since high school and I couldn't be happier to be back together again.

"God that smells good," I said as I heard my stomach rumble.

"El Rancho," Jess said with a wink. "We got all your favs."

The setting sun was a fiery pink ball on the horizon, bathing the airy room in gorgeous light. While I, *personally*, might not have been disinfected until today, my house was immaculate. I'd done a whole lot of cleaning to avoid writing. We could probably eat off the shiny cherry hardwood floor.

Resting my elbows on the granite countertop of the

breakfast bar and my chin in my hands, I sighed with relief and happiness. Sunshine was a lovely thing.

"Hear me out on this. This one is good. Questionably legal, but worth exploring," Mandy said, passing out the Mexican food while Jess made frozen margaritas in the blender. "It's a bar that has babysitting—a mini gym, tumbling mats, stuffed animals. Brilliant. Right? I'd call it Kiss My Glass."

"Not real sure about that one," I said with a laugh, digging into the guac with glee. The guacamole from El Rancho was so delicious people drove for miles to get their fix. "That sounds like a lawsuit waiting to happen."

Since Mandy had been a stay-at-home mom for the last few years, she'd come up with a never-ending list of side gigs. It was very clear how much she adored her little girls, but she'd always been a career-minded gal. Hell, all three of us were.

Mandy took a slug off of the drink Jess handed her and continued to plead her case. "Nope. No lawsuits. I'd hire a car service with baby seats and boosters. No wasted mommies would drive. Period. It would be open from three to five—just in time for mommy to arrive home and hand off *all* of her children to her husband who knocked her up with triplets. He could make dinner and do bath time while mommy takes a nap. I tell you this could work."

"I think you might be getting fantasy mixed up with reality," Jess pointed out with a laugh, munching on a chip. "Although, if you do it, I think that everyone should have to wear a t-shirt that says, *I don't get drunk. I get awesome.*"

Mandy laughed. "Or how about, *Less thinking. More Drinking?*"

"*Candy is dandy, but liquor is quicker,*" I added, dousing my spicy chicken taco with hot salsa.

Jess took a quick bow. "I believe I'm the winner," she announced preemptively. "*Beauty is in the eye of the beer holder.*"

I laughed. Mandy groaned.

"Of course you win," I said with a mouthful. "You're the wildly successful owner of a greeting card company. If you didn't win, we'd be in trouble."

"True that," Jess agreed with a grin.

"Kiss My Glass is a shitty idea," Mandy admitted, digging into her burrito. "I rarely drink—only when I'm with you two fabulous dummies. I just need something to do that doesn't involve Care Bears, Pull-Ups and applesauce. I need to use my brain a little more."

Jess's eyes narrowed. "Is David not helping with those beautiful babies?"

Mandy sighed. "David is the best daddy and husband ever—never complains and loves the little stinkers to the moon and back. He does dishes, helps with the laundry and makes sure my big O comes first. And on top of all that, after twenty years, he still makes me laugh."

"Wow," I muttered, envious but thrilled for my buddy. "Keep him."

"Obviously," Mandy said. "I'm just a little lost. Finding me lately has been impossible—like the magic got sucked out somewhere. I'm not sure I'm anyone except someone's mother. I mean, it was so damn hard to have them. IVF sucked, but I'd do it again in a heartbeat."

"Wait," Jess choked out. "You're not actually *doing it* again, are you?"

Mandy grunted out a pained chuckle. "Hell to the no. I'm forty-five with four-year-old triplet girls. I'm so done."

"Can you imagine when they're all going through puberty at the same time?" I blurted out, then slapped my hand over my mouth. "Sorry," I whispered between splayed fingers. "That was entirely uncalled for."

"Don't think I haven't had nightmares about it," Mandy said, taking an enormous bite of her burrito. "Honestly, I wouldn't trade a second of it, but I'm getting to the point where I need a little more for me to be better for them."

It was so incredibly normal and good to hear my best friends feel free to unload. They'd treated me like spun glass for the past four months. The sunshine was peeking through. Purple Gal was onto something, even if she had been hired by my scummy soon-to-be ex.

"Do you want to go back to the law firm?" I asked. "I bet Mr. Ted would take you back in a hot second."

Mandy nodded. "I've thought about it. Mr. Ted said he'd work with me on flexible hours."

Jess wrinkled her nose. "Wait. Do you actually call him Mr. Ted at work?"

"I do," Mandy said with a giggle. "Not in front of clients, of course, but when it's just him and me, I can't help it."

"Habits," I said, repeating Jess's earlier assessment of our failure to move on from childhood patterns. "Habits are hard to break."

"Agreed. Anyhoo," Mandy went on. "David's all for anything that makes me happy and whole. I want my girls to see me work. I saw my mom work and it made an important impression on me. Plus, Mr. Ted is thinking about retiring."

"When?" I shouted, horrified. The chicken taco felt like a lead cannonball in my stomach. "Not soon, I hope."

"Not soon," Mandy promised quickly. "And trust me, Mr. Ted wants to take Darren down just as much as we do."

"Speaking of small dicks, Darren wants half of all Clementine's future and backlist earnings," Jess announced.

"Is Mr. Ted aware of this?" Mandy asked.

"Not sure," I admitted. "I have an appointment in the morning at ten."

"How do you know Darren wants half your future royalties?" Mandy asked.

"An email from the asshole," I replied, grabbing my laptop and opening it.

Before I could close the doc with my marketing expenses, Mandy was all over it.

"What is that?" she asked, pointing at the screen with interest.

"Marketing expenses for the last ten years," I told her.

My legal-eagle bestie read the spreadsheet over my shoulder. "Why did you pull that up?"

I'd pulled up the files after Mustard Man's cryptic message. *Figure out your expenses... time is of the essence.* He'd said it could get me out of my troubles, but, frankly, I was still slightly unsure that he or even Purple Gal were real. No way I was sharing that with Mandy or Jess. I didn't have the energy to listen to my friends debate my mental state. This was the first evening I'd felt like my old self in forever, and I didn't want to ruin it by clueing my besties in that I might have a hallucination issue.

So, I shrugged. "No particular reason. Just having a look."

Mandy stared at the screen for a long moment as a devious little smile pulled at her lips. "Okay," she said, grabbing a pad of paper and a pen from her purse. "If I'm reading this correctly, you spend about fifteen to twenty percent of your gross income on marketing and advertising yearly."

I squinted at the screen. "Yep."

Jess whistled. "That's a lot of dough."

Mandy continued to take notes. "Gotta spend money to make money," she pointed out. "I recall you took out a monster loan to expand your business, Jess."

Jess gave her a thumbs up. "Smartest and scariest thing I ever did."

I grinned and shook my head. "I offered to lend you the money—interest free."

"Yes, you did," Jess said, kissing the top of my head. "That was a beautiful gesture. However, I don't like to mix best friends and big bucks. Never ends well."

"Amen to that," Mandy said, still taking notes from the screen. "Can you forward this to me?"

I nodded and did as she asked. "Will it help?"

Mandy compressed her lips. Her wheels were spinning. It was fascinating and kind of terrifying to watch. "Not sure. But I have an idea."

"Is it legal?" Jess asked, topping off everyone's drinks.

"Define legal," Mandy shot back.

"Oh shit." I took a healthy sip.

"Kidding!" Mandy giggled. "It's far more legal than reporting Teeny Weenie to the country club for wearing a collarless shirt... six times."

"Shut up!" Jess squealed. "I reported him for speeding in his golf cart at the country club. I understand he was fined."

"Beat you," Mandy said, waggling her brows. "I have photographic proof that the asswad didn't pick up after his dog."

"Wait, Darren has a dog?" I asked, appalled but enjoying the wonderfully awful things my besties had been doing.

"Weather Hooker has a dog," Jess confirmed with an eye roll. "From what I heard at the salon, Bouncy Tits is getting a little put out that Darren the Dickless doesn't have a job. She's getting tired of footing the bills so she's making him walk her dog."

It kept getting better and better. "He has money," I told them. "Mr. Ted put both of us on an allowance until the particulars are worked out. One hour after I caught him banging Weather Hooker, I froze the bank accounts and canceled all the credit cards. But even so, his *allowance* is large."

"Apparently, he went through it like a hot knife through butter," Jess said. "Weather Hooker has expensive tastes."

I rolled my eyes. I was shocked that the revelations weren't painful—they stung, but it wasn't debilitating. Maybe taking a shower had worked. "Why haven't you guys told me any of this?"

Mandy and Jess exchanged glances. "You weren't ready," Mandy said, grabbing my hand and gently squeezing. "Is this too much? We can shut our pie holes if it is."

I thought about it. Was it too much? It wasn't exactly fun, but it wasn't dreadful either. It was liberating that I hadn't curled into the fetal position and started to cry. "It's weird. I almost feel like we're talking about someone I don't know," I admitted, much to my own surprise. After as many years as I'd spent with Darren, it was sad that I was beginning to realize I didn't know him very well. "And I have to thank you for your brazenly unethical loyalty. I would like to go on record and promise the same semi-legal favors in return if they are ever needed—which I hope they're not."

"We can stop," Jess said, coming up behind me and resting her chin on my head. "You smell good."

"Thanks to you and Purple Gal," I said, then froze.

"Purple Gal?" Mandy asked, looking at me strangely. "Who is Purple Gal?"

Well, crap. The cat was out of the bag. Lying was off the table. There was too much honesty going on to screw up the chi.

"A woman in a purple regency gown broke into my house and ate my Grape Nuts this morning," I told them, staring at the remainder of the taco on my plate. "She was concerned about my hygiene."

"I'm sorry, what?" Jess asked, wrinkling her nose and squinting at me. "There was so much wrong with that statement, I don't know where to begin."

"Did you call the cops?" Mandy asked the logical question.

"Umm... no," I said sheepishly. "She was very polite. And Clark Dark stopped over on his own—he's a detective... I think. I guess someone else reported the break-in."

"I am so confused," Jess said, sitting down next to me. "Why in the heck do I know the name Clark Dark?"

"He's the main character from my Darkness series," I explained with a wince.

"The werewolf?" she asked.

"Yes," I replied.

Another more pointed look was exchanged between my friends.

"Hang on before you have me committed," I insisted. "I think Darren hired both of them to freak me out. The guy who called himself Clark Dark actually resembled the character I created. I didn't think Darren was that imaginative— hell, I didn't know he read my books. I have no clue who the woman was. She never gave her name. They were both harmless and very polite."

Mandy stood up and growled. She was freaking scary. "That son of a bitch is trying to frighten you. Make you think you're losing it. I'm going to tear his ass to shreds. Tomorrow, I'm going back to the firm. I want to legally take that bastard down."

"Darren's an ass," Jess said, shaking her head and pointing a tortilla chip at me. "But Clementine, you can't let people you don't know into the house. It's dangerous. Do you remember the crackpot who thought she was married to your character Damien?"

I shuddered. The deranged woman had flown from Canada to Kentucky to find her *demon husband* Damien and bring him back home with her… at gunpoint. At first it had been a polite yet bizarre exchange on my front porch. However, when I'd tried to gently explain that Damien wasn't a real person, she'd lost her mind and the gun had come out of her purse. Darren had missed the entire episode. He'd been golfing… like he always was.

"I do remember," I whispered. The particular event was burned into my brain. "And that's why no matter how many times Thick Stella tries to bite me, I won't complain."

My vicious cat had attacked the woman. And when I say attacked, I mean *attacked*. There was blood everywhere. It was a shitshow of epic proportions. At one point, I thought I might hurl from all the blood. The woman dropped her gun into the bushes when she tried to remove a rampaging Thick Stella from her face, then ran like the devil was on her heels. My cat howled like she was on fire and literally chased the woman for a mile.

The cops had picked up the psycho running down Main Street screaming like a banshee about killer cats and kidnapped demons. After she'd been arrested and claimed that I had been hiding her *husband Damien* from her, so she'd needed to kill me, they'd caught on fast. Apparently, I had many fans on the force who'd read *Exotic*.

She had been tried and convicted. After she'd served her time, she'd been deported back to Canada and not allowed to step foot in the States again.

Good times.

"Jess is right. No one in your house except people you know. Period. And next time, you call the police. Immediately," Mandy instructed in her take-no-bullshit voice.

54

"I promise," I told her.

She nodded, satisfied. "So, tell me again why you pulled up your financials?" she asked, pacing around the kitchen, still trying to work off her anger.

"Clark Dark told me to," I admitted.

"You think he was a real cop?" Jess pressed, still trying to wrap her head around the strange news.

"Doubtful," I said with a shrug. "He was just a guy who looked like my character. Might be an actor."

"Scum," Mandy barked. "Darren is scum."

"Understatement," I agreed. "You can really do something with those financials?"

Mandy paused her pacing and slapped her hands onto her hips. "Maybe. Before I lay it out, let me make sure I'm right. Clark Dark might have saved the day."

"The irony of that statement is absurd," Jess said with a laugh.

Right now, the irony of my life was absurd.

At least I had good friends to share it with.

CHAPTER FIVE

"I NEED TO GET A DANG PERM," AUNT FLIP SHOUTED.

Yanking the phone away from my ear, I winced. I hadn't talked to my nutty aunt in years, yet she'd called me at 9:15 AM to tell me she needed to get her hair done.

I was exhausted. I'd been up until four AM writing. About three good chapters rolled from my brain through my fingers and onto the page. It was liberating. Damien and Sasha were burning up the pages and the sheets. My imaginary muse Chauncy never showed up, but I found I didn't need him. I didn't need any man—not Chauncy and definitely not Darren. It was time for me to stand on my own two feet.

"Mmmkay," I said, trying to pull myself together for the meeting with Mr. Ted. "Is there a reason you wanted me to know you need a perm, Aunt Flip?"

She huffed into the phone, and I grinned. My entire

childhood I'd giggled over Aunt Flip's bitching and moaning. She and Granny used to argue constantly about the most ridiculous things. They'd lived to go at each other and had enjoyed the hell out of it. One fabulous smackdown that I recalled was over the Burt Reynolds mostly naked centerfold in *Cosmopolitan* magazine. Granny's more conservative senses had been wildly offended. So, of course, Flip bought forty copies and had taped them up all over the house. When I'd first moved into the Victorian they used to share, I'd found a naked Burt taped to the wall inside the foyer closet.

I'd left it up. It made me smile.

"Course there's a reason," she grunted. "Looked in the mirror and saw my dang scalp. That's unacceptable. I'm too attractive to go bald. My hair's gettin' thin, and it makes me feel old. Not likin' it."

Far be it from me to remind her she was eighty-five. "Okay," I said, slipping my feet into sparkly flip-flops. They were semi-acceptable footwear and they were comfortable. I'd been sporting sweatpants for four months. I was taking baby steps back into the world of fashion. I was nowhere near the heels stage yet. At least I'd put on a cute dress. I'd considered yoga pants, but Thick Stella had literally hissed at me when I went to pull them on. Deciding it would be better to make it out of the house without a bloody gash on my leg from my cat, I opted for the dress. "Do you need me to make you an appointment?'

"Why in the hell do you think I'm callin' you?" she bellowed.

Between Aunt Flip and Nancy from the law firm, I was going to go deaf.

"Honestly, I'm not real sure why you called," I told her, checking the time.

I could literally hear the old geezer rolling her eyes. I grinned.

"I need you to tell me when the dark of the moon is," she informed me, still using her outdoor voice.

"Because?" I asked, grabbing my purse. So much for slapping on a little makeup. There wasn't time.

"Beeeeeeeecause I have to get my perm during the dark of the moon. It'll hold better. *Everyone* knows that."

"Actually, *everyone* doesn't know that," I said with a laugh. "But how about this? I'll check into it after my meeting with Mr. Ted and let you know."

"You finally dumpin' that turd knocker?" she asked with a cackle.

"Who? Mr. Ted?" I asked, messing with her.

Aunt Flip screamed with delight and laughed so hard, I joined her.

God, I missed the kooky woman. I knew she never came around because she didn't like Darren, but Daren was no longer in the picture. I was fairly sure she knew that already.

"I'll take you to your appointment once I figure out the moon stuff."

"Dark of the moon," Aunt Flip said ominously. "If I don't land it right, I'll end up bald. That would suck."

"It most certainly would," I agreed.

59

"How are your mom and pop?" she asked.

"Great. Still in Florida. Still loving it."

"Hate Florida," she snapped. "Everybody looks like a piece of used leather. Do you watch *Dancing with the Stars*? Love that show."

"Umm... nope," I told her, grabbing my keys and my travel mug of coffee. "Should I?"

"Hell yes," she said. "You should make your demon people, Damien and Sasha, go on a dance show. It would sell like a mother humper. And I think Sasha's stepmother should get eaten by pigs. That's a real thing, Clemmy."

"That's seriously disgusting," I said, gagging. "But I'll keep it in mind."

"Well, you're welcome. If I wasn't so busy growin' weed, I'd write a book too," she said. "Gotta go water my pot. Call me later. I don't wanna go bald."

She hung up before I got a goodbye out.

Aunt Flip was certifiable... and possibly just what I needed.

She was the only family I had left in the area. My parents were as happy as clams in Florida and they did not look like used leather. Aunt Flip was clearly lonely, and I hadn't been a good grandniece.

I was changing everything up. Darren was out, and Aunt Flip was back in.

"Sunshine, here I come."

∾

THE INTERIOR OF WALTERS AND WALTERS WAS SLEEK AND impressive. While I might live in a small Kentucky town, it was peppered with famous Thoroughbred farms. Old money mixed with new money mixed with farmers and all kinds of neat people. The binding factor was Southern charm… and nosiness. I was thankful I hadn't run into anyone I knew on my way to the meeting. Talking to people again was going to take some practice. I was starting with Mr. Ted. He was kind, and I was paying him to help me. Win-win.

The leather couches and oak hardwood floors were lovely against the gorgeous and subtly hued area rug. The furniture was heavy and dark, juxtaposed with oil paintings of lush green rolling hills and beautiful horses. It felt formal, but because of Mr. Ted it also felt safe and welcoming.

Nancy was nowhere to be found. I'd arrived with six minutes to spare, and I spotted a stack of my books on her desk in the reception area. I thought about grabbing and signing them, but I could feel two little eyes boring into the side of my head.

I was pretty sure the young lady—who couldn't have been more than six or seven—wasn't waiting for an appointment with Mr. Ted, but who knew? Was she Nancy's daughter? I'd thought Nancy's kids were grown. She'd married her high school sweetheart when we'd graduated and had kids immediately. Maybe Little Blondie was her granddaughter.

"You're very stylish," the child said, pointing at my feet. "I think wearing two different shoes is risky, but well worth the effect."

Wait. Was she six or twenty-six? With a wince of horror, I glanced down at my feet. Little Blondie was correct. I was wearing a pink sparkly flip-flop and a purple sparkly flip-flop. And if that wasn't bad enough, my sundress was green and blue. I was a fashion don't today.

"Umm… thank you," I said with an embarrassed laugh. "I got dressed kind of quick this morning."

"I like it," she said, nodding as her blonde curls bounced. "I'll be copying that. I think it's beautiful. I think *you're* beautiful."

I smiled and took her in. She looked like a doll. Her eyes were an unusual cornflower blue and her blonde curls were a tumbled and adorable mess. Her outfit rivaled mine, and I immediately understood why she was impressed with my haphazard ensemble.

Her red cowboy boots were adorned with glittery pink daisies. A bright yellow sleeveless shirt was paired with a lavender tutu and blue jean shorts underneath. The topper was the rhinestone crown she wore on her head. It was definitely a risk, but she was winning big in life.

"Well, I think you're beautiful too," I told her.

"What's your name?" she asked.

"My name's Clementine."

Little Blondie pointed to the books on Nancy's desk. "Did you write those books?"

I nodded. "I did."

"That's very beautiful too," she commented, swinging her cowboy-boot-clad feet.

My little buddy had an affinity for the word beautiful… it was beautiful.

"Thank you." I was curious about her name and why she was here, but I was an adult who she didn't know—no matter how *beautiful* she thought I was.

I had to admit, her compliments made me feel great. After being lambasted for being stinky, hearing I was pretty —even from a child—was good for my wounded ego.

"Do you want to guess my name?" she asked.

I glanced around. Where were her mom and dad? While I was actually enjoying the conversation, I was a little concerned. "Are your parents here?" I asked.

"My daddy's in there," she said, pointing to the closed door of Mr. Ted's office. "It was super boring. I left. I told them I was done listening to stuff that made me sleepy, and I needed to pee."

"Umm… okay," I said, biting down on my lip so I didn't laugh. Little Blondie was going to grow up to be a ball buster.

"Nancy's having lady problems in the bathroom. I told her I would handle the clients," she explained completely serious.

"And Nancy said that was cool?" I asked, fascinated by the little old soul.

"Yep," she confirmed. "As long as I don't answer the phone."

"Right." I nodded. It would be a little off-putting to call and chat with a six-year-old at a law firm. "Okay, is your name Cinderella?"

She giggled. "Nope. Good guess though. I think my crown might have confused you. I'm not actually a real princess."

"Good to know," I said. "Is your name Goldie Locks?"

She giggled again. "Nooooooo, it's not Goldie Locks. Do you give up, beautiful Clementine?"

"I do," I said, grinning.

She hopped up, crossed the room and seated herself right next to me on the couch. She smelled delicious—Ivory soap and cherry Chapstick.

Leaning in, she lowered her voice. "My name is Cheeto."

I squinted at her in surprise. "Cheeto?"

"Yep," she said, crossing her little arms over her chest and daring me to disbelieve her. "Cheeto."

"Okay, Cheeto," I said, very seriously. "I like it. Fits you."

"That's what I told my daddy," she explained, relaxing since I bought right in. "Took him a while to catch on, but we're getting there."

"What about your mom?" I asked, then wanted to punch myself in the head as her face fell and her pretty eyes filled with sadness.

"She died," she whispered. "Long time ago."

I felt like an ass and wanted to cry. "I'm so sorry, Cheeto."

"It's okay," she said, leaning on me and making herself very comfortable. "You didn't know. I'm very busy looking for a new mommy for me and my daddy. Are you available? I notice you're not wearing a wedding ring."

Again, I marveled that Cheeto wasn't in her twenties. "Umm... no, I'm not available."

"That's too bad," she said, crawling onto my lap. "I think you would make a good mommy, and you would call me Cheeto."

The feel of her light little body on my lap did something to my insides. When I was at Mandy's, I was all over the triplets. I adored kids. It hadn't been in the cards for me. This moment with Cheeto was wonderfully bittersweet.

"Thank you, Cheeto. That was a kind thing to say."

"You're very polite, beautiful Clementine," she pointed out, twisting my wild dark curls in her little fingers. "My daddy is very handsome. He makes a good salary and knows how to cook. He's a very good catch."

It took everything I had not to burst out laughing. Cheeto was a piece of work. "Well, he must be very handsome to have a beautiful daughter like you."

"True," she said absently, continuing to play with my hair. "The offer is open to marry us. You know, in case you change your mind."

I heard a noise in the background. I was so taken with the little princess on my lap, I barely noticed. "The offer to marry you and your daddy is a very tempting one, but I'm going to have to pass."

"Oh my God," I heard a deep male voice groan in embarrassment. "I'm so sorry, ma'am. Cheeto, you cannot ask nice ladies to marry us. That's not how it works."

Cheeto pulled my face down to hers and gave me a wet, sloppy kiss. Turning toward the male voice, she giggled. "Well, you're not doing a good job of it, so I'm just helping. And Clementine said no. That's sad because she's beautiful, I like her shoes, and she calls me Cheeto."

"No worries…" I began—then choked on my words.

My mouth dropped open as I made eye contact with *Cheeto's daddy*, and I forgot my name for a brief moment. It was mortifying and ridiculous. If I wasn't mistaken—and I wasn't—my stomach filled with butterflies on crack doing the samba. It was as if I'd dropped myself into the meet-cute of one of my novels. Except I wasn't looking cute, this wasn't fiction and I'd met this person before, albeit a few decades ago. Plus, I wasn't available. Even if I was, I was not in this man's league. Not to mention I'd recently starred in a viral internet video, throwing dirty mop water on my naked husband who was banging another woman.

Aaaannnnd, *Seth Walters* wouldn't be caught dead with a woman wearing mismatched flip-flops to a meeting with her lawyer. I was sure of that.

"Holy shit," I muttered, then slapped my hand over my mouth in horror that I'd just sworn in front of a child. Could it possibly get worse?

Probably.

Cheeto giggled and I closed my eyes. Maybe all of this was a hallucination. That would be terrific.

"Don't worry, pretty Clementine," Cheeto said, patting my makeup-free cheek. "My daddy says that and other potty words."

"Thank you, Cheeto," Seth said with a chuckle.

"Welcome, Daddy," she replied.

Not a hallucination. Crap.

Opening my eyes, I was barraged with unfair beauty. The man had aged like fine wine. He was staring at me with open curiosity, his head tilted to the side.

My secret high school crush and the man I'd modeled my fictional heroes on was just as gorgeous as he'd been in my memories—more so now that he'd matured. His sandy-blond hair was a little too long to call professional, but his suit was immaculate and very expensive. Score one for Cheeto reporting her daddy made a good salary. The man's eyes matched his daughter's and his lashes were stupid. I knew plenty of women who paid good money for lashes like that.

"Seth Walters," he said with an apologetic smile as he scooped up Cheeto from my lap. "So sorry for any inconvenience. Miss..."

"Roberts," Cheeto said, pointing at the books on Nancy's desk. "Beautiful Clementine Roberts writes books."

Recognition sparked in his bright blue eyes for a moment, and I felt like a goddess. That lasted for ten seconds.

"Right," he said, nodding at me kindly. "You're my father's client. I'm joining the firm, and we just talked through your case."

I went from goddess to wanting to crawl under a rock and die in a matter of seconds.

"Awesome," I said, standing up and trying to maintain a tiny bit of dignity. "I appreciate that. You have a lovely daughter."

Walking across the room to Mr. Ted's office took five thousand years—my mismatched shoes felt like concrete blocks attached to my unmanicured feet. I cataloged all my feelings like I always did. This would be fabulous in a book. The sad fact that it was my life was hideous.

"Nice to see you again, Clementine," Seth said as I reached the door of his father's office without screaming in horror or collapsing to the floor.

"Again?" I asked, turning back to the Greek God who clearly knew I'd been thrown over for a Weather Hooker.

Seth smiled. "You might not remember, but we went to high school together."

I was speechless. Nothing came out. He knew who I was back then? It was kind of thrilling, yet the mortification of the present erased any tingles I might have gotten from the news.

As hard as I tried to say something quippy or clever, I remained mute and stared at the man like he was a serial killer. I was a writer, for the love of God. Why didn't I have words?

"Well, good seeing you," Seth said after an awkward silence, putting Cheeto down and taking her small hand in his large one. "I'm sure we'll see you around."

"Have a great life," I said, literally diving into Mr. Ted's office. Honestly, it would have been far better if I'd stayed silent.

I was a loser in different-colored flip-flops that didn't match my dress.

Whatever.

Even if I was available, which I wouldn't be for at least a decade, I would never date a good-looking man again. They couldn't be trusted, in my experience. Darren, for all his bad qualities—and there were many—was a very handsome man. Not Seth Walters handsome, but few men in the world were Seth Walters handsome.

He was probably an asshole.

Actually, he probably wasn't an asshole. He was a widower who was raising a really neat little girl. And I was a woman in the process of finding herself again. I didn't need a man. I simply needed me... and my divorce to be final so I'd never have to think about Darren the schnauzer dick again.

Onward and upward.

CHAPTER SIX

"I'M HOPEFUL WE CAN SETTLE THIS OUT OF COURT EVEN though Darren's demands continue to mount, Clementine," Mr. Ted said, closing the folder in front of him after our half-hour chat.

I studied his face. He was an older version of his son as far as looks went. The man was kind and steady and had an intense stare that made me feel like he could see inside me.

"That would be good," I replied, sighing with relief. "I'd prefer not to have to watch the footage of Darren and Weather Hooker... Oh God, I mean, umm..." Crap. For the life of me, I couldn't remember Weather Hooker's real name. I'd called her Weather Hooker for months.

"Jinny Jingle," Mr. Ted supplied.

I thought he might be biting back a smile, but I couldn't be sure. Mr. Ted's poker face was excellent.

"Right," I said, feeling my cheeks heat up. "My bad."

Jinny Jingle had to be a made-up name. If it wasn't, she

should smack her mother in the head. Weather Hooker was better than Jinny Jingle. My God, if Darren ended up marrying Weather Hooker, her name would be Jinny Jingle-Bell. I'd kept my maiden name, Roberts. That had been a point of contention with Darren and me, but now I was delighted that I'd insisted.

I grinned and tried to swallow back a laugh.

I failed.

"Something funny?" Mr. Ted inquired.

"Umm… no," I said, thinking I'd already pushed the limits of mature adult behavior by referring to Jinny Jingle as Weather Hooker. "So, what's the next step?"

"Interestingly, Mandy called me with some potentially pertinent information. She's coming in this afternoon and we're going to take a look at it. Since she's not technically with the firm right now, I need your permission to speak with her about the case."

"Yes," I said quickly. "I trust Mandy with my life. And just so you know, I think she wants to come back."

Mr. Ted smiled. "That's what I'm hoping. Would you like to know a little secret?"

"Is it legal?" I asked, raising my brow.

He chuckled. "Quite," he replied. "I'm going to add an in-house daycare. We have a large conference room that isn't being used and we have a nice outdoor space in the back. My granddaughter and son have moved back home and it makes splendid sense. Mandy can have her girls here, and I can have my granddaughter."

"Does Mandy know this?" I asked.

"She does not," he said, pushing a catalog across his desk

to me. The page was open to swing sets and sandboxes. "What do you think?"

I shook my head and grinned. "I think you're a brilliant man, and I'm happy you're my lawyer."

"As am I. Why don't you make another appointment with Nancy for Friday? I want to take a look at what Mandy found and discuss it with her."

"Will she be a lawyer on my team?"

Mr. Ted shook his head. "No. As good as Mandy is, I'm not sure she can contain her ire for Mr. Bell. If you're comfortable, I'll continue to represent you."

"Yes, that makes me very comfortable. Just *you*, right?" I asked, feeling a little sick to my stomach.

I assumed since Seth had said he was joining the firm that he was a lawyer as well. Having him on my case would not work for me. I'd just humiliated myself in front of the man I'd modeled all of my heroes on. I felt bad enough about myself as it was. I didn't need to be represented by someone who made me a tongue-tied idiot.

Mr. Ted looked at me quizzically for a moment. I could swear he was reading my chaotic mind. Explaining what I meant would only add to my embarrassment. Not going there today.

"Only me," he assured me, then moved on. "How's the writing going?"

"It's going." I was relieved he didn't press for more information as to why I only wanted him on my case.

"And you?" he inquired kindly. "How are you?"

How to answer that... "Well, I'm getting there," I told

him truthfully. "I'm kind of a work in progress right now. I'm searching for sunshine."

"There is always sunshine after the rain, my dear."

A tingle shot through me, and I was glad I was seated. I almost asked him if he knew Purple Gal but swallowed the words right before they spilled from my lips. It wouldn't do to have Mr. Ted think I was losing it. That was private information. Of course, he was aware I was pretty sure Darren had sent two people to my house to scare me, but I'd left out the part about the disappearing coins. That was difficult to explain. Mr. Ted had been as stern as Mandy and Jess about calling the police if anyone else stopped by.

I nodded and smiled. "I hope so," I told Mr. Ted. "It's been raining long enough."

"MR. WALTERS HAS AN OPENING ON FRIDAY AT ELEVEN," Nancy said, looking pale and exhausted.

"Are you okay?" I asked, signing the last of her books.

Nancy groaned. "Early menopause sucks all kinds of ass," she griped. "I have to bring extra clothes to work because I sweat right through everything—just awful."

"I'm so sorry," I told her, meaning it. I knew my mom's menopause had been easy and I hoped mine would be the same. "Can I do anything for you?"

"You can kill Sasha's stepmother violently," she informed me with a giggle. "It would replace me needing to kill my husband."

Nancy was obsessively invested in my characters. I seriously hoped she was joking about her husband's untimely demise. Jim was a nice guy from what I remembered.

"My aunt Flip suggested Sasha's stepmom get eaten by pigs," I told her with a wince.

Nancy considered it. "I like it. Messy, but fabulous. Not sure how many pigs live in Manhattan near Sasha's penthouse, but I'm sure you could make it work."

Everyone was insane... made me feel a little better about my own state of mind.

"I'll see what I can do," I promised her.

Nancy leaned across her desk and lowered her voice. "Is your aunt Flip still *gardening?*"

"Umm... possibly. Why?"

Nancy grabbed her purse, dug around inside it and slapped a soggy wad of cash into my hand. She wasn't kidding about the sweating. "I'd like to order some *flowers,*" she whispered. "I read that *flowers* might help with hot flashes. It's the only thing I haven't tried yet. Can you help me out?"

I choked back a giggle. Basically, a drug deal was going down in my lawyer's office. While pot was still illegal in Kentucky, medicinal marijuana was allowed for restricted use. I wasn't sure menopause counted, but I wasn't about to ask. Aunt Flip didn't grow acres of pot, just a few plants as far as I knew. Although, I hadn't been up for a visit in a long while. I was kind of shocked that Nancy was aware of Flip's hobby.

"I'll talk to her," I told Nancy, handing the money back to her.

There was no way in hell I was going to the pokey for

being the middleman in a pot deal. Aunt Flip was cranky and out of her mind, but she was also incredibly generous. She'd be delighted to share her *flowers* with someone in need.

"You are a lifesaver," Nancy said. "And I think Flip was onto something with the pigs."

I disagreed, but Nancy was feeling murderous. Instead of debating why a pack of pigs in Manhattan was an alarming idea, I simply nodded. I was just getting my life back. I didn't want to lose it by having an argument about a fictional character getting eaten by pigs.

"Alrighty then," I said. "I'll see you Friday. Take care, Nancy."

"Friday," Nancy said, clasping her signed books to her sweaty chest. "And if you happen to see your aunt, let her know I'm dying for some *flowers.*"

"Will do," I said, hustling out of the door before she asked for anything else.

Stepping out into the sunshine, I took a deep breath. The metaphorical rainstorm had lasted for four months and six days. It had been violent at times and devastating at others. I'd almost let myself be washed away in the deep puddles.

But I hadn't.

I was still here. I was breathing. I had friends. I had a lovely home and a job I was passionate about. The viral video was old news.

Everything was relative. I'd lambasted myself for feeling hopeless since I was a fortunate person in the scheme of things. I had to let that go.

Pain was pain. Burying it was counterproductive.

Wallowing in it for the rest of my life would also be counterproductive. Four months might be excessive, but I wasn't going to sweat it. It was what it was. I was ready to move on.

Walking to my car in my fashion disaster of an outfit, I felt free. I wasn't quite there logistically, yet, but I was close. The words were flowing, and I'd return my agent's multiple calls today. I'd avoided talking to Cyd for weeks. I didn't have anything to say that she would want to hear.

Today was different. It was a new day. The first day of the rest of my life. I was winning.

"Hello, Clementine," a terse male voice said. A very familiar voice. A voice I didn't want to hear. "We need to talk. Do you have a moment?"

My stomach tightened. I hadn't seen Darren since I'd doused his naked ass with filthy mop water when he was nuts deep in Weather Hooker on our kitchen table that I'd given away. I'd paid a visit to Jess when he'd gone back to the house to get his clothes and other belongings— including his six sets of top-of-the-line golf clubs. Mandy had been at the house to greet him and followed him around to make sure he didn't do anything shitty.

Like banging the blonde where we had eaten dinner for decades wasn't shitty enough.

Darren had insisted on staying at the house until he realized he wasn't going to get a piece of it. He'd been furious when his lawyer had explained the stipulation of the house's ownership set in place by my grandmother and aunt. For a few weeks he'd tried to dispute it, but Granny's will was ironclad.

"Two minutes," I said coolly. "Speak."

Darren seemed a bit taken aback at my tone. I'd always been so damned agreeable. It had been easier.

"It's about my money," he began.

I rolled my eyes. "You mean my money."

He reddened slightly and his eyes narrowed. "I supported you," he hissed. "You couldn't have written those trashy books without me. Half of your money belongs to me. Half of that house belongs to me. Hell, all of it should be mine, but I'm not that much of an asshole."

Actually, he was. How had I stayed with him all these years? I barely recognized him. I mean, he looked the same, but his insides had rotted. What in the hell had happened? Was this somehow my fault?

Nope. This shit was all on him.

"I'm sorry," I said through clenched teeth. "How exactly did you help me write books? By playing golf? By taking ten vacations yearly without me? By getting hair plugs? By banging women young enough to be your daughter? Explain to me how you were instrumental in my career."

Darren seemed shocked by both my words and tone. He recovered quickly. To be honest, I was surprised by myself. Confrontation wasn't my thing in the old days. However, it was no longer the old days.

"I was a *house husband*," Darren said with a devious smile that I was tempted to slap off his handsome face. "I cooked. I cleaned. I devoted *my* life to the advancement of *your* career. I dealt with your craziness. You would be nothing without me. I earned *everything* I'm going to take from you, Clementine."

I laughed. I couldn't help it. The sound was brittle and high-pitched. Darren had never lifted a finger to do a damn thing. Ever. Even in the beginning, I'd done it all. Darren was all for traditional roles in marriage. I was stupid enough to buy into it. That was on me, not him. I'd learned the hard way that an equal partnership was a healthier way to go. Mandy and David had taught me that. Jess's self-worth was also in the right place. She'd never married, but she'd had some terrific relationships over the years. She was friends with her exes. That was not in my future.

Once I'd started making a little money, we'd hired help. Connie had cooked and cleaned for us for the last fifteen years. She was like a second mother to me and had helped out Granny and Aunt Flip for years. I adored her. I was still paying Connie even though I hadn't had her come over in months.

She was pissed as all get out that I insisted on paying her for work she wasn't doing, but I knew she needed the money. Having anyone around feeling sorry for me wasn't working. We'd tried it for a few weeks, and it made me feel worse. Connie called weekly and left silly messages. The woman was golden to me, and I was definitely ready to have her come back. She was going to be delighted at how clean the house was. My agent Cyd, might have a different opinion, since I'd cleaned instead of finishing my book.

Baby steps. I was getting there.

"Glad you find it amusing," Darren snapped. "My lawyers will be in touch."

"Awesome," I said with a thumbs up. "Can't wait for my lawyers to touch back."

I had no clue what Mandy had up her sleeve, but I hoped to hell and back it was good. Darren was a shit. Mr. Ted had offered Darren's lawyer an absurd settlement that I'd agreed to readily. I had just wanted it to be over. He was offered an amount that he could live on for years if he was smart, plus a retirement fund, the five cars he'd amassed and the membership to the country club. The asshole could also get a damned job…

And yet, he wanted more. He wanted everything.

Darren seemed confused by my words and my gesture. Whatever.

"I'd say it was nice to see you, but it wasn't," I said with a polite smile. "And you can stop sending your people over. It doesn't scare me."

Darren glared at me like I was nuts. He behaved as if he had no clue what I was talking about. If I didn't know what an assbag he'd become, I might have believed him. I didn't believe him. I'd come a long way in four months and six days.

"See ya. Wouldn't wanna be ya," I said as I walked away.

CHAPTER SEVEN

"GIVE ME A WEEK OR TWO. I CAN FINISH IT," I SAID TO CYD over the phone. She was breathing like she was having a panic attack.

She wasn't. My New York agent was all bark and no bite. Cyd loved to refer to herself as Drama Mamma. It was accurate. She was also brilliant. Cyd Staples was six feet tall and had a rack that defied gravity, spikey gray hair and lovely deep-set dark brown eyes. She actually made me feel short and petite. My agent had had a few nips and tucks over the years, but she'd gone to a great plastic surgeon. I'd never seen her looking like she'd just walked out of a wind tunnel. We'd been together since my first book. Cyd's input was crucial and I adored her. She didn't like me much at the moment, but I knew she still loved me.

"You're killing me, Smalls," Cyd whined, quoting *The Sandlot*. Quoting movies was her favorite hobby and a conversation rarely went by that she didn't fit in at least a few. "The sales on the first three books are through the roof. I need the fourth. Yesterday."

"And you'll have it soon," I promised, filling Thick Stella's bowl with the wet food she preferred. "I'm finally able to write again."

"Thank God!" she shouted. "Nobody puts Baby in a corner."

"I prefer Clementine," I told her, rolling my eyes.

"Yep, but 'Nobody puts Clementine in a corner' would have ruined my *Dirty Dancing* reference," Cyd explained. "If you're gonna do it, do it right."

"Got it," I said, glancing down at my feet and realizing I was still wearing mismatched flip-flops.

It was beautiful.

"Tell me to shut my cakehole if I'm stepping into Shitsville, but how's the divorce going?" Cyd asked.

"Ongoing," I said, sitting down at the breakfast bar and glancing over at the spot where the kitchen table of sin used to be. "It's moving forward, but Darren's trying to Jerry McGuire me now."

"Lost me," Cyd said, perplexed.

"Seriously?" I asked with a laugh.

"Wait!" she squealed into the phone. "He's pulling a *show me the money?*"

"Bingo."

Cyd groaned. "Men are shits except for my Marty. He's a mensch. I love that sweet bastard. He puts up with me and that's a miracle."

"I put up with you too," I pointed out.

"And I put up with you," she shot right back with a

chuckle. "We're a good team. Take the time you need. I'll deal with the higher-ups. Just send me a damned good book."

"I promise."

"And please kill the living hell out of Sasha's stepmother," Cyd added. "Make it bloody."

"Umm... okay." Clearly, I'd created a villain everyone loved to hate.

"Great!" she yelled. "And remember if you write it, they will buy it."

"That was a bastardized *Field of Dreams* quote," I told her.

"I know. But it was nice. Huh?"

I grinned. "It was nice. Love you."

"Back at you. GET TO WORK."

And on that deafening note, she hung up on me. I seriously needed to remember to put everyone on speakerphone from now on. My eardrums couldn't take the volume much longer.

MY FINGERS SPED ACROSS THE KEYBOARD. MY POSTURE sucked, I'd downed two full-sugared sodas and I was in heaven. When the puzzle pieces started to click it was almost as good as an orgasm. I hadn't had one of those in a while so getting lost in a story was going to have to do.

"Thick Stella," I said, squinting at the screen. "I'm running into a snag with Sasha and Damien. Would make-up sex be a bad choice for the initial bang?"

It was seriously hot, but it didn't feel completely right.

"Maybe I'll off Sasha's stepmother and then go back to the smexy stuff," I muttered, grabbing a sharp pencil and a yellow legal pad. "But I hate writing out of order. My mind gets jumbled. You feel me, Thick Stella?"

"If you kill me with a pack of pigs, I will haunt you till the day you die," a woman said silkily. "Trust me, that would not be pleasant."

"What the hell?" I screamed, slamming my laptop shut, throwing the pad of paper into the air and backing myself up against the wall in my office.

The woman was dressed from head to toe in champagne-pink Chanel. Her vivid green eyes bored holes into my head, and I wanted to kick my own ass. My damn cell phone was in the kitchen. I could make a run for it, but I'd have to knock the intruder out of the way. That was iffy. She was older than me but had on really pointy stilettos that could take an eye out with ease. If she slipped one off and used it as a weapon, I was a goner. That was a semi-ridiculous scenario, but I wasn't going to count out anything right now. Not to mention, the woman was terrifying.

"Who are you and how did you get in my house? The doors are locked," I said, trying to keep my voice steady. It wouldn't do to let her know she made me want to pee my pants. She looked seriously angry.

"I don't use doors," she said, eyeing me like I was beneath her. "And you are quite obviously adverse to using a mirror."

I didn't like that one bit. I was wearing my yoga pants and a Sponge Bob t-shirt—my work uniform. I'd kept on the mismatched flip-flops because they made me happy.

Normally it was Ugg boots or running shoes. She was lucky I was wearing pants at all. Occasionally, I wore men's boxer briefs—not Darren's, mine. I kept a drawerful because they're comfortable and didn't ride up my ass.

The impeccably turned-out grand dame clearly didn't approve of my ensemble. Screw her. This crap was getting old fast. It was time to put an end to it.

"Did Darren send you?" I demanded, grabbing the scissors off my desk and wielding them like I knew how to use them as a weapon. I didn't, but that was for me to know and her to hopefully not find out.

"Don't be ridiculous," she said, sitting down on my couch and crossing her long shapely legs. She wasn't fazed in the least that I was holding pointy metal. "No man has ever told me what to do and no man ever will."

She was ballsy. I liked that in a woman, but she was not supposed to be here. It also didn't bode well that she wasn't afraid of a person in yoga pants with a pair of scissors gripped in her hand.

"What's your name and why are you here?"

Ignoring my question, she removed a cigarette from her Prada clutch and put it between her full ruby-red lips that had to have been enhanced, then waited expectantly. The intruder sighed audibly at my perceived rudeness and eyed me with disgust. "Do you have a light?"

"No can do," I snapped. "There is no smoking in my house. Period."

"How bourgeois," she said dryly, tucking the cigarette back into her bag. "I should have guessed."

I'd had enough of being judged by people I didn't know.

85

Although… she did look kind of familiar. Shit. Not going there again. This was getting absurd.

"Look, lady," I said, keeping my voice steady when all I wanted to do was climb out of the window and get as far away from her as I could. She was not a pleasant woman. "I don't know who you are or why you're here, but you have to leave or I'll call the cops."

"Go ahead," she said, raising a perfectly plucked brow. "I have a few on payroll."

Ballsy was an understatement.

She had to be in her later fifties. She was incredibly well preserved—too well preserved. Her skin and makeup were flawless. Her sable brown hair was thick and fell in shiny layers below her shoulders. Not an inch of excess fat on her long, lean frame. The woman was truly stunning and probably truly insane. While I didn't get a killer vibe from her, she looked like she could do some major damage. Her words were like sharp little daggers.

"Here's the deal," I said, trying again. "If you leave now, I won't report you. But you need to tell Darren to cut the shit. I'm over it."

She pointed a manicured finger at me, stabbing the air with vengeance. "You are an idiot. A simpering fool. I find it shocking that you're the one. I would have assumed it was someone much more cosmopolitan. Someone with style… panache. Not… *you*. This will end in disaster."

"Oh my God. You're heinous," I shouted, narrowing my eyes at the awful piece of work. "You broke into my house, tried to smoke and insulted me. That's not working. Out.

Get the hell out or I will plant the scissors in the middle of your Botoxed forehead."

Would I? No. But it sounded good.

"At least you have a little spirit," she said with an eye roll. "It would have killed me if you were a total dishrag. Honestly, with a spa day, a shopping spree and a salon visit you could be stunning. Not as riveting as I am, but then, no one is."

"I would love to kill you," I muttered, wondering how in the world to get her to leave.

"I'm quite aware of that," she said with a sneer on her lovely face. "However, as I stated plainly when I arrived, if you dare to kill me with a pack of pigs, I'll make your life and afterlife a living hell. Am I clear?"

"Are you insane?"

She smiled. It wasn't pretty. "If anyone would have the answer to that question, it's you, Clementine."

My mouth fell open. The sensation of rabid mice skittering up my spine made me shudder. Cataloging the woman from head to toe, I felt my entire body break out in an icy sweat.

I recognized every single inch of her.

This wasn't happening. It wasn't possible. How had I not known who she was? I'd freaking created her. She was just as gorgeous and vile as I'd written her.

Wait.

This was bullshit.

It had to be a setup.

Cassandra La Pierre was fiction. She'd come from my

ROBYN PETERMAN

imagination. There had to be a rational explanation. Darren must have sent someone who was the spitting image of my character to freak me out again—but Darren didn't know about the pack of pigs. Who knew about killing Sasha's step-mother with a pack of pigs? It had been Aunt Flip's sugges-tion. Aunt Flip wouldn't screw with me like this. She loved me. Yes, she was certifiable, but there wasn't a mean bone in her little body. There was no way in hell she would send a Cassandra La Pierre look-alike to mess with my head.

Who else? Who else knew?

Oh. My. God. Nancy. Dammit, Nancy knew about the pigs. I'd told her this morning at the law office. Could she be the one setting me up to look crazy because I'd cheated off of her spelling test in the third grade? Random, but possible. It had to be her. Although, if it was, she'd worked seriously fast. Nancy seemed to know my characters better than I did. Was she also trying to get me arrested for dealing weed? God, the heinous possibilities were endless. Had Nancy banged my husband too? Was he paying her to screw with my mind?

"Are you going to throw up?" the woman inquired, annoyed. "You look a bit pale."

"Name," I whispered. "Tell me your name. Now."

Again, she rolled her eyes. "This is tedious," she muttered. "You named me, Clementine. What do you think my name is?"

"Cassandra La Pierre?" I choked out, pinching my arm to see if I was awake or dreaming.

Unfortunately, I was awake and would be sporting a bruise on my arm later.

88

"Bingo," she purred. "You've been warned. Do not kill me with a pack of pigs. Am I clear? I'd prefer a more dignified death—one in which I'm not disfigured."

Dammit, I'd carried that exact thought in my head for a week. How in the hell did she know I wasn't going to disfigure her? It wasn't written anywhere, and I hadn't told a soul. I nodded at her. I was afraid if I spoke, I would start screaming and be unable to stop.

"Excellent," she said, rising gracefully to her feet. "I shall let myself out. Remember... I'll be watching you."

Her stilettos clicked sharply on the hardwood floor as she walked out of my office in a huff. I didn't breathe until I heard the front door slam behind her. My legs felt like wet noodles as I slid down the wall and landed with a thud on the floor.

"That didn't happen," I whispered, clasping my hands together so they'd stop shaking. "It's not possible."

I had no clue how long I sat on the floor. It could have been a minute. It could have been hours. The ringing of my cell phone in the kitchen yanked me out of my state of shock. Crawling through the house because my legs were still iffy, I answered the call.

"The dark of the moon is here for the next three days," Aunt Flip shouted with excitement. "Need to get my perm."

"What are you talking about?" I croaked out in a voice that sounded ragged and foreign to my own ears.

"What's wrong with you, Clemmy?" she demanded. "Sounds like you swallowed your dang tongue."

"I... umm... I—" I couldn't form a coherent thought or speak a single word. But I could cry, and I did.

"God durnit," Aunt Flip bellowed through the line. "Somethin's wrong. I'm drivin' in. Be there soon."

"I'm insane," I whispered.

"You're in pain?" she yelled, misunderstanding.

"No. I think I've lost it."

"Nah," Aunt Flip yelled. "You're gonna be fine. Nothing that a little toke and a talk can't solve. Shoulda talked to you sooner. Don't you go nowhere. Aunt Flip is a-coming."

"Okay," I said as I hung up and curled into a ball on the floor.

If Cassandra La Pierre was real, maybe Clark Dark was real. That meant demons and werewolves were real.

No. Freaking. Way.

Was it possible that Purple Gal was from the shitty Regency I'd written at the beginning of my career? I didn't have the energy to search my shelves for the paperback to find out. Maybe being alone in my grief for four months had sent me over the edge. Maybe Darren had won.

Thick Stella plopped herself down by my head and purred. It was the nicest she'd ever been to me. The world was definitely ending.

Sleep. I'd take a quick nap on the kitchen floor with my cat and when I woke up, I'd realize all of the madness had been a dream.

Probably not, but one could hope.

CHAPTER EIGHT

"So, you say Clark in the Dark is a werewolf?" Aunt Flip asked, perplexed, sitting at my desk.

"Yes, but he was in his human form. He was very polite. I tried to give him money and he wouldn't take it," I replied, not bothering to correct her on his name. She already called him Bark Fark and Nark Hark. The name was irrelevant. The fact he had been here, or that I *thought* he'd paid me a visit was the issue.

"And he bit you?"

"Umm... no. He lied to me... I think. Cassandra La Pierre threatened me."

"*She* bit you?"

I blew out a frustrated sigh and wanted to take back everything I'd just overshared. The conversation was going nowhere fast. "No one bit me."

"Well, now, I don't see the problem if you weren't bitten,"

she said. "And from what I recall, Pepe Le Pew is a skunk. I'd suggest not tangling with a polecat."

About to give up and commit myself somewhere, I tried three more times to explain to my aunt what had been happening—or what I *thought* had been happening. However, when I listened to the words leave my lips, they were so absurd, I laughed. The laughter verged on hysteria, but it was better than crying or rocking in a corner. Getting a full sentence out was impossible. Aunt Flip laughed right along with me even though she had no clue what I was talking about. Hell, I wasn't sure what I was talking about.

"I'm thinkin' you've got the woowoo juju," Aunt Flip said, still chuckling while rolling a joint on my desk.

It had taken her thirty-two minutes to get to my house. She lived an hour away. Aunt Flip had to have driven ninety miles an hour. The old woman had clearly rushed out of her house since she was wearing an orange floral muumuu that swallowed her small frame, pink socks and brown Birkenstock sandals... or maybe it was how she always dressed. It had been a while since I'd seen her.

My brain was so muddled, I was sure I'd misunderstood what she'd just said. At least, I hoped I had.

"Are you high?" I asked, shaking my head in confusion.

I knew my aunt was whacky, but woowoo juju was a little much even for her.

"Course, I'm high," she said, offering me the joint.

"No thanks," I said, holding up my hand. "Could you define woowoo juju? Is it a disease? Is it contagious?"

Aunt Flip cackled like I'd just told a hilarious joke. She removed a large plastic container of brownies from her oversized hemp bag and put them on the desk. She carefully took one out and began to nibble on it.

"Kinda hard to explain woowoo juju. Hits all of us different."

"All of us?" I asked, tempted to grab a brownie. I was sure they were pot brownies, so I refrained. Being stoned wouldn't be helpful. I was already losing my shit.

"Your granny and me... and now you. Passed your mamma right up. That one had no imagination at all," she said with a little shrug. "Thought if you were gonna have the woowoo juju it would have shown up before now. It hit your Granny and me when we turned thirty."

Taking the brownie from her hand and putting it back into the container, I squatted down to eye level. "I'm seeing the characters I've written in my books come to life... I think. Does that count as woowoo juju? Does it mean I hallucinate?" I asked, wondering why I was treating this as a serious conversation. Although, any excuse other than I was bonkers would work for me right now. I wasn't sure woowoo juju was any better than being certifiable, but it was something. It had a name. It could be defined and hope-fully cured.

"Hooooo weeeee!" Aunt Flip said, raising her bony hand up for a high five. "That's a new one. Never heard of that."

I slapped her hand weakly, then walked over to the couch and flopped down on it. "I was sure Darren was sending people to scare me, now... I'm not as sure."

"That son of a bitch is a suppressor," Aunt Flip said, nodding her head. "Probably why it's startin' for you now."

"What?" I asked, needing to understand. "*What* is starting for me?"

Aunt Flip spoke slower and louder—like I was five or hard of hearing. "The... woo... woo... ju... ju," she yelled.

"Got that," I said with a wince. Aunt Flip was a complicated old gal. She was also high. Getting a straight answer from her was going to take some work. "So, umm... you and Granny had woowoo juju?" I felt silly, but let that go fast.

"Yep," she said, firing up her joint. "I still got it."

While I'd told Cassandra La Pierre that there was no smoking in my house, Aunt Flip could do whatever she wanted as long as she helped me figure out what was going on and told me how to put an end to it.

"Mmmkay." I was hoping for a little more of an expansive answer. "And how does this woowoo juju affect you?"

Aunt Flip eyed me for a long moment while holding her breath to make the most of her toke. "What do you know about psychic abilities, Clemmy-girl?"

"I wrote a vampire series where they could teleport," I told her. "One of them could set fires by blinking her eyes."

"Nice," she said with an approving nod of her head. "Coulda helped you with that one."

This wasn't going well. Either Aunt Flip thought she could start fires with her eyeballs or she was trying to tell me she could astral project herself. Neither were possible. The weed had messed with her brain cells.

I nodded and decided I was on my own in Crazy Town. If I kept talking to Flip, I might buy property and stay. Trying a hypnotist was a potential plan. I'd have to go a few towns over since I didn't want word of my mental demise getting out. The problem was with me. Darren hadn't sent people to scare me. I was imagining them. From what Flip was saying, it obviously ran in the family. Awesome.

"Okay, then," I said, giving up and reaching for my cell phone to call the salon and make a perm appointment. "You want to stay over? I can take you to get your hair done in the morning."

"You don't believe me," she said, raising a brow. At least I thought she did. She exhaled at the same time and was eclipsed in a cloud of smoke.

"Does it matter?" I asked, feeling incredibly tired.

"Nah," Aunt Flip said. "Don't matter a bit, Clemmy." She stood up and tucked her brownies back into her bag. "I'd love to stay the night. I'll make hotdogs for supper. Be just like old times."

I smiled. As kooky as she was, I adored her and I'd missed her. "Umm… Aunt Flip?"

"Yep, sugar?"

"Could I give some of those brownies to a gal going through menopause? She's having a heck of a time with hot flashes," I explained. "She's willing to pay."

"Absolutely, and I don't want no money," Flip said, pulling the container back out and putting it on my desk. "Tell her to go easy. These are some strong brownies."

"Will do." I got up and gave her a hug.

She felt small and frail in my arms. While my mind might be spiraling out of control, this moment was real. Aunt Flip wrapped her arms around me and held me tight. It was beautiful.

"You're gonna be just fine, Clemmy girl," she whispered. "Aunt Flip's back to make sure of it."

Unsure whether to sigh with relief or shudder in terror, I just hugged her back. You could pick your nose and you could pick your friends. Your family was what it was… and mine was whackadoo.

As odd as my aunt was, she didn't think I was nuts. That might be because she only had one oar in the water. But she was mine. I was keeping her.

"I'm going to take a quick nap," I told her, walking back over to the couch. "It's been a long day so far."

"Why don't you go on up to your bedroom?" she asked, gathering up her bag and putting her weed away.

"Better in here," I told her. "It's my safe place."

Aunt Flip nodded and smiled. "You got hotdogs?"

Did I? Probably not. Hotdogs weren't something Jess would bring over. "I don't think I do," I told her, grabbing a light blanket from the back of the couch and getting comfortable.

"No worries," Flip said. "Got a few customers in town I need to visit. I'll stop by the grocery store on the way back."

My stomach felt a little queasy. "Umm… is that smart?" I asked, wondering if I was going to have to bail her out of the pokey.

Aunt Flip laughed. "Don't you worry your pretty head about nothing," she assured me. "Aunt Flip is mighty good at what she does."

The fact that she'd referenced herself in third person several times was worrisome. The knowledge that she was driving into town to sell *flowers* was flat-out alarming.

"You're a criminal," I told her with a giggle.

"Only a criminal if I get caught," she said over her shoulder before she closed my office door behind her.

She had a point.

It wasn't exactly a good point.

But it was a point.

CHAPTER NINE

"I am in need of an Abigail," a woman fretted. "I must find one immediately."

"Get off of my face," I mumbled to Thick Stella, trying to pry open my eyes. I was slightly allergic to my cat, and she'd napped right next to my head on the couch. Who was talking? Had Aunt Flip left the TV on?

"Don't have apoplexy, Clementine. I am nowhere near your head. And if I was, I'm far too well bred to sit on your face. The constable would be bloody horrified," she cried out. "I'm so upset I could cast one up."

My eyes shot open and my body jerked to a sitting position. I knew that voice. Thick Stella hissed and took a swipe at me. My cat was an asshole. "Purple Gal," I snapped. "What are you doing here?"

Purple Gal was now Turquoise Gal. She'd changed her frock. It was as low cut and over the top as the last gown— full of taffeta ruffles and a bow at the back the size of a two-year-old child. If she was indeed from the Regency novel I'd written, her outfit was proof as to why it had failed. It was godawful.

"What do you mean?" she inquired, offended. Her hands fluttered nervously and her expression was forlorn.

Slowly getting to my feet, I approached her. If she was a figment of my imagination, she would not be flesh and blood. She backed away and eyed me suspiciously.

"I don't lean that way," she said.

"What way?" I asked, not following.

She sighed and pulled a pale turquoise hanky from her ample creamy-white bosom and dramatically fanned herself. "While I find you quite fetching, I enjoy the company of men."

"Oh my God. You think I'm hitting on you?" I asked with a surprised laugh.

"You're going to *hit* me?" she demanded, appalled. "I didn't think you would do such a thing, Clementine. I'm but a defenseless incomparable. My beauty is renowned. And yes, I can see why you would desire me, but alas, I am taken. Let it be spoken aloud, I am flattered by your misplaced desire. It's beyond obvious that I am quite alluring and a pink of the ton."

Letting my chin fall to my chest, I groaned. Her Regency speak was like a foreign language. If I'd written that crap, I deserved every shitty review I'd gotten. "I am *not* making advances toward you," I assured her. "I'm just trying to see if you're real or imaginary."

She threw her head back and laughed. Again, it sounded like bells. Again, I thought I heard birds chirping. Covertly, I glanced over at my floor-to-ceiling bookshelves. I was sure a copy of the Regency was over there somewhere.

"I'm quite real," she said. "And quite amiable."

Bingo. It was on the second shelf from the bottom in the middle. I nodded to amiable Turquoise Gal and casually walked over to the bookshelf. Pretending like I was simply browsing so it wouldn't be obvious I was trying to figure out what the hell her name might be, I pulled the book out in between a few others. If she got all butthurt again and started crying, I'd lose it. Since I didn't have much more to lose, I was playing it cool.

"Holy hell," I muttered. The title sucked as badly as the book had—*Scandalous Sensual Desires of the Wicked Ones on Selby Street*. Whatever. It was my first book in a genre I wasn't supposed to write. Keeping my back to Turquoise, I scanned the back cover looking for a damn name.

I giggled. "Really?" I asked myself. "I mean, *really*?"

Cyd should have dropped me as a client after this one, but I suppose she'd seen something worthwhile in me. Thank God for small favors.

"Is there a problem, Clementine? Your countenance seems amused."

"No," I said quickly, turning to face her and hiding the book behind my back. I weighed my options. If I called her by the name on the book jacket, and she answered to it, that meant I was insane. If she didn't answer to it, it meant she was insane and most likely a stalker.

Calling the police was off the table until I was certain which one of us needed help. It was a fifty-fifty shot in the dark at this point.

Here went nothing... "Albinia Knightley Wynch," I said, wincing at the awful name I'd assigned to my very first heroine.

Her face lit up with delight, making her even more ridiculously lovely than she already was. My face paled considerably and my stomach dropped to my toes. It was becoming increasingly clear I was the one with the mental imbalance.

"*Lady* Albinia Knightley Wynch," she corrected me with a deep and graceful curtsy. "I am at your service as long as there is no buggering involved. Horace Skevington would not be pleased."

"Wait. What? I named the hero *Horace Skevington?*"

"No, silly goose," she said with a shudder of delight. "The constable is named Horace Skevington!"

"I'm so confused," I said, sitting on the edge of my desk and scanning the blurb. "The hero is Onslow Bolingbroke. Why are you all atwitter about the constable?"

Albinia's face fell and big crocodile tears rolled down her attractively blushed cheeks. "You don't remember?"

"Don't cry," I said, shoving a box of tissues into her hands. "I've had a long day and it sucked. And in my defense, I wrote your story about fifteen years ago. I can barely recall what I ate yesterday. You feel me?"

She nodded and dabbed at her eyes with a tissue. "Yes, I see how that might be a quandary. Shall I enlighten you?"

I closed my eyes. I still wasn't sure she was real. However, if she stayed long enough, maybe Aunt Flip would get home from dealing pot in town and would see her. Or maybe only I could see her. That would be a bummer. But if

Flip could see Albinia, she might know how to get rid
of her.

"Sure. Enlighten me."

It was a statement I would live to regret.

Two hours later...

"So, let me get this straight," I said, pressing the bridge of
my nose to ward off the headache that was coming on.
Albinia had yacked nonstop. My mouth had hung open
through most of it. Only small bits and pieces came back to
me. There was a reason I'd blocked the book out. It was
horrifying. "I spent the entire novel having you flirt with the
hero Onslow Bolingbroke, accept his proposal and then at
the end, you left Onslow at the alter to bang Horace Skevington, the freaking constable?"

"Yes! The ending was a shock to all of us. But I must say,
while Horace may be cucumberish and a bit of a whippersnapper, he is excellently well-hung and quite the joy to
bugger."

"I only understood part of that sentence," I muttered,
wondering what the hell I'd been thinking to have the
heroine bang the constable. "So, are you still with Horace
Skevington?"

I couldn't help myself. My morbid curiosity got the best
of me. I had no plans to ever read the book again, but I
needed to know a few more things.

"Oh yes," Albinia said with a coy smile. "Unless you write
the sequel and tear us asunder."

"No worries there," I promised her. "That was a one and
done. What about Onslow Bolingbroke? Do you guys run
into him... wherever you, you know, umm... live?"

Albinia leaned in and whispered, "Not often. And it's incredibly awkward when we do. He's quite the zany and never yoked."

I glanced around in terror. Was Onslow Bolingbroke about to show up and rip me a new butthole for making him look like an ass and a zany—whatever that was? I sighed in defeat, then laughed. I had accepted the crazy with open arms. I was having a conversation with someone who'd come from my imagination. Maybe I was like Sybil from the novel by Flora Rheta Schreiber and had hundreds of personalities. Granted, I'd suffered no abuse whatsoever in my childhood. My parents were awesome if not a little on the boring side. But they loved their only daughter a lot.

Nope. I was just plain nuts… and kind of hungry. My stomach growled and I realized I hadn't eaten anything all day.

"Albinia, can I get you something to eat?" I asked. "Unless you ate all the Grape Nuts, I can fix you a bowl."

"Not to worry!" she said with a wide smile. "Your kindness is duly noted. I'm not at all famished since I indulged in a tiny nibble of the cakey chocolate squares whilst you snored in your slumber."

"I don't snore," I snapped.

"I beg to differ," she replied so politely, I refrained from headbutting her. "But I must say, the cakey chocolate squares were delightfully moist."

"Oh my God, do not use that word," I said, cringing.

"Cakey?" she asked, alarmed.

"No."

"Chocolate?" she tried again.

"No."

"Which word?" she inquired, delicately wrinkling her nose in confusion.

I rolled my eyes. There were only a few words in the English language that made me itch violently. *Moist* was one of them. "Moist," I choked out. "Do not say that."

"But it's such a lovely, descriptive word," she replied.

Pressing my lips together so I wouldn't swear at her, a devious little thought popped into my head. "Yes," I said, nodding slowly. "While it *is* descriptive, it doesn't mean what it used to mean."

"Oh dear," Albinia said, fanning herself with the copy of the novel she had starred in. "Whatever does moist mean now?"

"Adventuress," I lied, wildly proud that I recalled the meaning of a Regency word. "If you say moist, you're referring to yourself as a prostitute."

"How dreadful," she gasped out, paling. "I would like to thank you for your generous concern of my reputation."

"Umm... welcome," I said, then froze. "Did you say you ate a brownie?"

"I did," she nodded. "Delicious."

"How many?" I tried not to laugh.

She blushed and glanced down demurely. "I must say it wasn't very ladylike of me, but they were so moi... succulent, I indulged in three—just a tiny nibble whilst you slept then the rest while we had our lovely chat."

"Shit," I muttered. I hadn't even seen her eat them. Of course, my eyes were closed in agony as I learned of the plot

I'd written all those years ago. "Do you have to be anywhere in the next few hours?"

"No. Why?"

"You'll see."

Albinia had been laughing hysterically for seventy-four minutes. My head was pounding and Thick Stella had left my office in a huff. Albinia's formerly pristine turquoise gown was now a wrinkled mess. My new and possibly imaginary buddy was wearing the enormous bow on her head and had shredded the hem of her taffeta monstrosity by rolling around on the floor.

"Aunt Flip wasn't kidding when she said the brownies were strong," I muttered, eating potato chips and keeping an eye on Albinia so she didn't seriously injure herself. "You done yet?"

"Sooooooo silly," she squealed. "Thankyouforgivinghoracesuchahugemember. Soooooo silly! Woooooonderrrrful."

I was pretty sure she'd just thanked me for blessing Horace with an impressive man tool. Maybe I should read the book. And maybe not. I wasn't that much of a glutton for punishment. Having any kind of conversation with Albinia about why she'd shown up was impossible. The logical side of my brain wondered if I was summoning characters from my mind who could help me with my current situation. It didn't change the fact that I was losing it, but it was a much easier way to frame it.

"Moooooist," Albinia shouted, laughing so hard, I was sure she would choke.

"What did I tell you about that word?" I demanded. It was one thing to hang out with a proper Regency woman stoned out of her mind. It was entirely another to hear her say the icky word.

"Moooooist," she repeated. "It's woooooonderrrrful to say hoooorid words!"

"Well, that certainly backfired on me," I said, wondering if I could knock out a chapter or two while she was shrieking and rolling around. Probably not. I liked it quiet when I wrote.

"I feel like a chit," she snorted. "I'm spewing such bloody claptrap! The costermonger never sold such wonderful cakey chocolate squares. I must have the recipe! I would like to indulge in them when I'm next in the midst of my courses."

I couldn't be positive, but I was pretty sure she'd just told me she wanted to eat pot brownies the next time she was on the rag. Glancing at the time on my phone, I realized Aunt Flip had been gone for a few hours. She'd be shit out of luck if she was in jail. She'd have to wait for me to bail her out until Albinia was a little less high.

Wait. What the hell was the matter with me? Albinia wasn't real. She definitely looked real and she'd torn my office apart. There were books strewn all over the place. She was now wearing a lampshade on her head. From the same lamp I'd almost nailed her with on her first visit. She felt the bow was a little much for someone of her breeding and decided the lampshade was more fitting. I actually agreed with her. The bow was awful.

"Oh my," Albinia said, getting to her feet clumsily. "What a wonderful visit this has been. Do you mind if I take a chocolate cakey square to Horace? I think he would love it."

"Knock yourself out," I told her.

"Thank you, Clementine," she replied, tucking about five into her cleavage.

"Welcome." I was tempted to tell her that shoving pot brownies between her boobs was a bad plan, but her dress was such a mess now, it didn't matter.

"Toodaloo," she sang as she skipped out of my office. "And remember, apples never fall far from trees!"

"Is that supposed to mean something to me?" I asked. Albinia was full of annoying truisms.

"I have no clue," she replied, giggling. "Does it?"

"No."

"Then there is your answer," she said, making sure the chocolate cakey squares were secure in her cleavage. "See you soon."

"Right," I muttered as I began to pick up all the books she'd pulled out as the still high woman skipped happily out of my office and out the front door.

Where was she going? Did she somehow reenter the book? Was there a portal in the yard that sucked up my characters, then spit them back out when they wanted to stop by? I didn't think there were any ley lines in Kentucky.

I was losing it. Laying out a plot that I would use in a paranormal romance and applying it to my real life was not an activity a sane person should indulge in. Hence, I was cuckoo.

That was nuts. All of it. Pausing my cleanup, I grabbed my phone and took pictures of the evidence that Lady Albinia Knightley Wynch had been here. I had no clue what I'd use it for other than my own personal proof that she actually was in my office, stoned out of her gourd. There was still a chance she was a stalker. I didn't believe it, but I was hanging on to an explanation that didn't make me the batshit crazy one.

Good luck… to me.

CHAPTER TEN

"You want another weenie?" Aunt Flip asked, holding out a plate with eight burned hotdogs on it.

"No. I don't want another weenie, but thanks," I told her. It had been difficult enough to choke down one. They were literally crunchy.

Aunt Flip had gotten home about an hour after Albinia had made her exit. She'd complained about her bald spot the entire time she'd charred the hell out of the hotdogs. There wasn't a moment for me to get a word in. I wasn't sure that I wanted to share the tale of my latest visit from an imaginary friend, but it would have been nice to have had the chance.

"There's a sixty-seven percent chance that getting a perm will make all my hair fall out," Aunt Flip explained, snacking on a hockey-puck-like hotdog. "That's why I figure if we hit it during the dark of the moon, my follicles will survive."

I wasn't quite sure how to respond to that, so I didn't. I was still mulling over Albinia's unannounced visit. She had definitely gotten high from the cakey chocolate squares. If Albinia wasn't real, could she have gotten stoned? Had I *made* it happen since I knew they were pot brownies? The questions far outweighed the answers. Hell, there were no answers to be found.

Thankfully, Flip wasn't looking for a response from me.

"I do have a nice Cher wig I could wear, though," she said.

I squinted at her and tried not to laugh. "I'm sorry, what?"

"Cher wig," she repeated. "I look like a million bucks in it. Got a few Dolly Partons too, but since I'm a natural brunette, I look better in the Cher."

She was a solid, steely gray, but I wasn't going to point that out. Time for a change of subject. I was a little terrified that she might feel the need to sing "Gypsies, Tramps and Thieves." Being that she was tone deaf, that would be seriously bad. "So… umm… how did your *visits* in town go?"

"Fandamntastic," Flip assured me with a thumbs up. "Lots of good folks were mighty happy to see me."

"I'm sure they were," I said, shaking my head and grinning. There was only one Flip and the mold had been broken after she was born eighty-five years ago.

Flip scurried around the kitchen wrapping up the leftovers. I was tempted to tell her to toss the scorched weenies, but refrained. She seemed to enjoy them.

"Well," I said, standing up and feeling kind of lost. "I guess I should try to get some words on the page."

"Not gonna happen," Flip said, putting the runny baked beans she'd made into a Ziploc bag. "You're too wound up. Will you eat these beans tomorrow?"

"Probably not," I told her, taking them from her and putting them into a plastic container. The plastic baggie was a messy accident waiting to happen. I was proud of myself for not gagging. My aunt had put half a bottle of ketchup, a cup of maple syrup, six heaping tablespoons of brown sugar, an equal amount of white sugar, a full jar of bacon bits and cayenne pepper into the beans. It was the kind of concoction that would put a person on the toilet for half the night making deals with Jesus.

"I'll pop them in the fridge just in case," she told me. "Beans, beans they're good for your heart! The more you eat…" She waited for my participation with a wide grin.

"The more you fart," I said with a giggle.

"That's right! The more you fart…"

I rolled my eyes but let my inner second-grade boy come to the surface. "The better you feel. So, eat them beans at every meal," I finished.

"That's my girl," Aunt Flip said, grabbing my hand and dragging me to the living room.

When Granny and Aunt Flip had lived here, it was far more formal. After I'd inherited the house, I'd filled it with comfortable furniture—overstuffed chairs and couches in florals and stripes. Darren hadn't cared what the house looked like. As long as he had his golf, he was fine with whatever I chose décor-wise.

The once white plaster walls were now a washed forest green. The overall color scheme looked like a muted spring flower garden. It was peaceful and welcoming. I'd kept a few of Granny's antique tables and lamps. The soft, colorful afghans that Aunt Flip had made lived all over the place.

"What are we doing?" I asked as the tiny woman sat down on the couch and patted the seat next to her.

"We're gonna talk. Your knickers are in such a tight knot, you're gonna end up with another hole in your rump," she told me.

"That was an unfortunately descriptive observation," I pointed out, sitting next to her.

"You can have it for a book," she offered. "It would be a great line for Sasha to say to her stepmother."

I laughed. The expression on Cassandra La Pierre's face would be priceless. Of course, thanks to my insanity, I could picture the expression on her face.

Letting my chin fall to my chest, I sighed. I wasn't sure where to start. I'd already tried and it hadn't gone too well.

"Hang on," Aunt Flip said, hopping up off the couch and running out of the room. "Gonna make this easier for you, Clemmy."

"The easiest thing would be to tell me how to make it stop," I called after her. "You know, like undoing it. Maybe we could un-juju woowoo me."

"Not the way it works. And it's woowoo juju, not juju woowoo," she yelled from my office. "Holy shit on a stick. How many brownies did you eat?"

She walked back into the living room with a shocked expression on her beautifully wrinkled face.

"None," I told her. "Lady Albinia Knightley Wynch ate three and left with about five tucked into her cleavage."

"She's a witch, you say?" Aunt Flip asked, still staring at the half-empty container.

"Nope. Her name is Lady Albinia Knightley Wynch. She's not a witch. I'm not even sure she's real."

Flip set the brownies on the coffee table and sat back down. "Awful name. She should take that up with her mamma."

"That would be me in a roundabout way," I said, agreeing about the name. It sucked. Just like the rest of the novel.

"What in tarnation?" Flip shouted. "You had a baby and didn't tell me? I would have stopped you from givin' that child such a shitty name. And I must say, I find it a little surprising that you'd let your baby eat weed brownies."

I blew out a long breath, grabbed a brownie and decided to loosen up a little. The cakey chocolate squares had certainly loosened up Lady Albinia Knightley Wynch. "No, I didn't have a baby. Darren's swimmers didn't swim very well. Albinia is one of my characters. She's imaginary."

Aunt Flip scratched her sparsely haired head. "That's debatable," she said. "Did Alhoona get high as a kite?"

"Affirmative," I said, declining to correct the name. Alhoona might have been a better choice than Albinia... or not.

"Welp, she's real then."

Taking a huge bite of the brownie, I sat back and waited for it to kick in. If I was going to have a ridiculous conversation, I needed some chemical help.

"You're gonna want to take a bigger bite," Flip suggested.

"For real?" I asked, taking another.

"Two more bites," she told me. "We're gonna get deep."

"How deep?" I asked.

"Real deep."

I shoved the entire rest of the brownie into my mouth. "Fine. How long till this crap kicks in?"

"Give it fifteen minutes."

Nine minutes and forty seconds later…

"HOLY SHIT! I can't believe I thought these were disgusting," I said with a mouthful of charred hotdog. "Little hard to chew, but really tasty."

"What you need to do is take a sip of soda, then take a bite of the weenie with the soda still in your mouth," Aunt Flip advised, showing me her method. "The carbonation in the soda helps break down the crunchy outer layer. Let's you get right to the goodness inside faster. And you won't chip a tooth."

The technique was outstanding. I was able to eat two more weenies without choking and my teeth were perfectly intact.

It was hilarious—the most hilarious moment of my life thus far. Not really, but it sure as hell felt like it.

Flip had wisely supplied snacks. When the pot kicked in, I was so hungry I could have eaten my own hand. After laughing hysterically for fifty-two minutes straight about the dust bunny under the couch—who I named Bubba—I had almost worn myself out.

"Aunt Flip, how much weed is in the cakey chocolate squares?" I wheezed, laughing and trying to stop myself from floating out of my body.

"A lot," she replied with a cackle. "You feelin' good now?"

"Sooooo good," I told her, thinking I needed to pee but

couldn't recall if I had indoor plumbing. "Are my lips bubbled?"

Aunt Flip examined my face carefully. "Nope. Lips are good."

I touched them to make sure they were still attached to my face. They were. Everything was fine.

"Freeeeeee," I sang. "I'm freeeeeee!"

"Yes, you are, darlin' girl," Flip agreed with a chuckle. "You ready to talk?"

"About the wooju wawa?" I asked, trying to focus while the area rug rolled like gentle waves under my feet.

Flip grinned and nodded. "Close enough. Your granny and me always knew you had it, but it sure showed up late."

I took a bite of the cold, sugary beans. Damn, they were delicious. "You guys were thirty when you got smacked with the juju?"

"Yep, right after the pigpen accident," she confided as her eyes grew wide with horror.

"The pigpen accident?" I asked, leaning in so the walls wouldn't eavesdrop. Walls were notoriously nosey.

Flip ran her hands through her thinning hair and sighed. "Yep. Bad day."

"How bad?" I asked, wanting to hear the story yet knowing I would regret asking.

"Real dang bad. Suffice it to say, Roger the mailman lost one leg, part of his ass and most of his left hand," she whispered with a shudder. "Nastiest damn thing I ever witnessed. Pigs are evil. That's why we're eatin' turkey dogs. After the porcine bloodbath, I quit pig."

"Did he live?"

"Nah, after the killer pigs took some gnarly bites out of Roger, they decided to eat each other. It was a hot damned shitshow. Still have nightmares about that one even fifty-five years after the fact."

The visuals were not good. "Umm... I meant Roger. Did he live?"

"Sure did," she said with a relieved sigh. "He don't deliver the mail no more. But he's got him a nice fake leg and he can even tap dance on it."

"You still know Roger?" I was trying to imagine an old man with a fake leg tap dancing. It was kind of fabulous.

"Hell to the yes," Flip said. "Saw him this afternoon."

"Roger's a customer?"

She winked and shimmied. "Something like that."

I gagged a little on the beans and pushed the plate of extra-crispy turkey dogs away. My appetite had disappeared as fast as it had arrived. I was delighted for Aunt Flip's implied sex life with the man who her killer pigs had tried to murder, but didn't want the details. "Mmmkay," I said, sobering slightly. "What does Roger's dismemberment by pigs have to do with juju?"

"Everything," Flip said, sounding very serious. "Woowoo juju is often brought on by external disasters—like killer pigs."

I didn't have killer pigs. Shaking my head, I tried to think linearly. Having cannibal pigs stuck in my frontal lobe wasn't helping. I needed something logical. Something that could rationally explain my cray-cray.

"Can you define woowoo juju?" I asked, making a mental list and attempting to check off the important points.

"Magic—all different kinds," Flip said. "All women have it, but only some of us can access it. Woowoo juju keeps the world in balance."

"So, I can make it go away by deciding I don't want it anymore?" I asked, grabbing the last turkey dog and nibbling on it.

Flip's brow wrinkled in thought. "Nah, once you got the juju, you got the juju."

Dipping the weenie into the beans to give it a little kick, I sighed. "That's not good news."

"Course it is," she said, slapping me on the back. "It's a gift. Never look a gift horse in the ass."

"Mouth," I corrected her.

"Your mouth is fine," she assured me.

"No, I meant…" I started, then decided not to go there. It would be bad to look a horse in the ass as well as the mouth. Flip had made a solid point. "So, I just need to get used to it?"

"You're gonna need to embrace it," she said. "And I'm here to help you."

Did I believe in magic? I wrote about it daily. I'd created worlds with witches, vampires, werewolves and demons. I'd strayed from the traditional tropes about the supernatural world and built my own fantasy universes following my warped imagination. It was a lovely place to live and I adored my characters. I did truly feel like they were real. I just didn't think they actually were real…

"What's your… umm… magic?" I asked, feeling slightly ridiculous. If we were going to go there, we should go all the way.

Flip grinned. "I have a few tricks in my bag," she said. "Like?"

Flip stared at me for a long moment as if she was trying to gauge my proximity to the edge of the cliff. Clearly deciding that I wasn't going to jump off, she went for it.

"Fire is one of them. I can control it."

I laughed in disbelief. She didn't.

Pulling a rolled joint from her pocket, Flip held it up. Narrowing her eyes like she was pissed at the wacky tabacky, she stared at it. In a matter of seconds, the joint was lit.

My mouth fell open. How did she do that?

"Again," I insisted, pushing an orchid-scented candle on the coffee table towards her.

Flip chuckled and glared at the wick. It fired up just as fast.

"How?" I demanded, feeling antsy. "That's impossible."

"Magic is like faith, little girlie," Flip explained. "You can't always see it, but it's always there. Woowoo juju makes the world a little prettier."

I wasn't sure how being threatened by Cassandra La Pierre made the world a prettier place, but I couldn't deny what I'd just seen. Blaming it on the laced cakey chocolate squares would have been logical, but I wasn't stoned anymore.

I was just...

Hell, I didn't know what I was.

Pressing the bridge of my nose and feeling the high fade into exhaustion, I smiled at my nutty aunt. "I love you. I'm still not sure that I haven't lost my damn mind, but thank you."

Aunt Flip leaned over and kissed my cheek. "Your mind is a beautiful place to be," she whispered. "You're just gonna have to open it a little wider."

I yawned. I was pretty sure Flip might be as off her rocker as I was, but it was nice to have someone to talk to even if the conversations were mind-bogglingly bizarre.

"I'm going to sleep in my office," I told Flip, giving her a quick hug and blowing out the candle. "Can you stay for a while?"

"Sure thing, baby girl," she said, gathering up what was left of the stoned feast and walking it back to the kitchen. "You busy tomorrow night?"

I laughed at the question. Going anywhere except to see Mr. Ted had not been on the agenda for four months. "Nope. You want to have a gin rummy evening?"

Granny and Flip had taught me how to play cards when I was six. I loved playing cards to this day. My favorite was a contract gin rummy game called I Buy, but we needed more than two people to play.

"Liking the sound of that," Flip said. "I can make meat twinkies."

"I *really* don't want to ask, but what the hell is a meat twinkie?"

Flip cackled and shook her head. "Everyone knows what a meat twinkie is, Clemmy. Where you been?"

I racked my brain. Nope. No meat twinkies hiding in the recesses. "Everyone does *not* know what a meat twinkie is," I said. "Define, please."

"It's a corndog!" she yelled with glee. "Except I make my meat twinkies with turkey dogs on account of my swearing off the pig."

"Got it," I said. "Meat twinkies and I Buy it is. I'll see if Jessica can come over."

Aunt Flip held her hand up. "Not so fast. I wanna take you to a meeting before the cards and meat twinkies."

"A meeting?" I asked warily.

"It's a support group," she explained.

"For?" I pressed. Both Granny and Flip had always been famous for leaving out important details when it suited them.

"For woowoo juju," she announced, as if that was normal. "More like a club, but we call it a support group to get a discount on the conference room at the library."

"There are more insane people than just us?" I was shocked. Kind of happy but mostly terrified.

"You bet your bippy," she said with a wink. "It's a real nice bunch of gals. You're gonna love feeling not as alone."

I shook my head. "I really don't think that's a good plan. I'm not ready to admit that I'm batshit crazy in front of a group. You feel me?"

"Sure do," Aunt Flip said. "Just think about it. Six tomorrow evening. I'll be bringing the snacks."

That right there was reason enough not to go. A roomful of high-as-a-kite nutballs who claimed to have superpowers could end badly... like in-the-pokey badly. I'd had more bad press in one lifetime than a person should have to deal with. Making the paper for being wasted with people who believed they were magical was not on my bucket list. Ever.

"Mmmkay," I said, moving swiftly to my office before Flip could make me promise to join her. There was no way in hell I was going to the library to commune with deranged people. Right now, I was the most deranged person I could stomach. Adding to the stress was a terrible idea.

"Love you, Clemmy," Aunt Flip said, flicking off the lights and going up the stairs.

Pausing in the doorway of my office, I watched her climb the stairs. She had no difficulty at all. She was a wonder at eighty-five and as much as my world was imploding, I was so grateful she was here.

"I love you more," I told her.

"Not possible," she called out.

I smiled. She was a piece of work and she was mine.

Time to write all the words… or go to bed.

First a little nap and then the words. It was a good plan.

Of course, according to the poet Robert Burns, the best laid plans of mice and men often go awry…

I wasn't a mouse. I wasn't a man. And most importantly, I wasn't a killer pig. Hopefully the quote didn't apply.

CHAPTER ELEVEN

WEED WAS A PRECURSOR FOR NIGHTMARES—AT LEAST IT WAS
for me. My little nap had turned into a trip to Hades on
crack. While my real life had taken a tumble into Crazy
Town, my dreams had gone straight to hell…

*"I'd like to point out the glaringly obvious. If he was bitten and
turned, he'd live for an eternity. I don't think that's an optimal
plan," Stephano said with an eye roll, flashing his fangs at the rest
of the assembled group. He wore black Armani from head to toe.
The vampire was stupidly beautiful and incredibly arrogant.*

*I knew him well. He was the antihero in my Good to the Last
Bloody Drop series. He was my undead asshole with a heart of
gold.*

*"No one suggested turning the bastard," Mina hissed. The
witch matched the vampire in her choice of color. She wore a
fabulous black Prada sheath. Mina's wild red hair was twisted
into a messy knot and her eyes glowed a glittering gold. She was*

breathtaking. *"All you think about is biting people. It's getting incredibly old and boring."*

I was well acquainted with Mina too. She was the heroine in my *Magic and Madness* series. She was a badass with an attitude. Mina had a penchant for blowing shit up. Even though I knew I was dreaming, I seriously hoped she spared my house.

"I'm a vampire," Stephano shot back. *"Sue me... or do me."*

"In your dreams, bloodsucker," Mina replied coolly.

"Enough," Clark Dark said calmly, taking notes as usual. Clark had changed his rumpled suit for another rumpled suit. Both had mustard stains on the lapel. *"If any of you were actually thinking straight, you'd realize that the demise of the man isn't an option. If the son of a bitch dies, our girl would be the first suspect since the perp is trying to fleece her for dough."*

"I see no issue with that," Cassandra La Pierre stated. *"Send her to jail. It would deter her from her porcine obsession."*

"You wouldn't see an issue," Sasha snapped, tossing her long raven-black hair as her demon eyes turned a sparkling blood red. Her glare cast a red glow that illuminated my office. She was stunning—dressed in a form-fitted, crimson Stella McCartney strapless dress. The demon's body defied gravity. *"You're an evil bitch."*

"Thank you," Cassandra replied.

"I'm not quite sure since I don't know many demons," Stephano pondered aloud. *"But I'm going to guess that Sasha's statement wasn't a compliment."*

"It was not," Sasha confirmed, staring daggers at her stepmother. *"I'd suggest that when she opens her mouth, we all ignore her. She despises being ignored."*

"Ignore who?" Albinia inquired, entering my dream wearing a

horrifying hot-pink ruffled number. "Sorry I'm late. Horace ate too many cakey chocolate squares and tried to fornicate with the costermonger. Terribly inappropriate. I've locked him in his room —Horace, not the costermonger. The costermonger will most likely require therapy."

"I have no clue what the hell you just said," Mina said, flashing some cleavage at Stephano, who seemed to appreciate the gesture.

The move shocked me. Mina didn't usually go for the undead.

"Not to worry," Clark Dark said. "Albinia's intel is not relevant to the situation."

"Thank God," Cassandra said, pulling out a cigarette and waiting for someone to light it.

The bitch had big balls. I was abundantly clear with her earlier that she could not smoke in my damn house. Whatever. This was a dream. Too bad Aunt Flip couldn't walk into my dreams. She could have stared at Cassandra's ciggy butt and lit it up. It would be fabulous to freak the evil woman out.

"So, as I was saying," Clark Dark continued, ignoring Cassandra's silent demand. "Clementine is a disaster at the moment."

Wait. That was kind of rude. I'd showered and put on clean clothes. Clark was being somewhat unfair.

"I beg to disagree," Albinia chimed in, defending me... kind of. "If you'd seen her two days past, you'd have an entirely different opinion. Clementine was disheveled and she seemed quite dicked in the nob. I told her that unless she wanted to end up an ace of spades, an adventuress or, heaven forbid, an ape leader that she must attend to her hygiene. Aside from her fashion choice at the moment, I'd have to give her a passing grade."

"I'm sorry," Sasha said, wrinkling her nose in confusion.
"What are you?"

"I'm a well-bred lady," Albinia announced, curtsying to the
crowd. "Lady Albinia Knightley Wynch, at your service."

"Not what she meant," Mina said, eyeing her with curiosity.
"What are you? A vampire? A demon? A werewolf? A witch?"

"None of the above," Albinia told her. "I'm simply a lady who
loves the constable."

"The constable who humped the monster?" Cassandra
inquired, appalled.

"While some may call the costermonger a monster, I do not
think that eating with one's mouth open is a sin that should label
the man a monster," Albinia announced, further confusing the
group. "However, as to your original query, yes. I am in love with
the constable who made a valiant attempt to bugger the costermonger. It was the fault of the cakey chocolate squares. But alas,
in the end the blame is on me. For I am the one who fed Horace
the succulent squares of naughtiness."

"Does she have to be here?" Mina asked Clark. "Seems to me
that she might be a liability."

Sasha huffed. "No more of a liability than the bitch with the
unlit cigarette in her mouth. At least Altweeta is nice."

"Albinia," Albinia corrected Sasha.

"God bless you," Sasha replied.

Albinia was perplexed, but went with the flow and thanked
Sasha for her concern. I was beyond perplexed. I also never should
have named her Albinia. The name was as unmemorable as the
novel.

Never in my life had a dream been so real and lifelike.

"Back to the matter at hand," Clark said, giving everyone a

stern look. "If Clementine can't get her life back together, the end of the good in the world looms near."

"Unacceptable," Sasha shouted. "I haven't banged Damien yet. And she's still alive." Sasha pointed and hissed at Cassandra, who simply smiled and flipped her off.

"And I've yet to walk in the sunlight," Stephano complained. "I must walk in the sunlight without looking like a human hamburger with third-degree burns."

Human hamburger with third-degree burns? Oh my God. Had I actually written that? It was awful.

"And I haven't found the stupid grimoire," Mina bitched. "I mean, I know where the damn thing is. Clementine's making me go through bullshit tests to earn the right to use it. Sooooooo tedious."

"And I haven't been eaten by pigs," Cassandra announced archly, pulling out her own solid gold lighter and firing up her cigarette.

Her statement silenced everyone.

"For the love of everything ridiculous," I snapped. "You're not going to get eaten by a pack of pigs. I'm a better writer than that."

"Oh!" Albinia squealed. "We thought you were sleeping."

"I am," I told her with an eye roll.

Again, there was silence.

"I *am* sleeping," I repeated, trying to convince everyone, including myself. "Aren't I?"

Clark Dark gave me a warm and fatherly smile. "No, my dear. You are not sleeping."

"You're shitting me," I said.

"We shit you not," Mina replied.

This was not good. They were all lying. Or I was making them lie. Technically, I controlled them. I created them. None of them existed until I had put them on paper.

Right?

"Hang on," I said, grabbing a metal ruler off my desk. If I smacked my leg and it hurt, I was awake. If it didn't sting like a mother humper, I was asleep. Putting my leg on the desk, I lifted the ruler above my head. I'd considered stabbing myself with the scissors for a brief moment. However, on the outside chance that I wasn't dreaming, going to the emergency room for stitches in the middle of the night due to a self-inflicted stab wound seemed like a terrible plan.

"Whatever in the blazes are you doing?" Albinia cried out, alarmed. "You're a bluestocking, not a Merry Andrew!"

"Cake hole. Close it," I told Albinia. I had no clue what she'd just said, but I was sure I didn't want to hear it. "This is necessary. You feel me?"

"I'd rather not," she replied. "Horace wouldn't like it."

I rolled my eyes. "I wasn't being literal. But I will remind you that you just said Horace tried to bang the costermonger."

She nodded and sighed. "Yes, well, Dudley Albon Stopford is quite the blade. Even I have attempted to bugger Dudley."

Shaking my head and glancing up at the ceiling, I groaned. "I named a character Dudley Albon Stopford?"

"You did," Albinia confirmed. "Very buggerable. However, he is besotted with Peregrina Ashfield Vanden, the Abigail with the countenance of an abbess."

"What the hell did you just say?" I asked, squinting at her.

"May I?" Stephano inquired.

"You speak *Regency*?" I asked, confused. Stephano's series was set in modern times. There was no time travel and he was a youngish vamp. Some of my vampires were centuries old, but Stephano was only ninety, even though he looked thirty.

"My guilty pleasure is Regency romance novels," he admitted sheepishly.

"Why do I find that hot?" Mina muttered with a shudder. "I should not find that sexy at all."

I wasn't going to touch the fact that my characters from entirely different series and worlds were hitting on each other. "Translate, please," I told the vampire.

"She said that Dudley Albon Stopford is quite fuckable, but he is in love with Peregrina Ashfield Vanden—the lady's maid who has the facial expression of a mistress of a brothel."

"Seriously?" I asked. "I wrote that shit?"

"Yes," Stephano assured me with a wince. "I read the book. It was awful."

"Okay," I snapped. "I really do not need this. I'm aware that *Scandalous Sensual Desires of the Wicked Ones on Selby Street* might not have been my best work, but none of you freaks would exist if I hadn't written it. The reason I switched to paranormal romance was because I sucked at Regency romance. So, keep your opinions to yourself. They're like assholes," I explained, borrowing a phrase from Jessica. "Everyone has one, but I do not want to see it."

"Such a way with words," Cassandra said with sarcasm dripping off each syllable. "You should be a writer."

"Zip it and put the damn cigarette out or I *will* kill you with pigs. They'll dismember you one limb at a time and you'll be alive until they decapitate you... which will be last on the agenda."

Cassandra huffed indignantly and put out her cigarette in my favorite candle.

I had better be dreaming.

"I like it," Sasha said, nodding with approval. "Not sure there are many pigs roaming Manhattan, but if anyone can make it work, you can, Clementine. I also read *Scandalous Sensual Desires of the Wicked Ones on Selby Street.* While I found it wildly humorous—which I'm sure wasn't your intention—I did find it slightly moving and occasionally enjoyable."

"Thank you," I said. It was an insulting compliment, but it was far better than most of the reviews. "Now if everyone would back up, I need to prove to myself that I'm dreaming."

"By injuring yourself?" Clark Dark inquired with a concerned expression.

"Yep," I told him. "And since I'm dreaming, it won't leave a mark."

"Good luck with that," Mina said with a grin.

"Thank you," I replied.

Lifting the ruler high and slamming it down on my thigh with way more force than necessary, I grunted in pain.

I was not dreaming.

And it was definitely going to leave a mark.

"You're all real," I choked out, feeling faint.

"No shit, Sherlock," Mina said with a laugh.

"And I'm crazy," I whispered.

"In a good way," Sasha insisted.

"There's a good way?" I asked as my vision began to tunnel.

"Definitely," Albinia said, pulling a pink hanky from her abundant cleavage and handing it to me.

"Are you going to faint?" Stephano asked, taking my arm and leading me to the couch.

"Not sure," I wheezed out, leaning forward and letting my head drop between my knees.

"Not to worry, dear girl," Clark said, gently patting my back. "Just breathe. You're having a panic attack."

"Right. A panic attack or a complete mental breakdown." I gulped air as my body chilled and my limbs grew heavy.

It was all too much. I'd snapped. I could no longer discern reality from fantasy.

The last thing I saw before I passed out was Stephano copping a feel of Mina's ass right as she zapped him with a magical bolt that sent the vampire flying across the room and hitting the wall with a sickening thud.

My Regency romance reading buddy and I had something in common. Tomorrow we would both have a mark. Mine was going to manifest as a big bruise on my thigh and his would be a dent in his head.

Life had spiraled out of control.

And I had no clue who was driving.

CHAPTER TWELVE

"Don't talk to me or look at me You can breathe, but that's all," I told Thick Stella as I typed like a mad woman. When I'd woken up at seven AM, everyone was gone. I wanted to pretend they hadn't been here, but the massive bruise on my thigh, the pink hanky and the cigarette butt in my candle proved otherwise. Fine. I saw imaginary people who were not imaginary. Things could be far worse. Right now, I couldn't think of anything worse, but I was going with my illogical logic.

And since my logic had too many fatal flaws to decipher, I went with what I understood. Writing.

"I'm so close to the end," I muttered. My body tingled like it always did when the story came together. "Cyd is going to be thrilled and pissed."

Thick Stella growled. I shot her a glare. She'd been fed. I'd even tried to pet her. That had gone poorly. Next to the black and blue welt on my leg was a three-inch-long angry scratch. My cat was heinous.

Picking up a burnt piece of cold toast, I took a bite. Aunt Flip had made runny eggs and charred bread for breakfast. I ate all of it. As I asked for seconds, it occurred to me that the weed might still be in my system and making me hungry. Flip was delighted to watch me eat. She was worried that I'd lost too much weight during my months of depression.

"I'm not going to kill her in this book," I told Thick Stella. "While I'm fully aware that Nancy, Aunt Flip and Cyd want Cassandra La Pierre to die a violent, bloody death, I'm not ready to let her go. You feel me?"

My cat had fallen asleep. Worthless.

I'd debated with myself for two hours as I'd downed four cups of watery coffee compliments of Flip. Twice I'd killed the evil stepmother and twice I'd deleted what I'd written. The third attempt included killer pigs that had escaped from a meat truck in Times Square. I'd laughed for fifteen minutes at the chapter before I tossed it. The third time wasn't a charm in this instance. No matter what Sasha had said about me being able to make a pack of murderous pigs in Manhattan work, the beautiful demon was wrong. While the Exotic series had some clever humor, it wasn't slapstick. Cannibal pigs didn't work.

However, I hadn't deleted the scene. I'd taken it out and moved it to a folder called *shit pile*. I planned to use it to threaten Cassandra with if she crossed me or tried to smoke in my house again.

Was I insane? Yep. Was I smart? Debatable. Figuring the

only way to handle the evil woman was to outwit her, I felt that the pig material was excellent blackmail to keep her ass in line.

"Gonna plant some flowers for you," Aunt Flip announced in her outside voice, standing in the doorway of my office.

Today she wore a pink and purple striped muumuu, yellow socks and her Birkenstocks. She looked all kinds of wrong and all kinds of beautiful. I'd gotten her an appointment for a perm at one. There were still a few hours until we had to leave and I wanted to get more words on the page.

"What kind of flowers?" I asked suspiciously. I had no problem with Flip's hobby, I just didn't want an acre of pot growing on my property.

She cackled and did a little jig. "Pink peonies and a few purple lilac bushes. You need some beauty and some sweet scents floatin' around here, Clemmy."

"And is that all you're planting?" I asked, still wary. Flip tended to omit details.

"Yep. No weed," she promised, grinning. "The soil here ain't good for Mary Jane."

"Good to know," I said with relief. "Your perm is at one. I'm going to finish this chapter, then shower. Cool?"

"As a cucumber," Flip said as she waltzed out of the house and into the gorgeous spring morning. "I'm ready to get rid of my bald spot."

I crossed my fingers and hoped she didn't end up completely bald.

I stared at Thick Stella. She stared back at me. "Do you

want to know what would piss Cassandra La Pierre off more than anything?" I asked my fat furball.

She yawned and lifted her leg. Whatever.

"Redeeming her," I continued with a giggle. "Redeeming her by having her give up her money and her designer clothes… and joining a nunnery."

Thick Stella meowed and threw me some kitty-tude.

"Okay, you're right," I admitted. "The nunnery is a bit much, but…"

My fingers flew over the keys. My grin was so wide it hurt my face. I wasn't sure I was going to keep the words I'd written, but I was kind of in love with them… and a teeny-tiny bit in love with the new and improved Cassandra La Pierre.

She was going to be furious.

Life was looking up.

"Shower time," I told Thick Stella, who flicked her tail menacingly. At least she didn't lunge at me and take a swipe.

Like I said… life was looking up. I was embracing the crazy and opening up my mind.

Or I was falling off the cliff.

"There's always sunshine after the rain," I reminded myself, deciding that was my new mantra. While the shower wouldn't wash the crazy down the drain, it would make my imaginary friends proud. The fact that I cared what they thought about me was alarming, but it felt better to accept the inevitable than to fight it and live in a continuous panic attack.

Again, the logic was flawed, but flaws weren't always

fatal. Logic was left-brained. I was right-brained. It was time to live in my right-brained world.

THE GOSSIP IN THE BEAUTY PARLOR COULD BE VICIOUS. FROM out here it didn't look busy inside, but that didn't mean it wouldn't fill up with women. Occasionally, gals just stopped in to chat.

I'd showered and dressed with care. There was no way in hell I was wearing mismatched shoes in Curl Up and Dye. It would be all over town in a hot second. I'd chosen a casual fitted green sundress that matched my eyes and had made sure my sparkly flip-flops were the same color. I'd even straightened my damn hair. By the time I'd walked out of my house, I was sweating with all the effort I'd put in.

We were in the South. While appearances could be deceiving, they were also perceived as important. Normally, I didn't care, but normal had left my wheelhouse about four months ago. Today my hair, makeup and choice of fashion were my armor. It felt like I was going into battle… which was ridiculous. Generally speaking, I was well-liked in our little town. I was about to test that theory.

I hadn't really been in public since the video of my husband banging Weather Hooker had gone viral. The only positive thing was that since I was doing publicity for my book, I had been dressed to kill and my hair and makeup had been perfect. Even when I'd showered Darren's naked ass with filthy mop water, I'd been graceful—or at least that's what the rag mags had written.

"I'm nervous," I admitted, sitting in the car and wondering if I should just wait for Aunt Flip instead of going into the salon.

"Nervous about what?" Flip asked, putting on some bright pink lipstick in the same shade as her muumuu.

She'd gone dangerously outside of the lip line. Grabbing a tissue from my purse, I gently wiped off the excess that made her look like a clown. My aunt had also slapped on some blue eyeshadow and enough blush to make her look feverish. However, she was feeling it and thrilled with her look. Not many could pull off the bold fashion statement, but Flip was one of a kind.

"About seeing people."

"Screw 'em," she said. "You've got nothin' to be ashamed of, Clemmy. You hold that beautiful head high, and I'll sucker punch anyone who looks at you cross-eyed."

I sighed and rested my forehead on the steering wheel. Picturing my eighty-five-year-old aunt physically accosting women with foil in their hair was kind of fabulous. It was also not going to happen. I had no doubt that Flip would happily throw a left hook in my defense, but it was time for me to pull up my big-girl panties and fight my own battles.

"Aunt Flip?"

"That's my name, don't wear it out," she said, taking my hand in hers and squeezing it.

"Something you said has been floating in my brain."

"What's that, darlin'?" she asked.

"You said that Darren was a suppressor. What does that mean?"

Flip squeezed my hand again. "Someone like Darren has

no magic. He sucks the enchantment out of everything around him. That's why your granny and me wore black to your wedding. We were trying to help you out. I'm guessin' that once he was gone, your gift popped out. And the *way* he exited your life might have been the catalyst that made it pop."

"You mean that finding Darren testicles deep in Weather Hooker was my pigpen moment? My external disaster?"

"Yep."

Darren kept falling further and further from grace in my book. I suppose I should be grateful that cannibalistic pigs weren't involved. But honestly, man-eating pigs would have been kind of wonderful on that heinous day. It would have been far more dramatic and final than mop water.

Speaking of mop water and public humiliation…

"Maybe I'll wait in the car."

"Hidin' solves nothing," Flip said. "You've been holed up long enough, little girl. You might not be able to control what people are thinkin', but you can control how you react. If you let them see blood, they'll go for the jugular. But if you're the first one to the punch, they don't have nowhere to go."

I squinted at her. "So, you think I should walk in there and announce that it's no big deal that my husband of several decades banged Weather Hooker? And that I'm fine?"

"Good God," a familiar voice griped from the backseat. "Where are your balls and your self-respect?"

"What the fu…" I shouted, whipping around and

confirming that Cassandra La Pierre was indeed sitting in the back of the car.

"What?" Aunt Flip yelled.

"Do you see her?" I demanded.

"See who?" Flip asked, reaching into her hemp bag and pulling out a stun gun.

"Holy shit," I choked out. "Where did you get that?"

"On the internet," Flip said. "Do I need to use it?"

"Do you even know how to use it?" I asked.

Flip nodded. "I read the directions. It's not hard—just aim and shoot."

Carefully removing the stun gun from my aunt's hands, I put it under the front seat. Inhaling deeply as I imagined what could have gone down, I gripped the steering wheel until my knuckles turned white.

"Aunt Flip, shooting someone with a stun gun is a shitty idea."

"I should say so," Cassandra said.

"Zip it," I hissed.

"I didn't say nothing," Flip said, confused.

Well, there was my answer. If Flip couldn't hear Cassandra, she couldn't see her. That meant I was alone in my crazy.

"Not you," I told my aunt. "Cassandra La Pierre is in the backseat."

Flip turned around and looked. "Interesting."

"You see her?" I asked. Maybe she could see her but not hear her.

"Nope," Flip said, disappointed. "But I can feel the vibration. Kind of pissy and rude."

"You got that right," I muttered, eyeing Cassandra in the rearview mirror. "Is there a reason you're here?"

"I'm gettin' a perm," Flip reminded me.

"Umm... not you," I told her. "Cassandra."

"Right," Aunt Flip said. "My bad. Keep going. If you're gonna talk to me, use my name."

Shockingly, it wasn't *shocking* at all that Flip believed one of my characters had hitched a ride with us to the beauty parlor. It was par for the course right now and I was thankful for it.

"Cassandra, why are you here?" I asked.

Cassandra La Pierre sighed dramatically and fidgeted a bit. It was odd to see her not in complete control. "Because I thought you might need some help," she snapped.

"Wait. What?" I asked, shocked. "That's not normal for you. You don't help anyone but yourself. You're not a nice person."

"I know," she shouted. "I have no idea what's happening to me. However, you are a ball-less hot mess. If you need to take anyone down a few pegs, you will be a dismal failure."

"There she is," I muttered, recognizing the awful woman. Even when she was nice, she was nasty. "I have balls," I said. "I don't need your help."

Flip chimed in with a thumbs up. "Big hairy ones."

"Thank you," I said with a grin.

"But," Flip continued. "While your nuts are meaty, I think Conundra might have a point. She has some terrific and vicious comebacks."

"I do," Cassandra agreed. "And my name is Cassandra, not Conundra."

I shook my head. "I *wrote* those comebacks," I informed both women. "She wouldn't have said them if I hadn't thought them up and written them down."

"Clemmy has a point," Flip said, turning and talking to the backseat like she was having a conversation with Conundra.

Cassandra shrugged. "Fine. If you don't want my help, I'll wait in the car."

I gaped at her. "You thought you were coming in with me?"

"Of course," she replied with an eye roll. "I had planned to feed you biting insults to flatten any bitch who tried to cut you down."

The thought was incredibly tempting and possibly stupid. "Do any of the others know you're here?"

"Absolutely not," Cassandra hissed. "And if you tell anyone that I was nice, I'll deny it and haunt your dreams for the rest of eternity."

"What'd she say?" Aunt Flip asked.

"That she wants to cut a bitch in the salon if anyone comes for me," I told her.

Flip scratched her head and thought about it. "I vote yes. Corputa might be onto something."

I audibly blew out a long breath and weighed the pros and cons. The cons far outweighed the pros. If I accidentally spoke to Cassandra, that would be bad. However, my life had been a massive con for four months. What did I have to lose? I'd already lost my sanity.

"Fine," I said finally. "Do not ask me a direct question

because there's an excellent chance that I will answer you. Agreed?"

"Agreed," Cassandra said, rubbing her hands together with glee. "Anything else?"

"Yep. If you're screwing with me and make me look like an idiot, you'll regret it. The pen is mightier than the sword."

Cassandra rolled her head because rolling her eyes didn't convey how annoyed she was. "What? You'll kill me with pigs?"

I smiled. "Nope. Cannibal pigs are off the table."

"What then?" she asked, giving me a side eye.

My smile grew wider. "You get redeemed."

She paled considerably. "You wouldn't," she snarled.

I shrugged and said nothing. Since I knew I was heading that way in the story, I didn't want to lie to her by telling her I wouldn't do it. However, it put the fear of God in her and that was what I needed right now.

"You will not look like an idiot because of me," she ground out through clenched teeth. "You don't need me to look like an idiot. You do a fine job of that yourself."

I laughed. She was right.

"We ready?" Flip asked. "It's almost one."

Checking myself in the mirror, I nodded. "I'm not even remotely ready, but that won't stop me. Let's do this."

"That's my girl," Aunt Flip said, hopping out of the car and skipping up to the glass door of Curl Up and Dye.

"You'll be fine," Cassandra said tersely.

I turned and looked at her. "I'm still not sure why you're here."

She stepped out of the car and tossed her shiny brown locks over her shoulder. "Neither am I. I'm quite sure I shall regret it."

She probably would.

I just prayed I didn't.

CHAPTER THIRTEEN

"Ain't you a sight for sore eyes!" Sissy shouted as we entered the shop.

Aunt Flip checked herself in while Cassandra examined the hair products.

Sissy was pushing fifty and looked like a million curvy bucks. Her bottle-blonde hair was teased to within an inch of its life and there wasn't a wrinkle on her sweet face. She and Botox had a close relationship. It was her smile and her personality that made her gorgeous. I felt immediately at ease. Cassandra's assistance wasn't going to be necessary, thank God.

"Darren's a shitbag," Ann Aramini yelled. "And that Jinny Jingle is a whore."

Ann Aramini wasn't one to hold her tongue. She'd dumped her filter the day she'd turned seventy and hadn't looked back. She was a tiny Mack Truck of a woman. Crossing her would be a very bad plan of action. She was retired now, but she'd been my high school counselor. I'd called her Ann Aramini since I was fifteen. She'd insisted we all use her full name even back then—said it made her more relatable to the kids. Truth was she scared the hell out of all of us, but we knew she could be trusted with our adolescent secrets. Of course, people were wary of having her at gatherings nowadays because she said whatever came to her mind... and it was usually horrifying. However, today, I agreed with her wholeheartedly.

"See darlin'?" Aunt Flip crowed, waving at the gals. "You ain't got nothin' to worry about."

Sissy hustled over and threw her meaty arms around me. "We've been so dang worried about you. Connie said you won't let her come clean the house, but you've been paying her. She's just beside herself about that."

"Well," Ann Aramini said, marching over, shoving Sissy out of the way and hugging me so tight, I thought my burnt toast might come up. "That's because Clementine is a good girl. She was brought up right. Not like that black and decker pecker wrecker who fornicated with her no-good cheatin' husband."

That was a lovely new name for Jinny Jingle. I laughed. It came from deep inside and felt fantastic. "That's certainly descriptive."

"Use it in your next book," Ann Aramini insisted. "Free of charge. Just make sure you kill that Cassandra La Pierre big time."

"Good God, does *everyone* hate me?" Cassandra muttered with a wide and delighted smile on her stunning face.

I ignored her. "I'll keep that in mind," I said, snapping the back of Flip's cape. "We're here for a perm for Aunt Flip."

"I'm lookin' a little bald," Flip said, showing Sissy the problem.

"I can take care of that, doll," Sissy assured her. "It's the dark of the moon. It'll be just fine. Sit your butt in the chair and let me do my magic."

Did everyone know about the dark of the moon except me?

"Woohooooooo!" Flip yelled, dancing over to Sissy's station.

The salon wasn't large—four hair stations and a nail area. For a brief moment I thought about getting a pedicure, but I wanted to stay near Flip. The shop was a bright, sunny yellow and smelled of hair dye and acrylic nails. I loved the scents.

"You lost that bastard yet?" Ann Aramini asked, fluffing her short blueish-gray hair and removing her cape.

"Working on it," I told her, sitting down in the empty chair next to Flip.

"Good," she grunted. "You don't need trash like that in your life. Any dumbass who bangs a box for hire needs to be put out for the garbage collector."

"I like her," Cassandra said, checking out the nail polish display.

Thankfully, there was no one else in the shop bedsides Ann Aramini, Sissy, Flip, me… and Cassandra. I was slowly reentering society, and spending time with these women was a fine way to start.

"You got a book coming out soon?" Sissy asked as she began to roll Flip's hair into perm rods.

I smiled. "I do. I'm still working on it, but it's finally coming along."

"Good," Sissy said. "I miss that Clark Dark. You ever gonna add to that series? Such a sexy man."

I almost choked on my own spit. Clark Dark was a lot of things—brilliant, crafty, deadly when necessary and all-around lovable. He was not what I would call sexy. But that was the amazing, magical thing about books. Everyone saw something different. Once I was done writing, my stories became the property of the imaginations of those who read them. It was one of the reasons I didn't like to see my favorite books made into movies. They could never come close to what I'd imagined.

"Probably not," I told a disappointed Sissy. "Maybe a novella."

"Fandamntastic," she said, cheering right back up. "Just can't get me enough of that Clark Dark. I'd give anything if that man was real. I could go for a hot, mysterious werewolf."

It was on the tip of my tongue to tell her he was real... kind of. However, a sharp glare from Cassandra made me swallow the words. I was definitely going to pass along Sissy's compliments to Clark. He'd be tickled.

"I'm just glad to see you out and about again, Clementine," Ann Aramini said, shoving a wad of bills into Sissy's apron. "You can't let a mega-ho monster ruin your life. Darren Bell is an ass canoe and an idiot. If he wants a hooker, he deserves the sidewalk tulip."

Her language was colorful and cringeworthy. It was perfection. I'd have to remember the terms to share with Jessica and Mandy. They'd scream with laughter. While Weather Hooker was outstanding, black and decker pecker wrecker might have it beat.

"You need a haircut, sweetie?" Sissy asked me.

"Nope, I'm good. I'll schedule a trim soon. Today's all about Flip."

The bells on the door jingled. Little did I know that the *jingle* was a foreshadow—an ugly one.

"I'm back from lunch," a nasally, bored voice announced. "I've got two VIP customers coming in. Are they here yet?"

"Does it look like it?" Ann Aramini asked with an eye roll.

The girl glanced around and shrugged. "Nope. No VIPs here."

Sissy's hissed intake of breath made me aware that she wasn't real fond of her employee.

Cassandra's head shot in the young woman's direction, and her eyes narrowed dangerously. A little shiver skittered up my spine. Could Cassandra do physical damage even though no one could see her except me? That would suck.

The girl was rude and unpleasant, but that didn't merit dismemberment. Cassandra was a demon. She was capable of horrible things. I should know. I made her that way. It would be incredibly difficult to explain if she waved her hand and incinerated the nail gal.

"They always run late. They like to make an entrance," Nail Gal said in a snooty tone. "They're very important people. *Famous* people."

Note to self… get a pedicure somewhere else.

"Well, at least you finally have a customer," Sissy said. "I don't recall seein' any nail appointments on the books."

"Umm… last-minute arrangement. Page me when my VIPs arrive," the girl said as she quickly flounced back to the break room.

"Page my butt," Sissy mumbled.

"I tell you what," Ann Aramini grumbled. "I don't care if that shit-mouthed girl is your niece, you need to fire her."

"I'd love to," Sissy said with a put-upon sigh. "But my sister begged me to give her a chance. While it's real hard to like my rude niece, I love my sister."

"Your sister should have whooped some sense into that girl's ass a long time ago. Not to mention, her dang pants are so tight that if she farts it'll blow her boots off," Ann Aramini commented.

"Good one," Flip said with a laugh. "I always say 'her pants are so tight you can see her religion.'"

Ann Aramini cackled. "Write this stuff down, Clementine," she insisted. "This is some damn fine book material."

"What on earth does she think you write?" Cassandra inquired, taking the empty seat on the other side of Flip. "Slapstick porn?"

It was getting more difficult, but I ignored her. What I wanted to do was laugh. Cassandra was funny. Who knew?

"Will do," I told Ann Aramini. It wouldn't be productive to defy her. She was always right, according to her.

Grabbing a pad of paper and a pencil from my bag, I jotted down the notes. I was so busy writing, I missed the entrance of the VIPs.

No one else missed it.

Cassandra hissed like a feral cat. Ann Aramini stiffened up like she was in rigor mortis. Sissy swore under her breath and Flip growled. Literally.

Me? My stomach dropped to my toes and I felt icy cold. Had Darren walked into the salon to demand money in front of an audience? Had he seen my car and decided to go for it in public? Was he that much of a dick?

Only one way to find out. If Darren wanted to have a smackdown with witnesses, so be it. I had Cassandra with me. Even though I'd given her the words, she seemed a whole lot faster on her feet than me. Maybe I shouldn't redeem her. If she saved my ass from embarrassment, she should get what she wanted in her fictional world. I mean, *not exactly* what she wanted since that meant killing every other character in the book...

Slowly turning my head and preparing myself to spar with my soon-to-be ex, I gasped. It wasn't Darren. It was far worse.

"What a *wonderful* surprise," my so-called nemesis ground out, clearly lying. She was far too excited for me to buy that this was a coincidence.

"You're gonna need to leave," Sissy said curtly. "I don't have you on the books for an appointment today."

Jinny Jingle's eyes were glued to me. A victorious and unattractive smile pulled at her overly enhanced lips. "I'm here for a manicure," she announced. "I'm a VIP."

"Only if VIP stands for Very Impotent Piece of Shit," Cassandra said dryly.

Cassandra was good...

"I'm a VIP too," Weather Hooker's buddy snapped, also staring daggers at me. "God, this shop is full of *old* ladies today."

"Sure is," Jinny Jingle purred.

If I had to guess the plot here, I'd surmise I was set up by Sissy's niece. The plot line was messy and underhanded, but it was what it was. I just needed to rewrite the narrative.

"That's some ugly lip-flappin'," Ann Aramini said, eyeing the two *VIPs* with distaste.

Jinny Jingle shrugged rudely, her gaze still on me. "Truth hurts."

For a second, I considered letting Ann Aramini handle the situation. She could eat the two twenty-somethings for breakfast, then spit them back out. But that would make me a loser.

I was done being a loser. I wasn't a damn loser. I was only a loser if I let myself be one. Darren had not turned out to be a prize. It had taken me far too long to realize the sad truth, but as Weather Hooker had just said, the truth hurt.

"Well, bless your tiny heart," I said with a smile that didn't reach my eyes. If she wanted to go, I was ready. I hoped.

"No punching and no hair-pulling," Sissy said, laying out the rules.

"I think bitch-slapping should be on the table," Cassandra muttered as she walked over and stood by my side.

How was this my life? It was ridiculous. I wasn't sure exactly what was about to go down, but my heart raced like I was being taunted by the high school bully. Absurd didn't even begin to define the situation. What I should do is walk right out of the front door. I was above this. I was almost twice the black and decker pecker wrecker's age.

"You owe my man money," Jinny hissed.

"You owe her man money, bitch," her idiot friend mimicked her.

"Nope," Sissy snapped, pointing at Weather Hooker's overly made-up second-in-command. "No backup. This is a two-woman smackdown. I'll pick you up and toss your ass out of here if another word comes out of your nasty mouth."

Jinny's buddy rolled her eyes and stepped back.

"Good thing no one knows I'm here," Cassandra said with an evil smirk. "You need me."

"Not so sure," I muttered under my breath. "I think I can handle this."

"What did you say?" Jinny demanded.

"I do not owe anyone any money," I said flatly.

"You're mistaken," she shot back. "My boopy has a better lawyer than you. Just wait. You'll be left with nothing. And... I just loooove your house. Can't wait to live in it. Darren promised me it will be ours."

I smiled and winked at her. She looked wildly confused. "I really don't have the time or the crayons to explain this to you, but your *boopy* is going to have to get a job. And the house is mine. Period."

"Nice," Flip said, giving me a thumbs up.

Jinny smiled. It was not pretty. "Yeah, well, you're so old, your birth certificate expired. You got traded in for a much better model. And I *will* have that house. Darren said I would. So there."

We were going low? Fine. I could go low.

"Is your ass jealous of the crap that just came out of your mouth?" I asked in a polite tone.

Her eyes widened in surprise for a moment. She might not know it yet, but she'd just met her match and then some. She was going to get creamed.

Ann Aramini grunted out a laugh, pulled up a chair and sat down for the show.

"I'm not as stupid as *you* look," Jinny shot back, giving her buddy a high-five.

"Interesting," I said, standing up. If I was in for the senseless name-calling game, I needed to be on my feet. "Isn't it rather dangerous to use up your entire vocabulary in one sentence?"

That one went right over her dyed head. I was winning.

"If I had a face like yours, I'd sue my parents," she yelled.

Glancing over at her friend, she checked in as to how she was doing. Her friend gave her a thumbs down. She didn't like that one bit.

"Erase that one," she snarled. "I meant to say, you're so old, you were alive when the Grand Canyon was a ditch."

"Do you actually know where the Grand Canyon is?" I inquired.

She couldn't answer the question. Geography wasn't Weather Hooker's thing, apparently. Darren had wonderful taste.

"It's fantastic to see that you're not letting your education get in the way of your ignorance," I told her sweetly.

"You might not need me after all," Cassandra said

approvingly. Her confidence made my day. Granted it was a bizarre day so far, but I was on top of it.

"You know, Junky," I said, mangling her name. "I would have preferred a battle of the wits, but I see you came unarmed."

Jinny bared her big and very white teeth. "No wonder my man kicked you to the curb, Phlegmentine," she countered. "You're so old and stuffy, you knew Mr. Clean when he had hair."

"Is that all you have?" I asked with an eye roll. "*Old jokes?*"

"You sound like an idiot," she snapped.

"Of course I sound like an idiot," I said. "How else would you understand me?"

Sissy laughed and Flip clapped her hands in appreciation.

"Don't mess with a writer," Flip yelled. "It ain't gonna end well."

Jinny Jingle was flustered. I had no clue what she'd expected. Did Darren tell her I was a dishrag? Did she truly think she could intimidate me?

"You have this," her friend assured her. "Go for the kill."

Jinny nodded spastically. "You're so old, you have to get your weathered vagina checked by the dino-cologist."

"Gross," Cassandra said. "Your ex-husband clearly lost his sense of taste. She's low-class trash. One never uses the word *vagina* in a cat fight."

"Yep," I agreed, then zeroed back in on the woman who I'd assumed for months was better than me in every way.

She was not. I would never assume again. It had made an ass out of me for four long months.

"You're the human version of period cramps," I said. "If you have a problem with me, write it down on a piece of paper and shove it up your ass. I don't want Darren. You can have him. You can also support him. He doesn't like to work."

"You think you're so smart," she ground out. "Just for your information, men do not like smart women. Your only chance of getting laid is to crawl up a chicken's ass and wait."

Where were cannibal pigs when you needed them?

"Low blow," Cassandra pointed out. "Would you like a hand?"

I shook my head. I had this under control. I was done with this crap. It was time to end it. "You're the reason the gene pool needs a lifeguard. I might love to shop, but I will never buy your bull or Darren's."

"Whatever. You're so old—" Jinny began.

"Not done yet," I informed her, holding up my hand. "For your information, light travels faster than sound, which is why you might look bright until you open your mouth. Next time you speak, think about it first. It's far better to let others think you're an idiot than to open your mouth and prove it. You actually did me a favor. Darren isn't good enough for me. Unfortunately, it took seeing him banging your skanky ass on my kitchen table to bring me to that realization." I took a deep breath. I'd always been the kind of person to give credit where credit was due. I was a polite Southerner after all, and some credit was definitely due. "Thank you. My life is far better without having to deal with a man whose ego outsizes his *parts* by vast, enormous and gigantic dimensions. You expedited what had been coming on for a long time."

Jinny was so confused, I almost laughed.

"Umm… you're so old…"

"Shut your cake hole," I told her, crossing the salon and opening up the front door. "You've given me a headache. While some drink from the fountain of knowledge, you clearly only gargled. I'd suggest you and your VIP buddy leave now while we're both winning. You obviously think you won by getting Darren. And I *know* I won by punting him."

Jinny Jingle and her buddy exchanged wildly shocked and dumbfounded glances. She wasn't sure what to do. I helped them out.

"It would be a darn shame to let the TV station know you accosted someone," I said with a raised brow and a grin.

"I didn't steal anything!" she shouted.

Her stupidity was astounding… almost as astounding as the size of her silicone rack.

"When God gave out brains, he sure skipped her," Flip pointed out.

"You got that right," Ann Aramini agreed with a laugh.

"Darren will hear about this," Jinny snapped as she and her buddy scurried out of the salon. "This means he'll get the house and you'll be out on your ass."

"Good luck with that," I said, waving as they stomped down the street.

"I love sarcasm," Cassandra said, patting me on the back

with pride. "It's like punching people in the face with words."

Now *that* was a damn good line.

Marching back over to my pad of paper and pencil, I wrote it down. That was definitely going into a book.

"You won!" Flip squealed.

"I think I did," I said with a giggle. "While I wouldn't want to repeat that... ever... I think it had to happen. I feel kind of free."

"Darn tootin'," Ann Aramini said, slapping me on the back and sending me lurching forward. For a tiny gal, she was strong. "You've got class and sass. No one can take that from you—not Darren and not the black and decker pecker wrecker."

"Amen to that," Sissy agreed as her niece came slinking out of the break room with a guilty expression on her face.

"Did I hear my VIPs?" she asked, not making eye contact with anyone.

I'd been correct about the plot. The niece had been the coordinator of the *chance* meet-up.

"Yep," Sissy said, eyeing her niece like she was a cockroach.

"Where are they?" she demanded.

"Gone," Sissy said. "Just like you. Get your crap and get out. You're fired."

The girl turned red in the face and glared at her aunt. "I'll tell my mamma. You can't get away with this."

"Already did," Sissy said, holding up her phone. "Texted your mamma. She's itchin' to have a few words with you."

The girl's mouth dropped open. Grabbing her purse

from her station, she purposely knocked over the polish display and sauntered out of the shop.

We all were silent for about a minute. After just unloading a diatribe on Weather Hooker, I was now speechless. I felt bad that I'd been the catalyst for Sissy's niece getting fired, even if her niece was at fault. I knew how close Sissy was to her sister.

"I'm so sorry," I finally said, moving to put the polish display back together.

"Nope, don't you be sorry, Clementine," Sissy told me, leading Flip over to the dryer. "You just done me a favor. I've been tryin' to figure out how to sack that girl for two months. Today is a damn fine day."

"Sure is," Flip said. "Damn fine."

"I'd have to agree," Cassandra added. "Haven't enjoyed myself like that in quite some time. However, a little bloodshed would have been a nice touch."

I covertly glanced at her and smiled. Of course, she *would* want a maiming or two. She was a demon. I was not. I was a writer who was finding my voice. Not as a writer—I'd found that voice a long time ago—but as a strong woman. It was liberating.

Flip's perm came out great. Maybe there was something to the dark of the moon. And maybe not. What mattered most was that Flip was overjoyed. Her happiness was contagious. It was beautiful.

Damn. Fine. Day.

CHAPTER FOURTEEN

"Come on," Flip begged. "It's only an hour or so."

"No can do," I told her for the umpteenth time. "I have to write."

We'd been going back and forth with each other about the woowoo juju support group since we'd gotten home from the salon. Cassandra had walked out of the shop while Aunt Flip paid for her perm. When we'd gotten to the car, she was gone. Trying to figure out where my characters went when I couldn't see them was an exercise in crazed futility. I still couldn't explain why they had come to me at all.

"Awwww," Flip said, pouting. "I wanna show off my perm to my friends."

"You can," I told her. "Go to the meeting."

She sat down on the couch in my office and crossed her skinny arms over her chest. "Nope. If you're not goin', I'm not goin'."

"That's blackmail," I pointed out.

"I know. Is it working?" She giggled like a silly fool.

I sighed and tried not to laugh. I failed. "You don't need me to show off your perm to the woowoo juju clan."

"I do," she insisted.

"You don't."

"Do."

I groaned. Flip grinned.

"How about this?" she suggested. "I'll bring snacks minus the weed if you'll come."

I squinted at her. "You were going to get the group wasted?"

"They expect it," she explained. "I'll make up some to-go goodie bags and serve meat twinkies during the get together."

Scrunching my nose, I gagged. "Cold meat twinkies sounds like a bad plan."

Flip considered my statement. "I see what you're sayin'. Not to worry, I'll put 'em in the Crockpot to keep 'em nice and toasty. Might get a little soggy, but those gals will eat anything as long as there's catsup."

"You're not selling this adventure very well."

Flip giggled. "I'm not real good at sellin' anything. That was your granny's forte."

"Granny sold pot?" I asked, shocked. Although, I didn't know why I was surprised. Granny and Flip had been peas in a pod. As much as they drove each other batty they could finish each other's sentences and had adored each other. I imagined Flip was lonely without her sister. I missed Granny a lot.

"Hell to the no," Flip yelled, slapping her thigh and laughing. "Jumper never touched the stuff."

"Mmmkay," I said. "I'm not following. What did Granny sell?"

Flip leaned forward and waggled her brows. "Magic."

"She sold magic?"

"Nah, not sold per se... kept it alive," Flip corrected herself quickly. "She wrangled the woowoo group. Kept us all in line. She listened to her minions and spread the word on how to make the world a better place."

I was so confused. "Minions?"

"Yep. Rhett Butler and Scarlett O'Hara mostly. When she was talking to Baby Jane Hudson and her sister Blanche, things got a little iffy. Those gals are whacked, if you know what I mean. I generally preferred Dorothy Gale and Glinda."

Confused had left the building. I was now dumbfounded.

"Are you high?" I asked. It was the only rational explanation for the conversation.

"Nope. Not yet."

Bye-bye rational.

"So, umm... Granny saw and talked to Clark Gable and Vivian Leigh?" I asked, feeling ridiculous.

"Nope," Flip said, knowing she'd caught my interest. "Rhett Butler and Scarlett O'Hara. Big difference."

My mind raced. Albinia's words echoed in my brain. *Apples don't fall far from trees*. I didn't understand it then. But now? Now it might be making sense. Of course, making sense out of nonsensical things was fast becoming my norm.

Was Granny the tree and I was the apple? Did she see imaginary people too?

I eyed Flip. "If you're telling me what I think you're telling me, it might have been nice to know that a little sooner. You feel me?"

She just shook her head and laughed. "Puzzles have to be put together one piece at a time, Clemmy. Wouldn't have done you no good if you thought Jumper was as nuts as you were thinkin' you were. You needed to accept your people on your own."

Did she have a point? It sounded like it, but I couldn't be sure. Had I accepted my people? For the most part, yes. There was still a very small part of me that thought I was imagining them, but there was too much physical proof of their existence.

"Are you the woowoo juju wrangler now?" I asked.

"I'm not," Flip said, sounding sad and defeated. "I tried. We all gave it a shot, but none of us have Jumper's special gifts."

Tracing the pattern of the woodgrain on my desk, my need to know all kinds of crap that I shouldn't know gnawed away at me. Question after question bounced around in my head. My curiosity was going to be the end of me.

"Shit," I muttered, then just gave in. "Since there's no wrangler, what's happening to the woowoo juju?"

"It's dyin'," Flip said matter-of-factly. "We're all gettin' old. No new blood in ages."

"No younger gals have the woowoo?"

Flip shrugged. "I sense a few who might, but without Jumper's people to help us find them, we're a little lost."

"And that's bad?"

"Real bad," Flip said. "If there are no more woowoo juju gals, the end of the good in the world looms near."

Where had I heard that before? The sense of déjà vu was overwhelming. *Clark Dark.* Clark Dark had said the very same words in what I thought was a dream that wasn't a dream at all.

Wait. Was I really taking this seriously?

Yep. I had laid down roots in Crazy Town and bought some property.

"Aunt Flip," I said, trying to go at it from a logical place. "If there's woowoo juju here in our tiny town, there must be woowoo juju all over the place. Right?"

"That's what I thought," she replied. "Me and the gals took a few cross-country road trips last year to try and find some woowoo juju. Came back with nothin'."

"That doesn't seem right," I said, standing up and pacing my office. I was getting my panties in a wad over something I wasn't sure was real. Whatever. I wrote about vampires and werewolves. This wasn't that off base for me.

"It's not right," Sasha said, sitting behind my desk and reading what I had written. "There's more woowoo juju. It just has to be found. OH MY GOD!"

"What?" I asked, glancing around in horror just in case the demon mafia had shown up. They were terrible Underworld denizens. While I was fine with the characters who had visited me thus far, I didn't want the unsavory crew of demonic assholes to appear.

"What do you mean, what?" Flip asked, going for her stun gun and coming up empty-handed. Thankfully, it was still in my car.

"Not talking to you," I told her, pointing to Sasha.

"Somebody here?" Flip asked.

I nodded. "Sasha."

No Underworld mafia to be found.

"I am *not* okay with this," Sasha snapped, pointing at the computer screen. "Does she know?"

"What are you talking about?" I asked.

"Me?" Flip asked, confused.

"Nope. Sasha," I said. "I'll use your name if I'm saying something to you."

"Good plan," Flip agreed. "I can feel Sasha, but I can't see her. Pretty sure that gal ain't happy."

"I'm not," Sasha confirmed. "Cassandra is supposed to die violently, not be redeemed. This is unacceptable. I'll leave the book if this is the way the plot unfolds."

I squinted at her. She was kind of a spoiled brat. "And how exactly will you do that?"

I'd stumped her. She was not in control of her destiny. I was.

Sasha rolled her eyes. "Not a clue. However, debating you ruining your career by letting Cassandra La Pierre live is not why I'm here."

"And why are you here?"

She sighed and pushed my computer away. "You have to go to the meeting."

"What'd she say?" Aunt Flip asked.

"Nothing," I told Flip, who gave me the eyeball.

Sasha raised a brow and stood up. Her midnight-blue, daringly low-cut Prada dress was to die for. "You're a terrible liar," she commented. "Go to the meeting. Stephano has volunteered to join you. I think that's a craptastic idea, but he drew the longest straw."

"So, none of you wanted to come?" I asked, a little insulted. "The loser with the longest straw got stuck with me?"

Again, Sasha rolled her eyes. "We *all* wanted to come. The persnickety Clark Dark insisted that having all of us there would distract you. Alhootia has been sobbing for hours that she can't go. She is a freaking nightmare, by the way."

"Thank you," I said absently, wondering if I was going to follow the orders of a very well-dressed demon who only I could see.

"Wasn't a compliment," Sasha said, crossing the room and hugging me. "Actually, it's fine if you want to redeem Cassandra. It will piss her off. As long as I can finally bang Damien, I'm good."

"The sex scene is epic," I promised her. "I got horny writing it."

She grinned. "That's another reason you need to go to the meeting. Get yourself back out there. And PS... wear some damn heels. The flip-flops aren't cutting it."

"You're suggesting that I get gussied up and work off my horny with the woowoo juju gals?" I asked, horrified.

"None of them are gay," Flip chimed in. "But we can zoom on over to Louisville after the meeting."

I gaped at Flip. "Why would we drive to Louisville?"

"From what I understand there are some real nice girl bars there," she explained. "You could meet a nice lesbian and settle down. After Darren, I'd go for girls myself."

"Okay," I said, pressing the bridge of my nose while Sasha laughed so hard, she had to sit down. "While the suggestion is lovely, I'm not gay."

"My bad," Flip said. "Misunderstood. Kinda hard when I can only hear one side of the conversation. Is Sasha gay then?"

"Umm... no," I said.

Sasha was now screaming with laughter.

"Ain't nothin' wrong with bein' gay," Flip said.

"I agree," I told her. "However, I'm not, and I'm still married to a douchebag at the moment. So, even if I was looking to settle down with a nice lesbian, I'm not actually available yet."

Flip nodded and pulled out a bag of weed. "Then as soon as the divorce is final, we'll go to Louisville and find you a nice gal."

Explaining myself again was futile. Sasha was useless. She was now rolling around on the floor. I hoped she ripped her fabulous dress.

"Will you leave if I agree to go to the meeting?" I asked the demon.

Crawling to her feet and wiping tears from her eyes. "Yes. I'll leave if you agree to go. And I am so in for the Louisville trip."

"You're kind of a dick," I told her.

She grinned. "You made me that way."

"Touché," I said, giving up.

"So, you're comin'?" Aunt Flip asked, placing a rolled joint on the edge of the desk.

"I am," I said. "Why did you put that joint there?"

"It's for Sasha," Flip replied with a wink.

"But she..." I began—and then gaped at the desk. The joint was gone and so was Sasha.

"Rhett Butler liked his wacky tabacky too," Flip said with a chuckle. "I'm gonna change into a fresh muumuu, then get the meat twinkies ready. You wanna drive or you want me to?"

"I'll drive," I said, still staring at the empty spot where the joint had been. "Apparently, Stephano is joining us."

"The vampire?" Flip asked.

"Yep."

"Excellent! The gals will be thrilled."

Scrubbing my hands over my face, I laughed. What was I doing?

I was going to the woowoo juju support meeting at the library with my weed-dealing aunt and an invisible vampire.

Life couldn't get any stranger.

CHAPTER FIFTEEN

"Pretty sure I'm overdressed," I said, glancing down at my fitted, pale green dress and wedge-heeled sandals. I'd been wearing sweats for so long, normal clothes felt foreign.

"You look hot. Your knockers are juicily fantastic and you could pop a quarter off that ass," Stephano assured me. "If you weren't like a mother figure to me, I'd hit on you."

"That was a compliment?" I asked, glaring at the idiot with my mouth open.

"What did he say?" Flip asked, balancing the Crockpot full of meat twinkies in her hands as we made our way across the very full parking lot.

"You don't want to know," I muttered. "What's going on at the library tonight? I thought you said there aren't many woowoo juju gals."

"Only three. I make four," Aunt Flip said. "I ain't got no clue why the library is hoppin' on a Thursday night."

"This is a horrible idea," I said, pausing by a red pickup

truck. "What if the black and decker pecker wrecker is in there?"

"That cow can't read anything but a cue card," Flip grunted. "Why would she be at the library?"

She had a point. "Okay, but…"

"But what, baby?" Aunt Flip asked.

I pulled on my hair and sucked my lower lip into my mouth. "I feel wonky. If I get overwhelmed, I'm going to wait for you in the car."

"Woowoo wonky or general wonky?" Flip asked.

I blew out a breath of frustration. "I don't know the difference."

"I'll stay with you," Stephano promised. "It would be delightful to sit in the car and play I Spy and sing folk songs."

I glanced at him. The vampire's idea of fun was actually sweet—bizarre but sweet.

Flip turned around and walked back to where I stood frozen to the spot. She put the Crockpot down on the pavement and wrapped her arms around me.

"It's okay to be scared, baby girl," she whispered. "We don't gotta do this. I might be pushin' too hard. Jumper always said I was too bossy for my own good. If this is too much, we can get right back in the car and go home. We can have a meat twinkie feast and watch that show where people don't throw their garbage out."

Her arms around me felt like home. I was safe in Flip's embrace. She loved me. And yes, she was bossy, but she was often right. I was being silly. I'd handled Weather Hooker on my own. Meeting the woowoo juju gals would be a piece of cake—crazy cake.

Kissing the top of Flip's head, I fluffed her curly do. "While the thought of leaving is tempting, if we don't go in, your buddies won't see your beautiful perm."

"Perm's gonna still be there tomorrow," she replied with a chuckle. "You're my priority, not my sexy new hairdo."

"I vote that we go in," Stephano volunteered. "I've never been in a library, and I understand librarians are stacked and don't wear underpants."

Ignoring most of what he'd just said, I keyed in on the non-pornographic part. "You've never been in a library?"

Libraries were one of my favorite places in the world along with bookstores. I'd logged too many hours to count at the very library we were standing in front of while growing up. Mrs. Pringle, the librarian—who was definitely not sexy —used to allow me to check out more than the allotted number of books weekly. I was a voracious reader. I still was.

"No," Stephano said. "No libraries in the Good to the Last Bloody Drop series."

He was correct. I'd have to remedy that.

"We're going in," I said, straightening my shoulders and pushing away my fears. "I'm fine."

"Yesssss, you are," Stephano agreed. "And if you didn't hold sway over my life with your nimble fingers and wild imagination, I'd suggest a quick and sweaty bang against that wall over there."

"Stephano, you're going to need to tamp that shit back. It's not working," I told him.

He was shocked. "It's not?"

"Nope. Your lines suck," I pointed out.

Stephano took in my assessment with a defeated sigh. His chin dropped to his chest and I thought he might cry. "I'm no good on my own. I need you to put the words in my mouth," he admitted, kicking the pebbles on the pavement with his black motorcycle boots.

How were people who were not real making me feel bad? "Look," I said, patting him on the back. "It's not that your lines totally suck, you just come on a little strong. Maybe if you didn't feel so free to describe female body parts in graphic detail you might do a little better."

"You think I should eliminate the phrase juicy knockers?" he asked.

"That's a good start," I told him.

He nodded slowly. I wasn't sure if he understood what I meant or if he was trying to play it off. He wasn't the sharpest tool in the shed.

"So, instead of sweaty bang, I should have said vigorous shag?"

"Umm... no. That would not be better."

"Are you serious?" he asked, completely perplexed. "It's much classier. Sounds kind of British—you know, the shag part."

"How about this?" I suggested. "I'll write you a list of lines that will not offend women."

"You would do that for me?" he asked with a smile that was sexy and adorable. Vampires were very charming.

"Yes," I said. "To save myself and others from having to

listen to you wax poetic about knockers and sweaty sex against brick walls in public, I would do that for you."

"Is Stephano gettin' spicy?" Flip asked with a grin.

"He's trying," I told her, picking up the Crockpot off the ground. "He's failing at the moment, but we're going to work on it. You ready?"

"Question is, are you?" Flip countered.

"Nope," I said with a laugh as I walked toward the entrance of the library. "And for your information, Stephano… the librarian is a happily married seventy-one-year-old, and I'm pretty sure she wears panties."

"That's very tragic," he muttered.

I shook my head and smiled. My characters were like naughty dysfunctional children—deadly, beautiful, certifiably insane children.

Pausing at the front door, I eyed Stephano. "You can't actually bite anyone, can you?"

"Sadly, no," he said. "Is there someone you would have liked me to turn?"

"Absolutely not," I told him. "Just behave. I can't have you asking questions. It would look bad if I answered you, considering I'm the only one who can see you."

"I can see how that might make you look mentally imbalanced."

"The fact that I'm having this conversation already proves that," I assured him. "Just don't talk to me when others are around. Cool?"

"Cool."

"Actually," I said, thinking of all the things that could go horribly wrong—there were too many to count. "Maybe just hang out in the back of the room and be quiet."

"What if you need my help?" he asked, hurt that I was confining him to the corner.

"How could you help me?" I asked, wondering why Clark had let Stephano come. While the vamp was beautiful and deadly, he wasn't my most intelligent character.

He shrugged. "Advice on how to bite someone without killing them? Amorous gazes that will render your busty, evil nemesis into a state of intense horniness so you can shag her—which you both know you want even though you're on separate sides of the cartel. Ways to hide your fangs if you're in a fit of bloodlust? There are so many ways I can be useful."

I closed my eyes for a brief moment. The plot revealing itself had all the trappings of a disaster. Stephano was trying. I had to give that to him.

"Great," I said, careful of his feelings. I knew he could pout like a two-year-old. "If I need to know any of that, I'll ask."

Stephano bowed to me and walked right into the library.

"Is he still yackin'?" Aunt Flip asked.

"Nope, he's done," I told her with a shake of my head and a laugh. "He's more of a hot mess than I am."

"Maybe that's why he's here," Flip pointed out, taking the Crockpot from my hands.

"Not following," I said.

"If Stephano is a walkin' shitshow, you'll be so busy making sure he doesn't wreak havoc that you won't have time to feel wonky."

"That's absurd," I said, wondering how much havoc Stephano could actually wreak...

Flip grinned. "No more absurd than woowoo juju or the fact that an invisible vampire is lookin' for a librarian with no grundies on."

"Shit," I muttered, quickly entering the library and scanning the crowded lobby for my horny character. On the outside chance that the idiot could lift up Mrs. Pringle's skirt to check on her underwear status, I needed to rein him in and keep him within eyeshot.

"Dang," Flip said, pointing to a sign. "Too bad we have a meetin' tonight."

"Why?" I asked, unable to locate the randy vamp.

"Roger's doin' a tapdancing puppet show. That man is amazing with the kids. They just love him to bits."

"Roger?" I asked, confused.

"My one-legged buddy from the pig episode," she explained, waving at Ann Aramini, who was sporting a long purple cape, heavy black eyeliner and a pointed hat trimmed in purple feathers.

I swallowed back my shock at Ann Aramini's getup. She looked like she was dressed up for Halloween. "Umm... is Ann Aramini part of the puppet show?"

"Nah," Flip said. "Ann's got the woowoo."

"You're shitting me," I said.

"I shit you not, baby girl," she replied with a grin. "Ann Aramini can move objects with her mind, among a few other little nifty tricks."

I'd thought a sexed-up invisible vampire was weird.

Clearly, my definition of weird was incorrect.

"You good to go?" Flip asked.

"As good as I'm going to be," I told her, not believing my words but deciding to dive into the deep end with a semi-positive attitude.

"That's my girl," Flip said. "Just you wait. You're gonna have a great time."

I wasn't sure Flip's description of great matched mine, but it would definitely be memorable. Of that I was sure.

"OH MY GOD," I HISSED AS WE PASSED THE CHILDREN'S section. "Duck."

I yanked Aunt Flip down behind a towering display of princess books. Of all the people who could be here, I didn't need to see him.

"What?" Flip asked, dropping into a squat next to me. "Is the pecker wrecker here?"

"No," I said, feeling myself begin to sweat.

"Darren?" she tried again.

"Umm... no." What the hell was wrong with me? I wasn't in high school. I was a grown-ass woman who was here for a woowoo juju meeting. I had a vampire with me and my former high school counselor was dressed like a witch. My aunt had made weed-filled goodie bags for her buddies and was carrying a Crockpot full of soggy meat twinkies. If none of that phased me, why did a man and his adorable daughter?

"Why are we hiding?" she asked.

The question was incredibly logical. My behavior was not.

"I don't know," I told her truthfully.

"Okay," Flip said, acting as if what we were doing wasn't out of the norm. "You wanna try to figure it out? The meat twinkies are gonna dissolve if we don't eat 'em soon."

"That's really gross," I pointed out.

"Don't you worry about that," Flip said. "I've got a few bottles of catsup in my bag. Them gals won't even notice. We can hide as long as you want to."

"I don't want to hide anymore," I said.

She nodded. "Well now, that's up to you. I got good knees so I can squat for at least twelve minutes."

God, she was awesome. And I was pathetic. The library was crowded. There was no reason I would bump into Seth Walters and Cheeto if I was careful. And so what if I did? I was acting like a fool. The man was to-die-for handsome, but he wasn't on the market and neither was I. Not to mention, I was technically still married and Seth was out of my league. He was never in my damn league.

"I'm a dummy," I muttered.

"So am I," Flip said. "We're all dummies sometimes. Builds character."

I looked at my aunt. She was crouched down wearing a polka dot green and yellow muumuu holding a pot of mushy weenies. She didn't question my insanity and clearly loved me. She was every kind of wonderful.

"Okay," I said, reaching down deep for my confidence. "We're going to stand up. We will not make eye contact with anyone. If you don't look at people, they don't look at you."

181

"Good plan," she said. "Then what?"

"Where is the meeting room?"

"In the back left corner," she said.

We were on the right side of the lobby, which meant we had to cross through the crowd. Dammit. Whatever. "We walk quickly. Stop for nothing or no one. You feel me?"

"Got it," Flip said, excited. "It's like we're running from the law while we're carrying a shitload of weed."

I paused and raised my brow. "Are we?"

"Are we what?" she asked.

"Carrying a shitload of weed?"

"Hell to the yes," Flip announced with a wide grin.

The ways for the evening to go straight to Hades were increasing.

"Awesome," I said dryly. "Eyes down. Make contact with no one. Let's move."

"This is exciting," Flip whispered loudly. "I can feel the magic coming back already!"

She was nuts. All I felt was sweaty. If this was woowoo juju, it kind of sucked.

CHAPTER SIXTEEN

"Holy crap," I ground out. "This can't be happening."

Unfortunately, the tower of princess books crashed to the ground when Flip and I jumped to our feet. To me, it sounded like a bomb had exploded. The noise reverberated through my body and I wondered if my newly emerging woowoo included the power to render myself invisible. That would be awesome. I closed my eyes thinking if I couldn't see anyone, they couldn't see me.

It did not work. I was still here and everyone was staring. So much for being covert.

"Beautiful Clementine!" Cheeto squealed.

"Busted," Aunt Flip said. "I think we've been spotted."

"Ya think?" I asked with a wince, trying to gather up the books and remake the tower. "Hi Cheeto."

The little girl had upped her game. Her crown was still perched on her blonde curls, but her tutu was missing. Tonight, she wore a full-on sparkly, pink princess costume with mismatched tennis shoes. Cheeto had unicorn stickers all over her face and chocolate all over her mouth.

She was beautiful.

"Are you here for the puppet show?" she asked, bouncing on her little feet.

"Nope, I'm not," I told her, trying to keep my focus on her and not the man standing next to her. He was wearing jeans, tennis shoes and a blue Henley that matched his eyes perfectly.

He was gorgeous. So what? There were millions of beautiful people in the world. He was a dime a dozen. Pretty men were bad news. That was going to be my new mantra. My brain told me it was a brilliant motto, but the butterflies dancing in my stomach disagreed.

"Who's your little friend?" Aunt Flip asked, smiling at Cheeto.

"I'm Cheeto. I'm on a date with my daddy, Seth," she answered, touching Flips muumuu with delight and awe. "What's your name?"

"I'm Flip."

Cheeto grinned. "You're as beautiful as Clementine. Are you married? I'm in the market for a new mommy. Clementine is not available. Are you?"

Flip laughed and squatted down in front of the child. "I'm a little old for your daddy," she said. "I think it's impressive that you're helping your daddy find him a gal, but you might wanna let him work on that himself."

"He's terrible at it," Cheeto informed Flip with a giggle.

"Means he's not ready then," she said as the little girl caressed Flip's cheek.

"I'm so sorry," Seth said, embarrassed as he stared at Flip and me with a strange look on his face.

"No worries," Flip assured him. "I know I'm a looker with my new perm. Must be why I got the proposal."

Seth smiled. My tongue felt tied in a knot. The stupid-ass beauty of his grin made my knees weak.

"Your hair is lovely, Miss…"

"Just call me Flip," she said. "And I tell you what, if I was a few years younger, I'd have taken your little gal up on the offer. You're a fine-lookin' boy."

Seth chuckled. "Thank you, Flip."

"I would look pretty in a dress like yours," Cheeto said, admiring Flip's muumuu. "Can I come to your house, and we can make one for me?"

Seth scooped Cheeto up in his arms. "Cheeto, we don't invite ourselves to people's houses. It's not polite. Again, my apologies," he said to Flip and me with a perplexed expression.

"What's the matter?" Flip asked him. "Do I have meat twinkie on my face?"

"Umm… as far as I know, no," he said, clearly having no clue what a meat twinkie was. I was glad I wasn't the only one. "It's just that Cheeto doesn't speak to people much and she… she speaks to both of you."

I had a good idea why Cheeto might be withdrawn, but I hadn't seen any evidence. She'd glued herself to me immediately after we'd met at the law office and she'd talked my ear off.

Flip stared at Cheeto for a long moment, then winked at

the little girl. "She just needs some friends who understand her."

Cheeto laughed and reached for Flip. Handing me the Crockpot filled with disintegrating corndogs, she took the little girl into her arms. Seth was shocked. I was still wondering if my tongue worked. Hopefully not. Speaking words right now would probably not be wise. I was terrified I would tell him that his jeans made his ass look great. Or even worse, that you could pop a quarter off of his butt. Stephano might have come by his lines honestly. The thought was horrifying.

"I understand my daughter," Seth said tightly.

"Course you do," Flip said. "She just needs some other buddies."

"I want you," Cheeto told Flip. "And Clementine."

"That can be arranged," Flip promised the child.

"It can?" I choked out, sounding like a frog.

Seth shot me a concerned look. To be fair, it did sound like I was choking on my own spit.

"Sure can," Flip said. "Come on by tomorrow and I'll cut up one of my muumuus and make you a muumuu of your own."

"Can we daddy? Pleeeeeeease?" Cheeto begged.

"Well…" he said, looking at me, unsure of how to answer.

Think. I needed to think. This was a bad plan. I knew Seth wasn't interested in me. I wasn't interested in him. I was in the midst of an ugly divorce and nothing he'd done suggested he felt anything for me other than pity. However, the very real chance that I would embarrass myself beyond repair increased in his presence. The man made me stupid. I didn't like it one bit.

"Doesn't Cheeto have school tomorrow?" I asked, thinking I'd just neatly solved the issue.

"I'm homeschooling her right now," Seth admitted, uncomfortable. "She won't speak to others."

Flip's nose scrunched. "Finding that a little hard to buy," she said, tweaking a delighted Cheeto's cheek. "This little princess is a yacker."

Seth watched in relieved confusion as Cheeto reeled off her favorite foods and colors to a very attentive Flip. He ran his hands through his hair and smiled at me apologetically. "If it's not too much of an imposition, we would love to stop by at some point tomorrow. We won't stay long."

I was mesmerized by the movement of his mouth. I didn't hear a word he said.

"Tell him you want to lay him out on a stack of books and bang him until he doesn't know his name," Stephano whispered in my ear. "Then tell him you're not wearing panties and will ride him like a bull in a china shop. *That* is a good line."

"Are you insane?" I hissed at Stephano, as Seth's expression tightened.

"My apologies," Seth said stiffly, taking Cheeto from Flip's arms. "That was forward of me."

"No," I said about ten times louder than necessary. "I was umm... talking to..."

"Herself," Flip chimed in. "My Clemmy is an author. She talks to herself all the time. It's what creative people do."

Or crazy people.

"Right," I agreed quickly with a slight wince. It was definitely better to let Seth think I talked to myself rather than the out-of-his-gourd invisible vampire standing next to me. "What did you ask? I got lost inside the gaping hole of my mind there for a hot sec."

The more I talked, the more idiotic I sounded.

"Daddy asked if we could come over tomorrow," Cheeto volunteered. "Pleeeeeease say yes."

"Say yes," Stephano urged. "You can fornicate with him in the foyer closet while Flip makes the muumuu. Everyone wins."

Headbutting Stephano seemed like an excellent move. However, it would look really strange and be difficult to explain.

"Sure," I said. "We live—"

"I know where you live, Clementine," Seth said with a smile.

Coming from some people, his words could sound spooky and ominous. Coming from Seth's lips they sounded like freaking foreplay.

"We have a plan," Flip said, taking the Crockpot from me. "See you tomorrow. We gotta skedaddle or we're gonna be late for the woowoo juju meetin'."

Her eyes grew large when she realized she'd just outed us.

"Woowoo juju?" Seth asked, curious.

"Yes, umm… woowoo juju… it's short for… you know… work work jump jump," I said, lying through my teeth and making it up as I went along. I was a writer of fiction. How hard could this be? "It's for people addicted to Jazzercise."

"Exactly," Flip agreed.

"You know," I kept going, even though I should have put a cork in it, "we help each other to… umm… stop jumping so much."

"By sitting on each other," Flip added.

I laughed. It sounded forced but it was better than screaming in terror. "No, we don't actually sit on each other," I assured a wildly confused Seth.

"We don't?" Flip asked.

"I think the entire concept is very hot," Stephano chimed in. "Women sitting on top of each other gives me a boner."

"You need to shut your cakehole," I snapped, then slapped my hand over my mouth. Speaking through splayed fingers, I dug my grave even deeper. "I was talking to myself again."

My explanation was like a shitty first draft. This entire story was worse than my Regency novel. I wanted to sink into the floor and melt like the Wicked Witch of the West. Or it might be better if cannibal pigs ate me.

"Got it," Seth said with a grin. "See you tomorrow. And thank you."

I nodded. I couldn't risk speaking again after the crap that had just left my lips. We watched in silence as they walked away. Cheeto waved until they disappeared into the crowd.

"I think that went well," Stephano commented.

"Then you need your brain checked," I muttered.

"Could have been worse," Flip pointed out.

"How?" I asked.

She didn't have an answer. I didn't either.

"Fine," I said, trying to center myself. "Let's go work off our Jazzercise addiction."

Flip cackled and led the way.

So far, the evening had been a disaster. It had to go up from here.

"You can fly?" I asked Sally Dubay who was easily pushing ninety.

"Sure can," she said, filling a paper plate with meat twinkies. "Did you bring catsup, Flip?"

"Yep," Flip replied, pulling out two bottles from her bag and plopping them on the table next to the Crockpot.

"Wait," I said, taking the bottle of catsup from Sally and opening it for her. "Like a bird? In the air?"

"Sure can," she repeated as Ann Aramini stood behind her shaking her head frantically. "Would you like a demonstration?"

Taking my cue from Ann Aramini, who was now shaking her head so hard, purple feathers were flying from her hat, I declined. "Maybe some other time."

"You just let me know, darlin'," Sally said, emptying half the bottle of catsup onto her meat twinkies.

As Sally walked away, Ann Aramini leaned in. "Do not *ever* ask her to fly. Last time she tried, she hit a tree and had to be hospitalized. It wasn't easy to explain how a ninety-year-old woman hit a tree going fifty miles an hour."

"I guess not," I said politely, wondering if I was being punked. There was no way in hell Sally Dubay could move at fifty miles an hour. She walked with a cane. "Umm... when did that happen?"

"'Bout six months ago," Ann Aramini said. "Sally still has a dent in her forehead. It's amazing. You should feel it. She won't mind."

"I'm good," I said, looking around the small meeting room. There was a white table against the wall and a collection of nondescript black folding chairs.

The walls were white. The carpet was gray. There was little to no color or life in the room except for the group of deranged women—myself included. And colorful was an understatement to describe us.

While it was impossible to deny I saw my characters, since Stephano was leaning on the table next to the Crockpot, I'd have to say the other woowoo juju ladies might be truly off their rockers.

"Okay gals, load up your vittles and sit your asses down, we have a lot to cover this fine evenin'," Flip announced.

"About damn time you got with the program," Joy Parsley snapped, glaring at me.

Joy Parsley was not a joy at all. She was the gal who filed official complaints about everything and everyone. She sat on every single board in town. People turned and sprinted the other way when they saw her coming. I'd modeled several of my most annoying characters after her. I'd been so tempted to name one of them Joy, but I was very aware she read my books. She'd sent me a ten-page critique after the last one came out. Joy took umbrage at every single thing I'd written except the sex scenes. She liked those.

The cranky woman stood about five feet tall and had a

sour expression on her face twenty-four seven. I'd guess her age to be in her later sixties, but she'd pretty much looked the same her whole life. It was a little hard to believe that she had woowoo juju. I'd thought it was supposed to be about the good in the world.

"Joy, hush your mouth," Ann Aramini chastised her. "If you scare Clementine off, I will tie your boney ass in a knot."

Joy shrugged, grabbed an entire bottle of catsup for herself and stomped over to a chair.

"She's a little bitchy, but she grows on you after a while," Ann Aramini said.

"Like a fungus?" I asked before I could stop myself.

Ann Aramini laughed and pointed at me. "You watch that mouth or Joy Parsley will report you for something."

I gave her a thumbs up and considered waiting in the car.

"Stay," Stephano said. "I'm fascinated by these people."

"Sexually?" I asked under my breath, wondering if the vampire liked everything that possessed lady bits.

"Oddly, no," he said. "However, I do find the one in the cape and pointy hat somewhat enticing."

I walked away. It was too tempting to keep talking to the over-sexed, undead freak. Sitting down next to Sally, I kept my eyes averted from her plate. It literally looked like she was eating roadkill.

"Who wants to start?" Flip asked.

"Start what?" I asked, growing more uncomfortable.

"We're all gonna share stories about our gifts," Flip explained.

"So that way when you take over, you'll be up to speed," Ann Aramini added.

I felt a little light-headed. What the hell was she talking about? "I'm not taking over."

"Yep, you are," Joy informed me in a tone that didn't expect any backtalk.

She was going to report me for something. I was sure of it. I also didn't care. "Wrong," I said to Joy, whose eyes grew huge and displeased. "I'm still coming to terms with the fact I might not be insane. There's no way in hell I will be in charge of people who have bought in and embraced it."

"Did she just call us crazy?" Sally asked with a mouthful of meat twinkie.

"Yep," Ann Aramini said with a laugh. "And she got that right. We're all born crazy. Only the lucky ones get to stay that way."

Sally giggled and nodded. "I don't suffer from insanity. I enjoy every dang minute of it! Did y'all know that when I was a youngin', I thought plastic bags were parachutes? I jumped off the garage roof and broke my arm. Did it again the next day and broke the other one."

"Is there a point to that story?" I asked, happy she hadn't jumped off the roof of a two-story house.

Sally thought about it for a long moment, then shrugged. "I'm sure there is, but for the life of me I can't recall it."

"No worries," Flip said. "Ann Aramini, you wanna tell Clementine about the external disaster that brought on your woowoo juju?"

I seriously hoped there were no cannibal pigs involved.

"Yes siree," she said, pulling a chair over next to me and

straddling it. "You ever heard of Boston's Great Molasses Flood of 1919?"

"Can't say I have," I replied warily. If she was going to inform me that she'd lived through it and was over a hundred years old, I was out of here.

"Well, lemme tell you about it," Ann Aramini said. "At midday on a goddang cold January the 15th in the year 1919, a whole hell of a lot of sweet, sticky death flowed from a burst storage tank. Now you see, the tank was designed to hold fermented molasses, which was used in the process of making industrial alcohol for munitions and other World War I era weapons."

"Not the kind of alcohol you drink," Sally chimed in. "You'd end up with gut rot from that stuff. I stick to moonshine. Better for my arthritis."

That was a new one to me...

"Correct," Ann Aramini agreed. "So anyhoo, the wave that got released was forty feet high and over a hundred feet wide. It blasted through the streets of Boston faster than a knife fight in a phone booth.

"Faster than green gas through a goose," Sally said with a giggle.

"Faster than a one-legged man in a butt-kickin' competition," Joy grunted.

That one confused me a little, but I didn't want to get into it with Joy again.

"Faster than a hot knife through butter," Flip added, clearly not wanting to be left out.

"Faster than Leticia La Monet, the vicious, sexy gargoyle shifter with the enormous bosom who uses men like someone with gastric issues uses sanitary paper to wipe their ass," Stephano announced, delighted to be part of the group even though no one could hear him—which was probably a good thing.

"Okay," I said, holding my hand up. "I get it. It was fast."

Ann Aramini nodded. "Point is, it moved like lightnin'— at least thirty-five miles an hour. The sticky shit knocked down buildings and covered up cars, horses and people. It was a hot damned mess. Course, it was colder than a witch's tit at that time of year, so that viscous molasses turned rock hard, trappin' anyone who happened to be in its path. Killed 'em dead."

"Horrible story," Flip said, shaking her head. "Just dang awful."

I waited for the next part or at the very least a punch line. Neither came.

"Is there a point to that story?" I asked.

"Yep, while I wasn't alive during the Boston Great Molasses Flood, I *was* alive during the swampin' deluge of the Kentucky Maple Syrup Kaboom. It was just like the Boston tragedy,

'cept it wasn't winter, nobody died and it only moved about a half a mile an hour. Buzz Cooter was playin' with fireworks and blew up his pappy's syrup factory. I got caught up in it and got stuck to a cow feeder for three days before my mamma found me. She was pissed. She marched over to the Cooters' house and tanned Buzz Cooter's hide real good. He couldn't sit for a week. After they peeled me off the cow feeder, I got the woowoo."

I bit down on my lip so I wouldn't laugh. "That's a real thing?"

Ann Aramini had a very serious expression on her face. "As real as my saggy bosom," she stated.

"I rather like the witch's hooters," Stephano commented. "While they're not exactly perky, the left one appears quite solid. I would love to take a bite out of those knockers."

"That's it," I said, whipping around and glaring at Stephano. "What did I tell you about talking about women's body parts?"

"Not to call them juicy," Stephano said, looking quite pleased with himself.

I gave up. "Go sit in the car. You're grounded," I told him. "You cannot take a bite out of anyone's breasts."

"What if I promise to be good? Can I stay? Pleeeeease?" Stephano begged, giving me his best sad face.

I couldn't help myself. I laughed. "Fine. You have one more strike, then you're out."

"Is she talking to Rhett Butler?" Sally asked.

"Doubtful," Ann Aramini said. "From what I recall, Rhett wasn't a cannibal."

"Stephano is *not* a cannibal," I said, defending the asshat. "He's a... he's a..."

Oh my God. From now on, I was listening to my gut. I never should have left the house. I might never leave it again. The evening had gone from bad to disastrous.

"Vampire," Flip said, helping me out. "Stephano is a vampire."

Joy laughed. I'd never heard that sound from her before. "Well, I'll be damned. Flip, you were correct."

"About what?" I asked, still shocked that Joy could laugh.

"That you got the gift that Jumper had," Sally said, clasping her hands together with delight. "Everything will be okay. I feel it in my old bones! The darkness can be held at bay!"

Letting my chin fall to my chest, I groaned. Going to the car with Stephano seemed like an excellent plan, but my curiosity was piqued. My obsessive need to catalogue information that would require me buying myself a straight-jacket was most certainly my fatal flaw.

Standing up and pacing the small room, I tried to put my thoughts in order. Psychic abilities were not crazy. Many had been documented. There were people who helped the police on cases of missing persons. There were those who could commune with people who'd moved on to the after-life. There were palm readers and others who could see the future. I'd incorporated psychic gifts into many of my fictional characters... keyword being *fictional*. However, I'd never heard of people who could magically start fires, fly, or talk to people they made up in their imagination.

Flip had said that I not only needed to accept my woowoo juju, I needed to embrace it.

Fine. I was still going to decline the invite to lead the nutbags, but I wanted to know exactly what I was passing on.

"You," I said, pointing at Joy. "What's your superpower?"

"I touch objects, and I can tell you their story," she replied.

At least that was logical. I was expecting something far more bizarre.

"Tell her the good one," Flip insisted.

"When I drink five beers, I can render myself invisible," Joy added.

"It's a real hoot," Sally said with a giggle. "I tripped over her the last time she did it—couldn't see her. Dang near broke my leg."

So much for logical.

"Alrighty then," I said, shaking my head. "Is that all you do, Joy?"

Joy grunted. "I think that's pretty damn impressive. But if you really have to know, I also sing arias without moving my lips."

"That's considered woowoo juju?" I asked, still absorbing that she thought she could tie one on and disappear.

"No, but it's very difficult," Joy stated in her defense.

"I'd love to hear that," Stephano said.

If I was being honest, I would as well. However, that would take time. All I wanted to do was leave. My bullshit meter was blasting in my head, but my lack of self-preservation and sanity skills had roared to the forefront.

"Ann Aramini, spill it," I said, waiting to be surprised or, more likely, appalled.

"I can move objects with my mind, and I can shift into a house cat," she replied with a straight face.

Appalled for the win.

"Is there pot in the meat twinkies?" I demanded of my aunt.

"Nope," Flip assured me. "But I did bring some brownies. You want one?"

"No. No, I do not want one," I said, running my hands

through my hair and wanting to pull it out of my head. "Ann Aramini, that isn't possible."

She just grinned and shrugged. "See that over there?" she asked, pointing to a gelatinous glob under the table.

"Unfortunately, yes," I said, gagging a little.

"Hairball," she informed me with pride. "Puked it up about ten minutes before you arrived."

"Of course you did," I said with an eye roll. "What else do you have in your bag of tricks?"

"When in cat form, I can sniff out danger and suppressors of magic," she announced as the others bowed their heads in respect. "Over the years, my shnoz has alerted us to who we need to run out of town so the darkness can't settle here permanently."

"And that's where I come in," Joy said.

"By rendering yourself invisible while drunk?" I asked, squinting at her in disbelief.

"Nah," she said with a chuckle. "I just make their life a living hell by reporting them till they pack up and skedaddle."

"Are you telling me that *everyone* you report is a suppressor?"

"Umm… that would be a no," Joy admitted somewhat sheepishly with another chuckle.

I wasn't sure if I was more shocked by the fact that she'd just chuckled or that there was rhyme and reason behind her obsessive need to report people to the town council.

"And if that don't work, Joy gets hammered, goes invisible and rearranges their furniture till they think they're losing their marbles," Flip added, grinning from ear to ear.

"I can see how that might be unsettling," I said, then slapped myself in the forehead. I couldn't believe that I was taking any of this seriously.

"Flip, does Clementine know what you can do?" Sally asked.

"Some of it," Flip said, winking at me.

I dropped down onto a chair and eyed my aunt. "Tell me the rest."

"I can detect illness in folks," Flip said, sobering and sighing. "Breaks my heart."

"Maybe so," Ann Aramini said, putting her arm around my aunt. "But I'd be as dead as a doornail if you hadn't seen my cancer."

Flip hugged her friend and swiped at a tear. "You're the reason I amped up my hobby."

"And thankful I am," Ann Aramini told her.

"Wait," I said, as pieces of the warped puzzle began to click together. "You grow pot for people with illnesses? You're not a dealer?"

Flip grinned. "Never sold weed to anyone," she said. "Told you I couldn't sell nothin'. I give the Mary Jane away."

"Old Bertram Beetle has glaucoma," Sally volunteered, shaking her head with sorrow. "Flip's brownies have been a lifesaver for him."

"And Pootie Hughs is gettin' through chemo without the side effects 'cause of Flip," Joy added.

"Roger's been smokin' the wacky tabacky for years on account of the pig attack," Ann Aramini pointed out. "But that's only a small amount of the folks your aunt Flip has helped. There's Donna Deetle, Sean the Seafood Guy, Tiny Smith, Mr. Ted and so many more."

"Mr. Ted?" I asked. "Mr. Ted, my lawyer?"

"Yep," Flip confirmed. "Mr. Ted has shrapnel in his legs from Nam. That sweet man is in terrible pain."

The fact that we all called him Mr. Ted was surprising, but what I'd just learned about my aunt floored me.

My mind raced. Was I being hasty and selfish in saying no to helping the ladies? Had I finally lost my mind because I was considering joining the kooky brigade?

"I need to clarify a few more things," I said as the women exchanged delighted glances. If they thought they were being covert, they were sorely mistaken.

"Clarify away," Flip said with a wide smile.

"Okay." I moved back over to Sally. "Explain to me how flying helps people, please."

"Clementine's manners are lovely," Ann Aramini commented, going back for a second round of meat twinkies.

"I'd be happy to. Do you happen to recall the fire at the elementary school about ten years back?" Sally asked.

The woman had catsup on her chin. It was hard to stay focused on what she was saying. Grabbing a tissue from my bag, I gently wiped her chin.

"Thank you, darlin'," Sally said.

"Welcome," I replied. "And yes, I remember the fire. I was shocked that no one died. It was a miracle."

"Nope, it was Sally," Joy corrected me. "She flew on in and saved twenty-two little rug rats before the fire department even got there."

"And no one saw you do it?" I asked Sally.

She giggled. The sound was so sweet. "All children have the woowoo. They're born with it. Children haven't been jaded by common sense and the need to have a rational explanation for the beautiful things like pixie dust and magic. So yes, the little ones saw me and they never breathed a word."

"Most people lose their belief in woowoo juju by the time they're ten. They forget all about it," Joy pointed out. "It's only the special ones who get to keep the fairy dust forever."

I nodded. Somehow, this was all making sense to me.

"Do it," Stephano urged.

The fact that Stephano thought it was a good idea to take the job was worrisome. He also thought that snacking on Ann Aramini's knockers was a fine plan.

"Why?" I asked him.

"Because if the magic goes away, life will be the color of this room," he explained without a single reference to a female body part. "An existence with no color, no enchantment, no pixie dust, no ability to dream of the fantastical is tragic."

He was correct. And I was probably screwed.

After a long pause, I made my decision... kind of. "Trial basis," I stated firmly. "I'm kind of busy right now with a deadline and a divorce. What are the responsibilities of this job?"

"Adventure," Flip corrected me. "It's not a job. It's more like a calling."

"Fair enough," I said. "What are the requirements of the *adventure?*"

"None," Ann Aramini said.

"That sounds easy," Stephano pointed out.

"Too easy," I replied.

Sally stood up and flew around the room. It was shocking—especially when she crash-landed at my feet. "We just keep our eyes and our hearts open. When a need arises, we fill it with love and woowoo."

Helping her to her feet and making sure she hadn't broken a bone, I hugged the small woman close. "Trial basis," I reminded everyone.

"YEEEHAW!" Flip shouted, doing a little jig and handing out brownies. "With Clemmy at the wheel, I'm bettin' we're gonna find some more woowoo juju gals!"

"Darn tootin'," Ann Aramini said, biting into the pot brownie with gusto. "Screw the darkness, we got us a brand-new wrangler!"

"Can someone explain the darkness?" I asked.

The gals went silent. The joy was immediately sucked out of the room, and this time it wasn't Joy Parsley's fault.

"As the story goes," Joy said, sounding ominous, "there are those who recall having the woowoo as a child."

"And they remember it going away," Sally said with a shudder.

"Mostly they fixate on the loss of the woowoo juju. Normally, it's a natural progression from childhood into adulthood—no big deal," Ann Aramini explained. "But Rhett Butler and Glinda the Good Witch told us that some of those who remember the magic want it back… and will do anything to get it. When they realize they can't, they'll try to destroy those who do have the woowoo."

"Rhett Butler said this to your face?" I asked, wondering if it was the weed talking. "And Glinda the Good Witch?"

"Don't I wish," Sally said wistfully. "I don't care if he wore dentures, he was a looker. Rhett Butler talked to us via Jumper. The day that your sweet granny passed, Rhett, Scarlett, Dorothy and Glinda died with her."

"Baby Jane and Blanche kicked it too," Joy reminded everyone. "But that was probably a good thing. Those gals were insane."

"You got that right," Flip said with a little shudder. "After Jumper died, we were lost. I mean, we still find ways to use the juju to make other people's lives better, but we don't know how to protect it or find other woowooers."

"Woowooers?" I asked with a smile. "That's what you are?"

"We," Ann Aramini corrected, pointing at me. "*We* are woowooers. Some might call us witches, but we prefer woowooers or magic she-devils."

"I vote for voodoo hags," Joy said.

"Awesome," I muttered, picturing all of us in matching t-shirts with Voodoo Hags emblazoned across the front.

"You still in, Clemmy girl?" Flip asked hopefully.

I nodded. "I'm still in."

I was ninety-eight percent sure I'd live to regret the entire evening, but my body tingled with excitement. It was the same feeling I got when a book came together. However, even though it was a celebration of sorts, I did not indulge in the brownies.

Someone had to drive all the ladies home. And that someone was me.

I was officially—on a trial basis—the new woowoo juju wrangler slash magic she-devil slash voodoo hag supervisor.

May God help us all.

CHAPTER SEVENTEEN

"Do not eat them at work," I warned Nancy, handing her a baggie of Flip's special brownies. "You'll regret it and probably lose your job."

Nancy almost cried with joy and tried to hand me a soggy wad of cash again. "Tell your aunt I love her."

"No charge," I told her, holding up my hand. "Flip spreads her *flowers* for free to those in need."

"She's an angel on earth," Nancy said, tucking the brownies into her purse. "Mr. Ted will be with you in a bit. He's running just a tad behind this morning."

"No worries." I sat down, leaned back on the leather couch and closed my eyes. I was beat. Staying up most of the night writing didn't make for an alert gal. However, the words had flowed from my fingertips like magic.

I smiled. Absorbing all that had occurred over the last week was a challenge, especially Sally flying. Ann Aramini had offered to shift into a house cat when she was as high as a kite, but I'd forbid it. I was worried she wouldn't be able to shift back. Cats were not allowed in the library.

The ease at which I accepted the gal's *quirks* should have alarmed me.

It didn't.

I felt freer and more myself than I had in decades.

Stephano had a grand old time and made me promise again to write him a list of pick-up lines. I assured him I would. He definitely needed them. The vampire disappeared when I pulled into my garage after having dropped everyone home. Aunt Flip had fallen sound asleep. She'd worn herself out dancing and laughing like a loon. Her happiness and the other gals' exuberance had been contagious. An evening that had started out on a wildly embarrassing note had ended on a high one. Literally.

"How's the book coming along?" Nancy asked, looking hopeful for a few juicy tidbits.

I stared at her for a moment. I'd never used beta readers before. Nervous about my work being pilfered, I'd stuck with just Cyd's input over the years. My agent never steered me wrong. It was an incredibly productive, constructive and creative arrangement. But it seemed like Nancy knew my characters as well as I did—possibly better. She was a fan of the series...

"How would you feel," I began, as Nancy's eyes grew huge with shocked excitement and she leaned forward, "if Cassandra La Pierre didn't get offed?"

Nancy gasped, then compressed her lips in thought. "So, there are no consequences for her hideous actions?" she questioned.

"There will be consequences," I said, thinking it out as I spoke. "I just think it might be more shocking if she were…"

"REDEEMED," Nancy shouted, finishing my sentence. "Brilliant! But you have to send her to Hell or something like that to burn in fire for a decade or three. She can't get away with being such a heinous bitch without being incinerated for a while."

"Not bad," I said, thinking about the twist. "However, she had that thing with the demon mafia leader, Sven. Sending her to the bowels of Hell might not be a punishment at all."

"You make an excellent point," Nancy said. "But didn't she castrate Sven in a fit of passion in book two?"

"She did," I confirmed. "But demon body parts grow back."

"Even peckers?" Nancy asked, surprised.

"Even peckers," I said, grinning. The conversation was ridiculous and all kinds of awesome.

Nancy's expression turned positively naughty. "Send her to Heaven. She'll shit."

I was speechless. It was perfect. And Cassandra would be livid. Not that I wanted to piss her off, but if I let her off easy, my readers would revolt. Not to mention Cyd's head would pop off.

Nancy had just become my new muse. Chauncey was permanently fired.

"Have you ever had a book dedicated to you?" I asked, wondering if she would like that. Over the years, I'd dedicated my books to the people who were important to me— my parents, Granny, Aunt Flip, Jessica, Mandy, Cyd, my readers and, unfortunately, Darren.

Nancy screamed. I slapped my hands over my ears and half-expected stray dogs to come running into the lobby of the law firm.

"Ohmygod, ohmygod, ohmygod!" she squealed. "No, I have never had anything dedicated to me in my life... why?"

I was slightly terrified to tell her I wanted to dedicate the book to her for her amazing idea, due to the fact that my eardrums couldn't take another Nancy scream, but I went for it. "I'd like to dedicate *Exclusive* to you."

Nancy's mouth fell open. I quickly put my hands over my ears as a precautionary measure. However, she didn't scream. She cried. Her tears were happy tears—very snotty and very emotional.

"I'm so honored," Nancy blubbered. "This is the best day of my life. First the flowers to help with the fact that I sweat like a whore at confession six times a day and now... now I'll be immortalized in a series that I love by my favorite author in the Universe."

"That's a yes?" I asked with a laugh.

"Yes times all the hot flashes and chin hairs I have— which are a freaking lot," she said, blowing her nose. "Clementine, I realize you might not understand what you just did, but I have to tell you... I feel alive again—important —like someone sees me and values me. I'm just Nancy the secretary who sweats like a pig. I didn't matter... and now I do!"

I was a little thrown. I didn't know Nancy all that well, but it sounded like she didn't value *herself* very much. "Nancy, you matter. I matter. I've had a hard time believing that for a while, but I'm working on it. We all matter."

"I know," she said, still sniffling. "I do know. It's just that sometimes the dark clouds feel endless—like the sun will never shine again. Menopause sucks ass, Clementine. I hope you breeze right through it when your time comes."

"From your mouth to God's ears," I muttered, hoping for the same. The whole *whore at confession* thing wasn't appealing.

"Anyhow," she said with a big smile. "You truly made my day, my week and my year. If you ever want to brainstorm again, I'm here for you."

"I'll keep that in mind," I said, getting up and crossing the room to hug her. She was damp, but I hugged her anyway.

Being a woman could be some seriously hard shit. Support was crucial.

"We're ready for you," Mandy said, popping her head out of Mr. Ted's office with a wide grin on her face.

My smile came naturally and was as wide as my BFF's. "What are you doing here?" I asked, giving Nancy one last squeeze, then grabbing my purse.

"I work here," Mandy announced, waggling her brows. "And I have to say, I'm not sure I recognize you out of sweats. Lookin' good, sister."

I turned a circle and showed off my vintage skirt, cropped sweater and chunky wedges. I would never give up my sweats and sparkly flip-flops, but I was back in the real world. Looking cute never hurt anyone.

I was loath to admit it, but I'd dressed with Seth in mind —which was stupid. Hopefully, Seth and Cheeto would have come and gone by the time I got back home. I was still married to an asshole. And I wasn't going to jump into anything with anyone anytime soon. Not that Seth wanted to *jump* into anything with me. Cringing at the memory of the work work jump jump support group for Jazzercise addicts, I pushed the mortifying exchange away. He probably thought I was nuts.

Whatever. I liked myself better every day. It didn't matter if the man with the excellent ass thought I was batshit crazy.

All I needed was me, my friends, my work, my new woowoo juju clan and a divorce. My priorities were straight. Somewhat strange, but very clear.

"You ready for some good news?" Mandy asked, holding open the door to Mr. Ted's office.

"Hell to the yes."

I STARED AT THE PAPERWORK. MY BREATH CAME OUT IN SHORT spurts. Mandy and Mr. Ted watched me with interest.

"Explain again, please," I said as my heart raced.

Mandy pointed to the numbers at the top of the page. "This is what you spend on marketing and advertising yearly."

"It is."

"May I ask a question?" Mr. Ted inquired, examining his copy of what I was looking at.

"Shoot," I said.

"Why are you absorbing the costs? Why not your publisher?"

I'd asked myself the same question many times... "Well,

the industry has changed," I explained. "I'm not Stephen King or Nora Roberts. While there is an initial spend on the publishing house's part when one of my books comes out, there's not any financial support for backlist."

"So then in order to earn what you do, you have to make the investment to advertise the backlist. Correct?" Mandy asked.

"Correct," I confirmed. "I'd make less than half of what I'm pulling in if I didn't."

She nodded and put another page in front of me. "Gotta spend to earn. Get us up to speed on this."

"Audiobook expenses," I replied, feeling excited and light-headed. "Cyd, my agent, in an unheard-of move, got me my audio rights. I produce my audio and own it."

"That's expensive," Mr. Ted said, studying the numbers. "Quite a chunk of change."

"Worth it," I told him. "The audio helps sell the books and vice versa."

"This is looking prettier and prettier," Mandy commented, grabbing a calculator.

"It is?" I asked.

"It is," Mr. Ted said, smiling. "If Darren wants a piece of the action, he will have to pay dearly for the action to continue."

"For real?" I asked. I was glad I was seated. My knees felt like jelly.

"I believe so," Mr. Ted explained. "He would be far smarter to take the *overly generous* settlement you agreed to than to have to be a partner in the ongoing financial demand of selling the backlist and paying for half of the audio cost. He'd come out with very little to nothing to show for it."

"Yesssss," Mandy hissed, punching in numbers. "That shitbox will be broker than he already is." She paused in horror and glanced over at Mr. Ted. "Sorry."

Mr. Ted closed his eyes and tried not to smile.

He smiled.

"As long as you don't use the term shitbox in court, I'm fine with it," he told her.

"Fine point, well made," Mandy said, still blushing in embarrassment. "And I don't think this will go to court. Not when Tiny Darren hears what he'll be liable for. I think he'll settle."

"Tiny Darren?" Mr. Ted inquired.

"Scratch that," Mandy said quickly.

"Will do," Mr. Ted replied with a raised brow and a chuckle.

"He thinks he's getting the house, according to the black and decker pecker wrecker," I said, then let my head fall to Mr. Ted's desk in mortification. "I meant Jinny Jingle," I whispered, staring at the dark wood.

"Caught that," Mr. Ted said dryly. "Both of you can stop trying to edit your speech. We're in the confines of my office. Whatever you say is fine... and quite amusing, if I do say so myself."

"Do you realize what you're getting into?" Mandy asked her boss with a laugh.

"I have a fine idea," he replied.

"Actually, you don't," I told him, grinning.

"I was in Vietnam. Trust me, you young ladies can't scar me."

I bit down on my bottom lip. I almost asked him about the shrapnel pain. There was no reason in hell I would know about that. However, I let myself smile inside, knowing that Flip helped him deal with it.

As to letting Mandy and me talk filter-free... Ask and you shall receive.

"Weather Hooker ambushed me in Curl Up and Dye," I said.

Mandy was pissed. "How did she know you were there?"

"Sissy's niece—who got fired, by the way," I told her. "Anyway, she let me know that her *boopy* promised her that the house would be his, and I'd be out on the street."

"Her boopy?" Mandy asked with a snort. "More like droopy."

"Exactly," I agreed. "And microscopic. But as far as I know, that's not possible. Granny and Aunt Flip locked the house up tight when I inherited it."

Mr. Ted, who was now blushing, pulled the paperwork on the house. He'd gotten more than he bargained for. He didn't have daughters—just a son, who was hopefully at my house right now and would be gone when I returned home.

Mr. Ted cleared his throat. "The house goes to the historical society or a living relative when you die," he said.

My stomach tightened. My thoughts were completely screwed up, but... "So, since I'm still married to the assbag, if I died before we were divorced, he could claim the house?"

All three of us were silent.

"Possibly," Mr. Ted said tightly.

"The people," Mandy shouted, jumping to her feet. "The people Darren of the dwarf dick sent to scare you. Do you think they were supposed to murder you?"

The answer was a definitive no, but there was no way to explain that without sounding like I needed to be institutionalized. Crap.

"No. I really don't think so," I said, trying to come up with a reasonable way to make Mandy drop her logical assumption. "I think they were either hired to scare me or they were simply fans of my books."

"Stalkers?" Mr. Ted asked, looking worried.

I shrugged. I was in a little too deep here. "More like enthusiastic readers," I said. "No guns. No threats. They were actually quite polite."

Mandy and Mr. Ted exchanged glances.

I had to convince them or at least change the subject. "And I have a hard time believing that Darren would kill me over the house."

Mr. Ted pressed his temples. "You'd be surprised at what desperate people will do. It's a highly doubtful scenario, but I've seen all kinds of unsavory behavior during my career."

"I'm a little concerned now," Mandy said, sitting back down and running her hands through her hair in frustration.

"Why?" I asked.

She sighed. "Once the douchebag realizes that all he's getting is the settlement, he might snap."

I wanted to puke. I'd been married to Darren for over two decades. While he could be a sexist asshole, he wasn't a murderer. "How fast can the divorce be finalized after the settlement is agreed on?" I asked, feeling like I was plotting a book. The scary part was that this wasn't fiction, it was my life.

"Since there are no minor children, the court can finalize a divorce as soon as twenty days after the paperwork is signed," Mr. Ted informed me.

"A lot can happen in twenty days," Mandy muttered.

I stood up and paced back and forth. It helped me think. "Look, Darren is many things—a lazy jerk, a cheating loser, a sexist man-whore having a midlife crisis, a..."

"A man packing a schnauzer tail," Mandy added.

"I prefer dinky winky or wee nug," I said, all but forgetting Mr. Ted was in the room. "But with all of the things he *is*... I don't think *killer* is in the description. He'd lose his country club membership over that. Life without golf would kill him."

"You have a point," Mandy said. "But what if he made it look like an accident?"

"I think maybe you've been watching too many cop shows," I told her with a smile. "You really think he's that smart?"

She paused and thought. "I don't, but..."

"We hire protection for Clementine or she goes on a twenty-day vacation once the wheels are set in motion," Mr. Ted suggested. "I say we take no chances. Again, I believe the actuality of Darren trying to murder Clementine is far-fetched, but safe is better than sorry."

"I agree," Mandy said, glancing over at me to see how I felt.

It all felt ridiculous, but strange things had been happening as of late. Problem was, I was on a tight deadline for my book. I was a creature of habit. I couldn't write anywhere except at my house. I'd have to finish *Exclusive* quickly if I was going into hiding for twenty days so I didn't get offed. God, when was I going to catch a dang break?

I nodded. "Maybe Jess would come with me."

"Great plan," Mandy said. "She's been under a black cloud for a while. She needs to get away."

"She has?" I asked, shocked. I'd been so deep in my own depression, I hadn't noticed. I was a shitty friend.

Mandy looked a little guilty. "She has, but she insisted I not tell you. We've been worried about you."

"Stop," I said. "Stop worrying about me. I'm a big girl. Yes, I went through it, but in the scheme of things it could have been far worse."

I wasn't sure how much worse it could have been. Being infamous for catching my husband shagging the black and decker pecker wrecker wasn't fun, but I'd survived. And I was coming out on the other end better for it.

Now I just needed to make sure I lived through it.

"Deal," Mandy promised. "I'll stop worrying as long as you agree to leave town."

The logistics were complicated. Maybe Flip would stay at the house with Thick Stella. My vicious cat was my only responsibility. "I can make it work. When can we meet with Darren and his lawyer?"

Mr. Ted checked his calendar. "I have it on the books for Monday at noon. Do you want to be there?"

Today was Friday. I could stay alive for two days. Piece

of cake. "Yes. I want to be there. I wouldn't miss it for the world." I wanted to see Darren's face. I wanted to see the bastard get what was coming. And... I wanted to figure out if I was in danger. Darren wasn't subtle. He never had been and he never would be.

"That's my girl," Mandy said. "Your balls are impressive."

I laughed. Mr. Ted sighed dramatically.

"And on that descriptive note, I shall call an end to the meeting," he said with a laugh. "It has been informative."

"Beware of what you ask for," Mandy warned her wonderful boss.

"I'll remember that in the future," he replied, amused.

Today had been enlightening and very interesting. I needed the weekend ahead to be mundane and boring—no surprises.

I had to finish a book, and no one, not even my fictional characters come to life, was going to stand in my way.

CHAPTER EIGHTEEN

MY STOMACH LURCHED AND MY HEARTBEAT SPED UP. THE CAR
in the driveway was unfamiliar—a high-end, silver SUV.
Had someone come to kill me? Was Flip tied up with a gun
to her head in the house? Was she already dead?

Shit. Think. Think like a killer. I'd written lots of killers.

An experienced killer wouldn't have parked the car in
the driveway. If Darren had gotten him at a discount, that
was even worse. I was more familiar with killers who had
fangs and fur—not a cold-blooded human assassin who
wanted me dead so Darren could have my house. Sliding
down low in the seat and trying to spot if there was a
getaway driver, I put my hand over my heart so it wouldn't
beat out of my chest.

Was I being overly dramatic? Probably.

Was there a chance that I was correct in my assessment
of what was going on? Highly unlikely, but Sally Dubay
could freaking fly. Anything was possible.

"Dammit," I hissed. "I need to save her."

"Who?" Mina asked from the backseat. "Save who?"

I screamed. My characters needed to stop ambushing me. I'd end up dead from a heart attack. Forget about Darren murdering me. I had imaginary friends who could accomplish my demise much faster.

The gorgeous redheaded witch smiled and waved. She was sporting emerald green leather from head to toe. On anyone else, it would look ridiculous. However, Mina looked like she'd just walked off a runway.

"I have to save Aunt Flip," I told her frantically. Maybe Mina could help me strategize. The witch could throw fireballs and cast spells. I could not, but she still might have some useful knowledge. She was insanely deadly. "Darren might be trying to murder me for the house. There's a henchman inside. I'm pretty sure that he's taken Flip hostage and is waiting for me to get home so he can decapitate me. He'll either frame Flip or make it look like an accident. I need to get in there and save her. I have scissors on my desk in the office. I could stab him in the eyes. It wouldn't kill him, but it would buy time. However, I'll be screwed if there's more than one murderer in the house. So, I could call the cops, instead. That might be the saner idea." I looked at Mina. "Do you have a better plan?"

Mina rolled her eyes and laughed. I wanted to smack her in the head.

"Are you a fiction writer by any chance?" she asked.

"Are you a dick by any chance?" I shot back, looking for my cell phone. I'd call the cops first. I wasn't sure I could stab anyone in the eyeballs. Although, if Flip's life was in danger, I could do anything. Right now, I wished I had five beers and could render myself invisible like Joy.

"I prefer bitch," Mina informed me. "There are no murderers in your house. Just a very sexy man and a beautiful little girl."

My breath came out in such a relieved whoosh, I got dizzy. "My bad. I forgot about that."

"I should say so," Mina said with a laugh. "And if you're still looking for advice, I say go on in there and do that man. He's smokin' hot."

Letting my head fall to the steering wheel with a thud, I groaned. "All of you people are entirely too oversexed."

"Turning that back on you, babe," Mina said with a grin, tossing her wild red hair. "I'd argue that *you* might not be getting enough. All of your sexual frustration comes out in your stories. Mind you, I'm delighted with that. You write some incredible sex that I have enjoyed personally and *immensely*. However, I think it would do you good to get laid. Take him to the pantry, strip and snog the living daylights out of him."

"Not gonna happen," I muttered, hoping she would stay in the car. I didn't need her suggesting ways to bang Seth Walters with him and his daughter present.

"Your loss... and his," Mina said with a shrug as she disappeared.

For five minutes, I debated with myself about staying in the car until they left. It wasn't mature, but it was safer than me making an ass out of myself... again.

"Beautiful Clementine!" Cheeto yelled from the wrap-around front porch wearing a hot-pink muumuu trimmed in yellow sequins. "Look at me!"

I waved and pointed to my phone. It was brilliant. Pretending to be on a business call until they had to leave was sheer genius. If I couldn't speak to them—them meaning Seth—I couldn't stick my foot in my mouth and pull it out of my butt.

Win-win.

Not.

Cheeto sat down on the steps and stared at me as I yacked away to no one on the other side of the call. Her bottom lip quivered, and I could tell she was trying not to cry.

"Crap," I muttered, hanging up on the imaginary business person. Her tears would undo me. The little girl had cried enough in her life. Of that, I was pretty sure.

Thankfully, Seth was nowhere to be seen. He was probably getting an earful of God only knew what from Aunt Flip.

"You look fabulous," I told Cheeto, getting out of the car.

"Flip said that too," Cheeto said, sprinting toward me and jumping into my arms.

Swinging the squealing little girl in a circle, I laughed along with her. She really was delightful... magical.

"Are you super-sure positive that you aren't available?" she asked. "Me and daddy would take very good care of you and Thick Stella if you married us."

I sucked in a terrified breath. Ignoring the marriage proposal, I got right to the point. "Did my kitty try to bite you?"

She giggled. "Nooooo, silly Clementine. She licked me, and she scratched daddy."

"Did he bleed?" I asked with a wince.

"Just a little. Flip made you a muumuu too. It matches mine!"

"Awesome," I said, grimacing. Muumuus were not my thing, but I would probably wear it for Cheeto.

"Daddy is going to take all of us to lunch and we can wear our muumuus," she informed me with sparkling eyes.

Not happening. I'd never been so happy to be on a tight deadline in my life.

Cheeto kept talking a mile a minute. "We've been waiting for you. Flip has been telling us stories from when you were a little girl!"

"Are you serious?" I asked, feeling a little sick. I'd been a weird child.

"I'm Cheeto, not Serious," she said with a giggle.

"Right," I said, putting her down.

I had no choice. I had to go inside and stop Flip even if it meant gagging her.

"I'm hungry," Cheeto announced, running back up the porch stairs and into the house. "I'll get Flip and Daddy."

Following her in to make my excuses for lunch, I stopped dead in my tracks. I squinted to make sure I was seeing things correctly.

I was.

Flip was wearing a muumuu that matched Cheeto's. Mine was laying over the back of the couch in the living room. However, the real shocker was Seth. Biting down on my lip so I didn't scream with laughter, I slowly walked into the living room.

"Really?" I asked, grinning from ear to ear.

Seth turned his head to me and raised a brow. "I didn't have a choice. I swear to God."

"He looks fantastic," Flip insisted, gluing the yellow sequin trim to *Seth's muumuu*. "There are many cultures where men wear muumuus."

"Name one," I said, sitting down on the couch and crossing my arms over my chest. I was so tempted to snap a picture, but figured that was kind of mean since I didn't know him very well.

Flip's brow wrinkled in thought.

"Canada," Cheeto yelled, skipping in a circle around her dad.

"That's right," Flip said with a cackle. "Canada."

I laughed.

Seth rolled his eyes.

Most men would be emasculated by wearing a muumuu. Not Seth Walters. The damn man still looked sexy.

"I'd like to take you ladies to lunch to say thank you," Seth said.

"For the muumuu?" I asked.

"But of course," he replied.

"That's very kind, but I can't join you guys," I said. "I'm on a deadline and sadly, books don't write themselves."

"But you have to eat. Right?" he asked with a smile that made me a little breathless.

"She sure does," Flip said.

"We have food in the house," I insisted, eyeing my traitorous aunt. She was supposed to be on my side. "I really can't go, but you guys will have fun."

Cheeto looked crestfallen. I felt bad, but I really did have to write. Just in case Darren did want me dead, I needed to finish my book. Cyd would lose her mind if I was late again… or dead.

"Pleeeeease?" Cheeto begged.

"Oh honey," I said, playing with her hair. "Next time. Writing is my job, and I'll be in big trouble if I don't turn it in on time."

Seth again watched in fascination as Cheeto kissed me and wrapped her little arms around my neck.

I tried not to make eye contact with him. I didn't succeed.

Seth's eyes narrowed playfully. "What if I agree to wear the muumuu? Would you go to lunch with us then?"

My mouth formed a perfect O. He was nuts. I was fully aware that he was pressing the issue because of Cheeto, but it was fun to pretend for a second that he wanted my company.

"You lie," I said with a laugh.

"I do not," he shot back.

I stood up and approached him. "You would really wear a hot-pink muumuu trimmed in yellow sequins in public if I agree to go to lunch with you guys?"

He didn't miss a beat. "Absolutely."

I didn't believe him. I shrugged. "If you wear a muumuu, I'm in," I said, waiting for him to back down.

"Great," he replied, picking up his pants as Flip backed away to examine her handiwork.

Seth took his wallet out of the back pocket and folded his jeans and t-shirt. He then picked up Cheeto's discarded clothing and made a neat pile of it all. "We'll grab these when we drop you back at home."

"Shut the front door," I said with a grunt of laughter. "You're really going to do this?"

"I am," he said. "And so are you."

"Wait. What?" I asked, not following.

Flip handed me my muumuu and giggled. "The boy is fun! I just love him to bits. Go on and put on your muumuu. I'm starvin'."

"Me too!" Cheeto sang as she helped Flip clean up the mess.

"I'm *not* wearing a muumuu," I stated firmly. People in town were still gossiping about my national crash and burn. There was no way I was adding to the fodder.

Seth smiled. It was devastatingly beautiful. "I dare you."

My eyes narrowed to slits. His behavior was unacceptable. I'd never turned down a dare in my life. Jessica and Mandy could attest to the fact.

"Repeat," I ground out, wanting to slap the smile off of his face.

"I. Dare. You," Seth repeated with his grin growing even wider.

"Yaaaaaaaaay," Cheeto shouted. "Best day of my life. We're the muumuu club!"

"You are a dick," I whispered so Cheeto couldn't hear me.

"Been called worse," Seth said, still delighted with himself.

"I'm sure you have," I snapped, marching into my office to change into my hideous muumuu.

A dare was a dare.

"I'D SUGGEST A CORSET WITH THAT," ALBINIA VOLUNTEERED.

It took all I had not to scream, which would have been awful. I was standing in my office in a bra and a thong. I did not need Cheeto, Seth and Flip storming in to see what was wrong.

"What I'd like to do is burn it," I told my Regency buddy, who was wearing a bright yellow gown that matched the sequins on the heinous garment that I'd been dared to wear.

"Is that the latest fashion?" Albinia inquired, wrinkling her nose in distaste.

"Umm... no," I told her with a laugh as I pulled the monstrosity over my head.

Albinia circled me and examined the muumuu. "It's not that bad," she offered. "You're a very beautiful woman. I do believe you can pull it off."

"Thank you, Albinia."

"I'm going by Alhootweeta now," she informed me. "Cassandra La Pierre said the name fits me. Now that I'm a single strumpet, I need a new identity."

"Single?" I asked, surprised. "What happened with the constable?"

She sighed dramatically and sat down on the couch. "He was successful in buggering the costermonger. They're seeing each other. It's quite devastating. I was bamboozled. I did consider purchasing a barking iron a fortnight ago to end the whippersnapper, but alas I did not. I'm quite fearful I shall never be yoked now."

"The only part of that I understood was that the constable is dating the costermonger," I said, sitting down next to her and putting my arm around her. I knew the pain of finding out the person who was supposed to love and cherish you was a lying, cheating dick. "Are you okay?"

"Not at the moment, but I suppose I will be in time," she said, dabbing at her eyes with a yellow hanky. "Stephano offered to kill Horace, which was very kind."

"Please tell me Stephano didn't eliminate the constable."

"He did not," Albinia assured me. "I passed on the generous offer. Cassandra explained that revenge was far more satisfying than dismemberment and castration. She's guiding me now."

That was not going to end well.

"You might want to reconsider that route," I told her. "Do many people know about the... umm... breakup?"

I knew very well what it was like to have the world know your husband banged a hooker... or a costermonger, in Albinia's case. It sucked.

"Oh yes," she lamented. "The Ton has shunned me."

"Screw the Ton," I said, having no clue what the Ton was. "You hold your head high. It's not your fault that Horace Skevington banged Dudley Albon Stopford. They deserve each other with names like that. You don't need a damn man."

She was shocked. "I don't?"

"No," I said firmly. "You don't."

She pondered my statement with confusion written all over her lovely face. "So then going back and throwing myself on Onslow Bolingbrook's mercy is a bad plan?"

"Terrible plan," I confirmed. "I would never write that for you."

"Oh, thank heavens," she said. "From what I understand, Onslow is not packing an impressive man-tool. It would be devastating to bugger someone and wonder if you were being buggered at all."

"Tell me about it," I said with a pained laugh. "Look, before you fall for someone else, you need to stand on your own two feet. You feel me?"

"I'm not comfortable with feeling you," she reminded me.

God, she was literal. "Right," I said. "My bad. But I'm serious about you living your life for yourself and not for a man. You're a strong and capable woman,"

"Of what?" she asked.

"Not following."

"What am I capable of besides being lovely?" she asked very seriously.

Shit. Had I written her as a helpless damsel in distress?

"Well, I'm not sure. Is there something you like to do?" I asked, hoping she had a hobby that we could turn into a career for her.

"I love to bugger," she said dreamily. "I'm quite good at it."

That certainly wasn't going to work out.

"Okay," I said, kicking off my wedge heels and slipping into some sparkly pink flip-flops that went nicely with my hideous muumuu. "Hold that thought and let me think about it. I'm going to write Stephano some inoffensive pick-up lines. How about I write you a new life with a fabulous career?"

"Smashing!" Albinia announced with excitement. "I shall go share the fortuitous news with the others."

"You do that," I said.

"Oh, and Clementine?"

"What?" I asked, putting on a swipe of lip gloss.

"What you see is not always how it truly appears," she said.

"Would you like to be more specific?" I asked, thinking she was saying much more than met the ear.

"Most certainly," Albinia said with a curtsy. "A friend in need is a friend indeed."

I shook my head. "That didn't help."

She looked perplexed for a moment, then smiled. "Always follow your gut instincts."

"Seriously?" I asked, thinking she'd lost it. "Is that all?"

"For now," she said as she turned in a grand circle, then disappeared.

Pressing the bridge of my nose, I groaned. The truisms were getting tedious, but I grabbed a piece of paper and a pencil and jotted them down. Albinia spoke in code, but she was usually onto something.

"Are you ready, beautiful Clementine?" Cheeto asked, poking her head into my office.

"As I'm ever going to be," I answered.

If I had a bounty on my head, I was going out in style. Horrible style.

CHAPTER NINETEEN

"DON'T LOOK AT ME OR TALK OUT LOUD," CLARK DARK whispered as he appeared between Cheeto and me.

My swift intake of breath was far better than the scream that almost flew out of my mouth. Note to self—have a meeting with the gang about sneaking up on me. It was not working for me at all.

Staring straight at the back of Flip's perm, I covertly nodded so Clark was aware I'd heard him. Thankfully, I was in the backseat. Aunt Flip tended to get car sick, so I'd insisted she sit up front with Seth. Clark would have racked himself on the gear shift if I'd been in the front passenger seat. His balls got a reprieve due to Flip's penchant for puking if she rode in the back.

"You're in danger, Clementine," he said. "Something hinky is afoot."

I wanted and *needed* to ask why, but that wasn't exactly

possible unless I wanted to reveal my crazy to Cheeto and Seth.

"The trace evidence suggests that the darkness is near," he went on. "A soup sandwich is on the horizon. We got into a high-speed pursuit with the perps last night but lost them. Stephano was sure they were driving a STOLO, but the vampire is an idiot."

Squeezing my eyes shut, I tried to think of an excuse to stop the car and get out for a moment so I could actually talk to Clark. Would it be weird if I asked to pull over so I could pee in the woods?

Yes. That would be very weird. Crap. Should I pretend to get car sick? I *was* getting sweaty. It could look legit. Maybe I could feign a hot flash and say I needed to walk it off. If I was about to bite the big one and Clark had info, it didn't matter if Seth and Cheeto thought I had a few screws loose. I was pretty sure they already knew that—at least Seth did.

Clark continued talking. I continued freaking. "I was driving a U-boat so I was surprised that the Adam Henry knew I was a copper. You need to find more of your kind to build a Goodness Army. I'll continue to survey the subjects if I can find the rat bastards again. In the meantime, you need to watch your back."

What the hell was a Goodness Army? And the term "watch your back" was ridiculous. Unless I could Linda Blair my head, there was no way I could watch my damn back.

Wait. Clark Dark had the ability to mind-speak in the Darkness series. I had no clue if that might be in my bag of woowoo juju tricks, but it was worth a shot. Of course, I wasn't a werewolf, but I wrote about them. Hopefully that would be good enough.

"Umm... Clark?"

"I was curious when you would figure that out," he replied with a chuckle.

"It might have been nice if you'd told me I could do this instead of freaking me out," I snapped.

"Against procedure," he replied.

I rolled my eyes. *"There are rules?"*

"There are always rules."

"Rules are made to be broken. Every good writer knows that," I informed him. *"From now on if any of you know something that will help me, you have to spit it out. Deal?"*

"Deal," Clark said with an impressed chuckle.

"Okay," I said, so relieved we could communicate I almost started crying. *"Is Darren trying to eighty-six me for the house?"*

"No."

"He's not?"

"No. Darren is a spineless imbecile. The man doesn't have the testicles to commit murder," Clark said, much to my relief.

"Is he hiring someone to do the deed?" I asked, wondering if Clark couldn't tell me things I didn't specifically ask about. On the outside chance that this was the case, I was going to get in as many questions as possible.

"No."

I racked my brain for more questions. We were almost at the diner. *"What's a Goodness Army?"*

"*An army of witches or woowoo juju practitioners, if you will,*" he answered.

"*How many make an army?*"

"*Eight, but ten would be better,*" Clark told me.

Crap. Right now, there were five of us. Flip, Sally, Joy, Ann Aramini and me. How in the heck did I find more magic she-devils? *Why* I needed to find more voodoo hags was the more important question.

"*And I need a Goodness Army because?*" I pressed as Seth pulled into a parking spot.

"*To stop the impending darkness. It's getting closer... and more desperate. Desperation makes people do dastardly things.*"

On that cryptic note, Clark Dark disappeared.

"Y'all ready to show off our muumuus?" Flip asked, getting out of the car.

"Yes!" Cheeto yelled.

"No," Seth added with a chuckle. "But I'm doing it anyway."

I just smiled. Clark's words were banging around in my head. I needed to talk to the woowoo juju clan. I also needed to finish my book. But if Darren wasn't trying to kill me for the house, that bought me some time. I wasn't sure how I'd convince Mandy and Mr. Ted that I wasn't going to go on a twenty-day vacation, but I'd figure that out later.

"Are you okay, Clementine?" Seth asked.

I forced a smile. "As fine as I can be dressed in a muumuu."

Seth laughed. "You wear it well."

"I bet you say that to all the gals," I teased, pushing away the impending doom and focusing on the man in the hideous dress.

"You would be incorrect," he replied in a tone that I would swear was flirty. "But I want to seriously thank you." His tone grew soft and very serious. "Cheeto hasn't spoken this much in two years."

I nodded and internally reminded myself that the man was only interested in the fact that his daughter was happy around Flip and me. I needed to take the advice I'd given Albinia. I was a woman who needed to stand on her own. Silly high school crushes were sweet but not substantive.

"Will she be okay in the diner?" I asked, concerned.

Seth shrugged and ran his hands through his hair. "With you and Flip, she might be. I'm not sure. But lunch was her idea, so I'm hoping she'll do okay."

"She'll be fine," I told him. "And if she wants to be silent, we let her."

"Where did you come from?" he muttered, looking at me curiously.

"Venus," I shot back, not wanting anything to get too serious. "Men are from Mars. Women are from Venus. Although, in your muumuu, you can choose which planet you like better."

He laughed and I walked away. Seth Walters was dangerous for my sanity. Not that he would ever know, but I knew. I needed no complications in my life.

I had plenty as it was.

～

OF COURSE, VELMA'S VITTLES WAS PACKED. THE DINER WAS right off of Main Street near Curl Up and Dye. It was kitschy and fun. The décor was right out of a 1950s movie, complete with little jukeboxes on every table. The cheese-burgers and French fries were to die for, but Velma was most famous for her shakes.

"Deeeelicious," Flip said, slurping on a chocolate shake and casting a concerned glance at Cheeto.

Cheeto had clammed up the minute we'd entered the diner. Seth had been correct. It was heartbreaking. We'd chosen a booth in the back. Quickly standing up, I rearranged the seating. Flip and Seth followed my lead with no questions asked. Cheeto's back was now to the customers. She was sandwiched between Flip and me. Seth sat by himself across the table.

Cheeto smiled and rested her little blonde head on my arm. "Better."

"Good," I said, glancing over my shoulder for the waitress.

Sadie Hawkins had seated us and delivered our shakes. She was a doll and had taken shit for her name her entire life. Sadie had developed an excellent right hook during middle school and had used it often on the boys when they'd teased her about her name. The worst time of year for Sadie Hawkins was springtime—when the Sadie Hawkins dances went on at the middle school and the high school.

It was springtime. I was curious if she'd broken any noses this year.

I glanced around the diner and spotted Sally, Joy and

Ann Aramini sitting a few tables away. Sucking in a breath so I didn't squeak, I tried not to laugh. The gals had no clue, but Stephano had joined them for lunch. He had wedged himself nice and close to Ann Aramini, whose knockers he'd admired last night.

And the world kept tilting further off its axis.

"I'm gonna get me a cheeseburger and fries," Flip said. "What about you, Cheeto?"

"The same," she whispered, looking down.

"Good plan," Flip said, not making any fuss about the change in her personality. "I think you're a brave little princess."

"You do?" Cheeto asked softly, peeking up at Flip.

"Yep. Doin' shit you're scared of makes you brave," she told the little girl.

"Umm… probably not good to use the word shit," I said, then winced, realizing I'd just said it too.

"Did I say shit?" Flip asked, shocked.

"You did say shit," Cheeto said with a giggle, perking up. "It's a potty word. It means poopoo in a naughty way."

I glanced over at Seth, who shook his head and smiled.

"Good to know," Flip said with a twinkle in her eye that made me think she'd used the potty word on purpose to tickle Cheeto. "Next time I'll say poopoo."

Cheeto nodded and giggled again. "That would be better, Flip."

Flip kissed Cheeto's head. "Would you like to meet some of my best friends?"

"Are they like you?" Cheeto whispered, her eyes growing large and uneasy.

"Just like me. And just like Clementine," Flip promised the little girl.

My stomach began to tingle. My vision swam a little bit. Staring at Cheeto, I saw it. It was a slight golden glow around her little body. Quickly refocusing on Flip, I realized she had the same golden haze around her.

"Well, I'll be damned," I muttered, turning and glancing back over at Sally, Joy and Ann Aramini. Sure enough, the glow was there. How had I not noticed it before?

"You good?" Seth asked me.

Sucking back my shock at my newfound gift, I nodded. "As good as anyone can be in a hot pink muumuu. You?"

"Better than good," he said, tilting his head toward his daughter, who was chatting it up with Flip. Cheeto's voice was quieter, and she wasn't as animated as usual, but glimmers of the spirited little girl were still there.

"You two are magical," Seth whispered.

My head jerked to him and I almost choked on my shake. Did he know? There was no way he could know. Maybe he did. Had Cheeto shown him her gifts? I wondered what Cheeto's gifts were.

"Daddy? Can I go meet Flip's friends?" Cheeto asked, looking scared but excited. "They're right over there." She pointed to the table where the woowoo ladies were stuffing their faces with pie and banana splits.

God, those gals could eat.

Seth wasn't sure what to say. Reaching across the table, I put my hand on top of his. "The gals are amazing. I think Cheeto will be comfortable."

Seth looked down at my hand for a long moment. I felt the heat start at my chest, crawl up my neck and land on my cheeks. I quickly pulled my hand away. Why in the heck did I even do that? It was unnecessarily intimate. I was an asshat.

He caught my eye and my embarrassment. He winked. I wanted to die.

"Yes, Cheeto," he said. "You can go meet Flip's friends, but Flip…"

"I'll bring her right back over here if it don't go well," Flip promised. "But I'm tellin' you right now, it's gonna be just fine."

"I think I'll be fine, Daddy," Cheeto said, gripping Flip's hand tightly.

"I know you will, munchkin," Seth told her. "So proud of you."

As Flip and Cheeto went to meet the ladies, I squinted in disbelief. Right behind the woowoo gals, Cassandra and Albinia were seated at a table with a family who had no clue they had extra guests in their party. Glancing around wildly, I spotted Mina and Sasha sitting at the soda fountain counter. Clark was by himself at an empty table with his back to the wall and his eyes on the entrance—just like a cop.

"What the hell is happening?" I muttered.

"I'm sorry, what?" Seth asked, his eyes on his daughter and my aunt.

"Talking to myself again," I said, letting go of caring what he thought about me. With all my characters here, I wondered if I was about to die. Having a handsome man think I was batshit crazy was nothing compared to being six feet under.

"What in the ever-lovin' hell?" Jessica asked, sliding into our booth and staring at Seth and me in shock. "Who lost the bet?"

"Everyone," Seth said with a chuckle.

I didn't even see her come in. I was too busy freaking out about my invisible buddies all gathering in the same place. I cased the diner and looked for... I didn't know what I was looking for, but I looked.

"Dude, you okay?" Jess asked, concerned.

Pushing back the panic attack that was trying to escape, I focused on my best friend. "I am. Aside from the horrifying fact that I'm wearing a muumuu in public, I'm good. Are you?" I raised my brow and gave her a look.

She chuckled and shook her head. "Mandy blabbed."

"She did," I said. "You should have told me you were down. I feel like the shittiest friend in the world."

"Poopooist," Seth said.

"Right," I said with a laugh. "Poopooist."

Jess's glance went from Seth back to me, then back to Seth. She grinned. I wanted to headbutt her. She had gotten it all wrong.

"It's about time you talked to her," she said to Seth, nudging him with her elbow. "Took you long enough—like over twenty years,"

He glared at her. I was reminded that Jess's older brother had been friends with Seth in high school. I wondered if Jack and Seth were still close after all these years. Men were different than women. Although, from

Jess's brotherly familiarity with Seth, the answer was probably yes.

"Talked to who?" I asked, wondering what was going on.

Jess grinned. "You."

"Me?" I was confused. What had I missed?

"Zip it, squirt," Seth said flatly. "For real."

Jess made the international zip-the-lip sign and grinned from ear to ear. I'd get to the bottom of that later. Right now, I needed to figure out what was happening without anyone knowing I was trying to figure out what was happening.

My life was a roller coaster headed to hell.

"Tell me what's been going on," I said to Jess.

"Later," she promised.

I nodded. That was good. I wasn't sure I could give her my full attention since the Underworld mafia had just appeared.

"Shit," I said, standing up and practically falling out of the booth. "I have to umm... pee... no, make a phone call to my... you know, agent," I lied. "Be back in a sec."

As I made my way over to where Clark was sitting, I thought my lie was pretty dang good. Sitting down at an empty table and talking on the phone was a great cover for talking to an invisible werewolf. I'd considered mind-speak, but that would look bizarre. Being certifiably creative was coming in handy.

Cheeto was sitting on Joy Parsley's lap and singing her a song. Joy's face was lit up like a Christmas tree. I'd never seen the cranky old gal smile like that, but Cheeto was one of a kind. Sally, Ann Aramini and Flip were all besotted with the little girl. Even Stephano was happily clapping along to whatever she was singing.

Sliding into Clark's booth and pulling out my cell phone, I began to speak. It definitely looked more normal for me to be on the phone instead of talking to him in my head. "Why is everyone here?"

"Just in case," he replied.

"In case of what?" I demanded.

"If we knew that, we would have taken care of it," Clark explained. "Since we're unclear of what's happening, we're staying near you."

"And the Underworld mafia?" I questioned.

Clark shrugged. "My guess would be Cassandra called them in."

I eyed the ten demons dressed like wise guys and wanted to kick my own ass for creating them. They were gaping assholes with a penchant for blood and a love of chaos. "Can they actually cause harm?"

"Up to you," Clark said cryptically.

"What does that mean?" I ground out.

Clark sighed. "Clementine, a puzzle has to be put together piece by piece. If you dump all the pieces on top of each other, all you have is an undecipherable mess."

"In other words, I have to figure it out myself," I said.

"Bingo."

"Fine." It wasn't fine at all, but I could tell I would get nowhere fast with Clark once he'd made up his mind. The werewolf could be incredibly stubborn. I should know. I made him that way. "Tell me this, am I about to die?" I asked, keeping my voice low. I didn't need anyone to hear me. It was bad enough that I was wearing a hot-pink piece of fabric trimmed in yellow sequins.

"That would be incredibly unfortunate," Clark muttered as his gaze roved the diner.

That was a non-answer. I didn't like it one bit.

"What are you looking for?" I asked, feeling frantic.

"The darkness," he whispered. "I'm looking for the darkness."

"What does it look like?"

"That's the million-dollar question," he replied.

He didn't know. Awesome... If Clark didn't know, none of my characters did. I pictured a slithering, grayish-black mist. That was probably dead wrong. We were the blind leading the blind unless the woowoo gals knew what the darkness looked like.

Keeping my phone at my ear, I saw Nancy enter the diner. Her clothes were drenched. She looked like she'd just run a marathon in a rainstorm. Poor woman, I just...

"Holy shit," I said, staring at Nancy, who gave me a harried wave.

"What?" Clark Dark asked.

"Nancy has the glow."

"The glow?"

"The woowoo," I whispered. "Nancy's got it."

"Dude," Jess yelled across the diner to me. "Foods here. If you don't get your muumuu-covered butt back here, I'm gonna eat your fries."

"No freaking way," I choked out, gaping at Jessica. "Jess has the woowoo too!"

"How many does that make?" Clark asked urgently.

I counted in my head. Me, Flip, Ann Aramini, Sally, Joy, Nancy and Jess. "Seven," I told him, standing up to go back to my table. "Not enough."

"Did you include Cheeto?" Clark inquired.

"She's a child," I snapped, thankfully remembering to keep my phone at my ear.

"Children are the strongest," he said.

"Nope. Not happening."

I walked away and kept my eyes wide open. I had no clue if I would recognize the darkness. Needing to get back to Jess to test my theory that she had the woowoo, I hauled butt across the small diner.

I also wanted some of my French fries.

CHAPTER TWENTY

THE MANICURED HAND THAT GRABBED MY ARM WAS STRONG. The person on the other end of it was repulsive.

"Funny seeing you here," Jinny Jingle said, pulling me into her booth with the strength of a freaking man. "What in the hell are you wearing?"

Her bitchy VIP friend and Sissy's niece sat on the other side of the booth sneering at me.

Reaching into my pocket, I pressed the button to record on my phone. If she had something to say, I wanted to make sure Mandy and Mr. Tim could hear it. I was over her and Darren's crap.

"A muumuu and I'm rocking it," I snapped, removing her hand from my arm and trying to stand up.

"That dress is so ugly, I'd hire you to haunt a damn house," Sissy's niece commented, getting laughs from her buddies.

"She's so ugly, she didn't just get hit with the ugly stick, the old bitch got nailed with the whole tree," the nasty VIP gal pal added.

Again, they laughed. They *really* needed some new lines. I'd used those in elementary school. They'd sucked then and they sucked now.

"So, now we've graduated to ugly jokes? Pathetic," I said, shaking my head and moving to stand.

"I wouldn't leave so fast if I were you," Jinny purred. "You might regret it."

"Or not," I said, eyeing her like she was a diseased animal. "You got Darren. You're not getting the house. We've already done the old jokes and the ugly jokes, not sure what you want to chat about."

"I want what you have," she hissed.

I rolled my eyes. "You already got it."

"Hardly," she said. "Give Darren the house."

She was crazier than I could ever hope to be. "Nope."

Jinny leaned forward and got in my face. My fingers itched to smack her overly made-up head right off her shoulders. I knew I should get up and walk away, but yet again, I wanted to hear what she had to say. I was an idiot. My curiosity gene was going to get me into a bitch-slap fight... in public. It did occur to me that this could be my second viral video within four months if anyone happened to be recording. My only regret was that I was wearing a muumuu.

"I need that house," she snarled. "I know what's there. It belongs to me. If you don't give it up, I'll destroy you."

My eyes narrowed to slits. The black and decker pecker wrecker was the most money-hungry, sad excuse for a human being that I'd ever come across. She made Cassandra La Pierre look decent. I didn't have time for this crap. I needed to spot the stupid darkness when it showed up.

Pushing her farther into the booth, I grabbed her chin so she had to look right at me. "If you ever threaten me again, I'll wipe the ground with your ass in a court of law. You'll have no career left. I will leave you a broken woman."

Weather Hooker shrugged and laughed. What the hell was wrong with her?

"You are not getting the full picture," she said in a cold voice. "I got Darren, and I'll get the good-looking one you like now. I will make your life a living hell."

"Are you right in the head?" I asked. "What's the end game here?"

"Simple. To win," she said flatly. "I've waited too long. It could all be solved if you give me the house."

"Darren," I corrected her. "Not you."

She smiled. It was ugly. "When he gets the house, I'll marry the loser. Bing bang boom. The house is mine."

I'm sure Darren would love hearing that he's a loser. It was the only statement Weather Hooker had gotten right. Far be it from me to tell my soon-to-be ex that his girlfriend just wanted him for a house and not his prowess on the kitchen table.

"Why is the house so important?" I asked, trying to understand what most likely boiled down to sheer disgusting greed.

"Playing stupid is beneath you, Clementine," she said. "Give up the damn house or the fun will begin. And trust me. It *won't* be fun for you."

"Alrighty then," I said, standing up and feeling like I needed a shower after talking to the nasty excuse of a woman and her friends. "On that lovely note, I'm out of here. I'd say it's been a pleasure seeing you, but it hasn't."

As I walked away, Jinny and her minions got up and followed me. There was nothing casual about it. The Underworld mafia didn't like it one bit and swarmed around me. It was a little disconcerting to get back to my booth with ten visible-only-to-me, red-eyed demons on my ass, but a girl did what a girl had to do.

"What the heck?" Jess mouthed as I slid into the booth.

I shrugged.

Jinny Jingle stopped right at the end of the booth. Her buddies flanked her. The rancid woman eyed Seth like he was a piece of meat and she was extremely hungry. "Hi," she purred, reaching out her hand. "I'm Jinny Jingle, and you are gorgeous."

Seth nodded in confusion and took her hand politely. "Nice to meet you, Jinny. Seth Walters."

"I know," she replied, licking her lips.

"She's the weather girl," Sissy's niece chimed in. "She's famous."

I wanted to gag, but held it back. Watching Jinny in action was like watching a ten-car pileup in an ice storm.

"Of course," Seth said, still a bit perplexed. "I'll be sure to catch you on the news soon."

Jinny made a pouty face at not being recognized, then giggled. It was like nails on a chalkboard. "I'm looking for a lawyer to handle a few things for me. Do you happen to have a card on you? I hear you're a *tiger* in the courtroom."

I couldn't help myself. I rolled my eyes. If this was the shit Darren fell for, good riddance. It was grossly pathetic. And if I was being honest... it was pissing me off. I couldn't tell if Seth was into it or not. He was a man. He probably was. In my experience—which sadly consisted of my marriage to Darren—most men were led by their peckers. Seth was probably no different. Yet another reason I didn't need a man.

"Actually, no. I don't have a card on me at the moment," Seth said, his face completely neutral. "My muumuu doesn't have pockets. But I'm sure if you call the office, someone can help you out."

Actually, the muumuus did have pockets...

Jinny leaned across the table, tits to the wind. Pulling a card out of her cleavage, she handed it to Seth with a smile. "Here's my card. Don't share it please. My personal cell phone number is on it. However, *you* can call me whenever you'd like."

Seth nodded and took the card. Jinny slowly stood back up.

"Ready girls?" she asked her snickering buddies.

They nodded. Blowing Seth a kiss, she turned and sauntered out of Velma's Vittles. We sat in shocked silence for a few minutes.

"What the hell was that about?" Jess finally asked. "I thought that hooker was dating Darren the Dickless."

"She clearly likes to play the field," I muttered, all of a sudden not hungry anymore. "I really have to get home and write." I stood up and implored Jess with my eyes. "Can you give me a lift home?"

"Sure," she said, standing up.

"I can do that," Seth said quickly.

"Nope." I grabbed my purse and avoided eye contact at all costs. "You stay. Cheeto is having a blast. I'll see you around. Thank you for lunch."

Without another word, I hightailed it over to the woowoo juju table. I bent down and kissed Cheeto on the head. "I have to go home and write my story. Are you having fun?"

She giggled. "I am."

"Good," I said, then leaned over to hug Flip.

"Cheeto has the woowoo," Flip whispered in my ear.

I nodded and pulled her closer. "Jess and Nancy have it too. I don't know if they know it yet, but they have magic."

Flip's eyes widened with delight, and she glanced over at Sally, Joy and Ann Aramini, giving them a thumbs up. All the women immediately got giddy.

"You have news?" Sally asked.

"I do," Flip said. "We'll discuss it later back at Clemmy's house."

"Tomorrow morning," I said. "I need today to finish the book."

"Gals, tomorrow morning, nine AM sharp at Clementine's. Everyone bring a dish. I'll supply the catsup and beverages," Flip announced. "Does that work for y'all?"

The nutty ladies nodded and literally bounced in their seats.

It was a good idea—not the catsup, but getting together to talk. I did have to write, but pow-wowing with the women was high on the to-do list. Taking one last look

around the diner, I tried to see if I spotted the darkness—
whatever it was.

I didn't.

I just hoped I spotted it before it spotted me.

"SHOULD WE DISCUSS THE MUUMUUS OR LEAVE IT ALONE?"
Jess asked, driving to my house.

"It was Cheeto's idea," I said, glancing down at the pink
disaster. "And I was dared by Seth."

"Ohhh." She laughed. "You've never been able to pass up
a dare."

"Hence the hot-pink muumuu," I said dryly.

"You're working it, guuurl," she commented with a
laugh. "Also, it was good to see Cheeto having fun. That
poor baby has been through it."

My unhealthy desire to know stuff that was none of my
business gnawed at me, but I pushed it away. "Does Cheeto
talk to you?"

Jess nodded. "She does, but not as much as she was
talking today."

It made sense. The little girl seemed most comfortable
with those who had the woowoo. Jess had the woowoo. I
just needed to figure out a way to bring the subject up
without her freaking out, tossing me out of the car and
speeding away.

"Sooooo, you want to tell me what's going on?" Jess
asked as she pulled into my driveway and turned off the
ignition.

"I do. Do you?" I asked, turning it back on her.

She sighed and laughed. It sounded hollow and tired. "I'm not sure I can explain it without you having me committed to an asylum. You won't believe me."

Reaching across the console, I cupped her cheek in my hand. "You'd be surprised at what I will believe."

She shrugged. I knew she had no intention of confiding in me. However, if I confided in her first, I was pretty sure I'd get her to talk. Or she'd run screaming from my house.

"You wanna come in?" I asked.

"I thought you had to write," she said.

"I do. But talking to you comes first."

Jess looked a little like a deer caught in the headlights. "Clementine... I can't."

I nodded. "You don't have to tell me anything, but I could really use the ear of a best friend to let off a little steam. You in?"

"Like Flynn," she said, obviously relieved that she didn't have to come clean.

"Follow me," I said with a grin, getting out of the car. "I have potato chips."

Jess laughed. It was an awesome sound. "Well, that's a game changer. If I'd known there were chips, I would have already been in your kitchen."

"Dude, you bought me the chips," I reminded her as I saw Clark Dark and the others sitting on the porch waiting for us.

"Correct. And I got the good kind."

"You always get the good kind," I told her, taking a deep breath in preparation of revealing my crazy.

I took another good look at Jess to confirm I was right about the glow. I was. It amazed me that I'd never seen it until now. But then, maybe now was when I was supposed to recognize it.

"I'm not sure the best way to explain it, so I'm gonna jump right in," I told her. "I thought I was going insane. Stuff started happening and I was sure I'd snapped."

Jess nodded and looked intrigued—wary but intrigued.

"I see the characters that I write," I confessed. "They come to me and hang out."

Jess nodded, not even remotely shocked or even a little impressed. "That's probably normal for a writer," she said. "What did you want to talk about?"

Shit. This wasn't going as planned. Cassandra laughed, and I was pretty sure I heard Sasha snicker as well.

"No," I told her. "They're real. I see them. They talk to me. They eat pot brownies and get high."

"Wait a minute," Stephano shouted as his fangs dropped in fury. "I didn't get any pot brownies."

"You weren't here," I told him. "I'll let Flip know you're interested."

"Thank you," he said, mollified.

"Welcome," I replied.

Jess squinted at me. She looked up at the empty porch, then back at me. "Was that supposed to prove something?" she asked.

"Umm... yes," I said, feeling kind of dumb. "I was talking to Stephano. You can't see him. Only I can. He's upset because he didn't get a pot brownie."

"And I'm supposed to believe that?"

"Yes."

Jess wrinkled her nose and sat down on the front porch steps. "You're going to have to do better than that."

"Seriously?"

"Seriously," she replied.

I didn't fly. I couldn't drink five beers and disappear. All my woowoo juju was kind of hard to prove. "So far, my magic is hidden," I said, deciding to just let her rip. "However, the rest of the gals' magic is not."

"Rest of the gals?" Jess questioned, looking hopeful yet still extremely cautious.

"Yes. I know you have magic," I said, as she paled considerably. "I can see a yellow aura around you, just like I see one around Flip, Nancy, Sally Dubay, Ann Aramini and Joy Parsley."

Jess was now laughing. The chat was going to hell in a hand basket.

"Joy Parsley has magic?" she asked with doubt written all over her pretty face.

"She does," I insisted. "I thought it was bullshit too—especially when she told me she could drink five beers and render herself invisible."

"Shut the front door," Jess said, laughing harder.

"Sally Dubay can fly. I saw her do it. Flip can light shit on fire by looking at it. I also saw *that*. Flip has a gift where she can detect illness in people. That's why she grows weed. I was under the impression she was a dealer for years. She's not. She grows it mostly for medical purposes and gives it away. Ann Aramini says she can shift into a house cat. I'm going to have to see that one to believe it, but I was witness to a hairball that she claimed to have puked up."

Jess was no longer laughing. She looked as if she might faint. "All of that's true?" she whispered.

"All of it," I promised. "I swear on our friendship. Every bit of it is true."

Jess stood up, then sat right back down. "So, when you said you see and talk to your characters, you meant you *see and talk* to your characters."

"Yes." I was pretty sure she was starting to believe me.

"What about Chauncey? Is your muse actually a real person?"

"No," I told her. "He's a completely imaginary asshole. I fired him."

Jess nodded slowly, taking it all in. "Who's here now?"

I glanced up at the porch and grinned. All of them were watching with wide smiles on their faces. "Clark Dark, Mina, Sasha, Stephano, Cassandra La Pierre and Albinia."

"Who is Albinia?" she asked.

Albinia gasped in horror and started to cry. "Has no one read *Scandalous Sensual Desires of the Wicked Ones on Selby Street?*"

"Albinia is from my one and only Regency novel."

"The first book you wrote?" Jess asked. "The one with the shocking ending where the heroine went off with the constable instead of the hero?"

I winced. "That's the one," I admitted. "However, we're not talking about the constable right now. He buggered the costermonger and left Albinia. We don't like him anymore."

"Got it," Jess said, looking up at the porch. "And they're all up there? Now?"

"Yep."

Jess turned back to me and stared for a long moment. I held my breath. Was she going to call me an idiot and leave... or worse?

"Will you be upset if I ask for more proof?"

"Umm... no," I said, wondering how to give her more proof.

She smiled. "I'm holding up some fingers behind my back. Can Stephano tell you how many I'm holding up?"

I shrugged and hoped like hell Stephano knew how to count. There was a fifty-fifty chance. "Sure. Stephano, how many fingers is Jess holding up?"

"Two," he replied with a chuckle. "Two birdie fingers. She's flipping all of us off. Or possibly just you from behind her back."

"Horrible manners," Cassandra commented. "I heartily approve."

"Two," I told Jess with a grin. "You're flipping my posse the double bird, according to Stephano. Cassandra approves."

"Holy shit," she muttered. "Now how many?" She sounded lighter and freer than I'd heard her sound in a few years.

"Do thumbs count?" Sasha inquired.

"Do thumbs count?" I asked Jess.

"Yes."

"Five fingers on her left hand and three on her right," Mina supplied.

"Five on the left. Three on the right," I said.

Jessica's chin fell to her chest and she began to cry. "Oh my God, I'm not insane!"

Dropping my purse on the ground, I ran to her and wrapped my arms around her. "If you're insane, I am too."

Her sobbing grew louder, and her entire body shook violently.

"How long?" I asked, rocking her back and forth. "How long have you lived with your secrets?"

She looked up and me. Her body stopped trembling, but tears still ran down her cheeks. "Since the accident where I broke my leg in four places," she whispered. "At first I thought I was suffering hallucinations from the pain meds. I quit taking them even though the pain was hellish. But it didn't stop. It never stopped."

I nodded and tucked her hair behind her ears. "I feel you. I thought I'd snapped and couldn't tell reality from fiction. Magic comes on when people who naturally possess it have a traumatic event. Flip and the ladies call it an external disaster."

Jess took in what I was saying. Wiping her tears with my muumuu, she shuddered. "I'm not sure if I'm in a state of shock right now or just so damned relieved I feel nauseous."

"Probably both," I told her with a little giggle. "Let me know if you're gonna hurl. I can do a lot, but I'm not real good with puke."

"Roger that," Jess said. "I've hidden for four years. I wouldn't date anyone. I was terrified that… I was terrified of everything. If it hadn't been for you and Mandy and my work, I don't think I'd still be here."

My heart hurt for her. I couldn't believe that she hadn't broken. But I did have a question. "What are your gifts?"

She eyed me for a long moment, then stood up. Pointing to a dead tree that I needed to have removed, she asked, "You fond of that tree or are you going to get rid of it?"

"I'm going to get it cut down. I just have to call someone to do it. It's too big for me to take care of it on my own."

"Let me save you a few bucks," she said, raising her hands above her head, then wiggling her fingers.

The tree groaned and cracked. It swayed back and forth as if it was dancing in the wind. It was macabre and beautiful. Then, with an enormous crack, it fell to the ground with a loud thud.

"Now that's impressive," Clark Dark said.

"No shit, Sherlock," I said, staring in shock. "Clark Dark is impressed, and so am I."

"You're not freaked?" she asked, clearly worried.

"Not even a little bit."

"Wait a darn minute," Jess said, wrinkling her brow in thought. "The people you assumed Darren had sent to scare you… Darren didn't send them, did he?"

"He did not," I confirmed. "That's when I figured out that I'd lost my mind and then realized I hadn't lost it at all."

"So, it was Albinia who ate your Grape Nuts?" she asked with a laugh.

"It was."

"What the hell?" Stephano bellowed. "I didn't know you had Grape Nuts. I love Grape Nuts."

I ignored the vampire. It was Jess/Clementine time right now.

"Can you do other things?" I asked.

She nodded. "It's freaky."

"Freakier than drinking five beers and turning invisible? Freakier than flying and crashing into trees? Freakier than shifting into a house cat?"

"When you put it like that, it's not so bad," Jess said with a chuckle. "I can transport myself. Not far, but I can do it."

"You're shitting me."

She laughed. "I shit you not. Wanna see?"

"Is Journey the greatest band ever?" I asked with a raised brow.

"I do believe it is."

"Then there's your answer," I told her, feeling tingly and alive. "Transport your ass. Now."

Without a word, Jessica disappeared.

"I'm by the car," she called out.

I was speechless. She was standing by the passenger door.

In the next second, she was right back next to me.

"I think I got gypped," I muttered. "Your woowoo juju is way cooler than mine."

"Woowoo juju?"

"It's what the gals call it."

Jess nodded and reclined back on the stairs in exhaustion. "Woowoo juju. I like it."

"You want to take a nap while I write?" I asked her.

Her eyes were closed. She smiled. "That won't bother you?"

"Nope. Not a bit. I want you close right now. And Cyd will have my ass in a sling if I don't get the book done."

"Then the answer is yes. I'll nap and you will write... Clementine, I love you."

"Right back at you."

"I'm not crazy," she whispered in amazement as she stood up and walked into the house. "I just can't believe that I'm not nuts. What a great freaking day."

Even though I'd embraced my juju, I still thought I was a little nutty. However, if I had to be nutty, there would be no better partner in crime than my best friend. My unpleasant chat with Weather Hooker aside, I planned to focus on the positive.

It really was a great freaking day.

CHAPTER TWENTY-ONE

THANKFULLY, I WAS LOCKED IN MY OFFICE AND MISSED SETH
and Cheeto dropping off Aunt Flip after lunch. I was
rocking toward the end of the book and needed just a few
more hours. My body tingled and I felt a little like I'd
indulged in one of Flip's cakey chocolate squares.

"You hungry, Clemmy?" Flip asked quietly, popping her
head into the office as the sun was setting.

Jess was still asleep on the couch. She'd slept the entire
day away.

"Some burnt toast would rock," I whispered. Flip's
kitchen skills were lacking, but her toast was growing
on me.

"Does she know?" Flip asked, walking in the room and
carefully putting a blanket over Jessica.

"She knows," I said, looking at my best friend. "She
thought she was crazy for four years. Broke my heart."

ROBYN PETERMAN

Flip leaned over and lightly kissed Jess's forehead. "What can she do?'

"Transport short distances and knock trees down by wiggling her fingers."

"Sheeee-ot," Flip said with a soft whistle. "That girl's gonna come in handy."

"She is?" I asked, wondering why.

Flip nodded. "We're gonna need every hand on deck to beat back the darkness."

"Define the darkness," I said, moving over so Cassandra could read what I'd written.

The well-dressed demon had thrown a shitfit when she'd realized I was sending her to Heaven as a punishment. She'd argued with me for an hour that a heinous death would be far preferable—even by cannibal pigs. It had been Albinia who'd convinced Cassandra that she could wreak havoc in Heaven by infusing her own brand of demonic Hell into the mix.

While I hadn't been exactly sure of what that meant, it had calmed Cassandra greatly, and I'd been able to continue writing without the grand dame threatening my afterlife. Win-win.

"Well," Flip said, scratching her head and sitting down on the love seat. "In the past, we always recognized the darkness was comin' by black clouds in the sky, but the sky's been clear lately. Jumper would have a chat with Rhett Butler, and he usually knew who we needed to run out of town."

"Granny's *people* knew who had the darkness?" I asked, thinking mine had no clue. We might be screwed.

Flip nodded. "Yep, and Ann Aramini used to prowl the streets as a cat for backup. That gal has a sniffer like you wouldn't believe."

I still didn't technically believe Ann Aramini could shift into a house cat, but I was getting closer to throwing away all rational thought.

"So then, we're looking for people?" I questioned, realizing that my visions of grayish-black mist were indeed wrong.

"People who want the magic back and will go to great lengths to get it," Flip confirmed, pulling a brownie out of the pocket of her muumuu and taking a little nibble.

"Crap," I said as a thought hit me like a ton of bricks. "The black and decker pecker wrecker! Do you think Jinny Jingle could have the darkness in her?"

"Possible, but highly doubtful since she's as dumb as a box of hair," Flip said, pulling her cell phone out of her pocket and texting like a madwoman. "In my recollection, most of 'em have been real smart who remember the woowoo from childhood."

"What are you doing?"

"Gonna have Joy report the skank to the town council for something and then have her tie one on and rearrange Weather Hooker's house tonight. Also lettin' Ann Aramini know she's gonna have to go prowlin' this fine evening on the off chance that the darkness has gotten stupider than an idiot with a brick for a brain. If so, we'll suss it out."

"Good," I said. If being smart went hand in hand with the darkness, Jinny Jingle was not a suspect. She was just a money-grubbing hooker. "Maybe have Ann Aramini sniff around the community college. Lots of smart professors over there."

"Good plan," Flip said, texting the message. "I'll tell her to make a round at the library too."

"And the hospital," I added. "Doctors are smart."

"On it," she said. "You done with the book?"

"Almost," I told her with a tired smile. "A couple more hours."

"You wanna let Jess spend the night on the couch?" she asked, glancing over at my still sleeping bestie.

"I'll check in with her when I'm done," I said. "I'll let her do what she wants."

Flip eyed me curiously. "You gonna be okay sleepin' in your bedroom? You've been snoozing on that there couch for a few months."

She was correct. The answer was, I didn't know. "Won't know till I try," I told her as Thick Stella hissed at me.

Flip chuckled. "That fat feline thinks it's a good idea," she pointed out. "I say give it a shot, Clemmy."

"I think I will."

"The freaking end!" I said with an exhausted grin. Ninety-five K in the bag and ready for edits.

"I love it," Sasha gushed. "Every single last word."

My characters had been reading over my shoulder for the last couple of hours. Thankfully, they'd been silent. I needed quiet to write. Stephano had been put in time-out a few times but finally got with the plan. The vampire hated being left out of anything.

Cassandra examined her manicure. "It's acceptable," she conceded. "However, I want to have an affair with an angel in the next book and destroy his reputation. I'd also like to tear a hole in the lining of Heaven and let the demon mafia in. It would be thrilling and wildly unexpected."

"I think you should fornicate with Sven on an altar up there," Stephano suggested. "Maybe a strip tease at the Last Supper or something fun like that."

I rolled my eyes. "I don't write time travel, but I'll keep all of that in mind," I promised with my fingers crossed. Stephano should never write a book. Ever.

I hit send. The manuscript was on its way to Cyd. She'd be knocked over sideways that I was early. I just hoped she didn't have a hemorrhoid that Cassandra was still alive.

A thought I couldn't push away had been forefront in my mind. If I killed Cassandra La Pierre in the book, would she disappear from my life? The answer was a mystery. I wasn't going to take any chances. She was growing on me in surprising ways. I wasn't ready to let her go.

And yes. I was aware that I was crazy, but when in Rome...

Clark Dark cleared his throat. "Clementine?"

"Yep?"

"It's seems we don't have the same knowledge as this Rhett Butler character who was in cahoots with your granny. I'm concerned that we're not of value to you."

"I call bullshit," Stephano announced. "I am very valuable. Clementine will need tutelage when she is ready to bang the handsome man in the muumuu. I plan to share all my knowledge with her."

"If brains were dynamite, you couldn't blow your nose," Mina told Stephano with an eye roll.

"Thank you," he replied, bowing low to her.

She squinted at him and shook her head. "All the knowledge that you have about snogging came from Clementine," she reminded him. "The only reason you have any *knowledge* —and I use the term very loosely—is because she wrote it."

"I'm confused," the vampire said with a panty-melting smile.

Mina slapped herself in the head. "Why do I find that hot? There's something very wrong with me."

"As I was saying," Clark continued. "I'm unsure that we're helping you sufficiently."

I thought about what he said. While it was true that they were different from Granny's people, I was different than Granny. We were a work in progress. I was still getting used to everything.

"I think you're wrong," I told Clark. "I think our path is ours and ours alone. We're figuring it out as we go. Together."

"You're saying that since we're beau monde with sensible bone boxes, it would be terribly premature to send us packing with a chum ticket in hand," Albinia said, confusing the hell out of everyone except Stephano. "While we may appear dicked in the nob, we are quite the opposite. I say we have a hot flannel and celebrate our motley joining."

"Stephano?" I asked. "Did you get that?"

He nodded enthusiastically. "And yet another reason I

am useful." He winked at Mina, who flipped him off. "I can understand Allhoowhompa."

"I'm going by Alhootweeta now," Albinia told him.

"My mistake," Stephano said politely. "What Alhootweeta said was that since we are fashionable people with good heads on our shoulders, it would be fucking stupid to send us packing with pink slips in our hands. And while we may come across as idiots—myself excluded— we're the very opposite. Alhootweeta would like to share a drink with everyone that consists of beer, gin, eggs, sugar and nutmeg—best consumed hot—to celebrate our unusual working relationship."

"Is that what you said?" Mina asked Albinia.

"I have no clue," she replied. "I didn't understand a word of it."

I laughed. "I'll take a pass on the drink, but we're a team. I have no clue how we're supposed to work together or what the hell we're supposed to do, but all of you have helped me so far whether you know it or not."

"Works for me," Sasha said. "And I'll pass on the drink as well."

"Would you like our presence in the morning when the woowoo juju gals are here?" Clark asked.

I nodded. "Absolutely. I need you."

Clark gave me a shy, pride-filled smile. He really was an adorable man.

"Okay," I said, yawning. "I'm hitting it. I'll see you people in the morning."

With smiles and waves, my *people* disappeared. I didn't even try to wake Jess. She was sleeping like a baby. I was positive she hadn't slept this well in four years. Knowing for sure you hadn't lost your mind was a relief that was difficult to explain.

Crossing the room and tucking the blanket more securely around her, I kissed her cheek. She was going to be okay. I was going to be okay. The woowoo juju would be okay.

How? Not a clue. But if I was woman enough to accept my crazy and wear a muumuu trimmed in sequins in public, I was going to make sure of it.

There was no other choice.

CHAPTER TWENTY-TWO

"Okay," I said, taking in the ragtag crew of gals sitting in my living room. "From what Clark Dark told me, we need to form a Goodness Army."

Joy was sitting on the sofa with Flip and Sally. They had platefuls of unidentifiable breakfast casserole squares covered in catsup. Jess sat in the overstuffed armchair with a cup of coffee and a few pieces of Flip's burnt toast. Ann Aramini paced the room and kept coughing like she was about to hurl up a hairball. I really hoped she didn't. The catsup was about as much as my gag reflex could take this morning.

Cassandra, Clark, Albinia, Stephano, Sasha and Mina were scattered about the room watching everyone eat.

"If you guys are hungry, go make a plate," I told them.

"We'll pass," Cassandra said, eyeing the gals' plates with a pained expression.

"I'm good," Sasha said quickly. The rest nodded. I

guessed they weren't fans of catsup or bizarre breakfast-bakes.

"What's a Goodness Army?" Joy asked with a mouthful of something seriously unappetizing.

Looking away from her so I didn't puke in my mouth, I explained. "It's a group of woowoo juju gals who join together to fight the darkness. An army of eight is needed. Ten would be optimal."

Ann Aramini counted the attendees. "We're screwed. We've only got six magic she-devils."

"Seven with Nancy," Sally pointed out.

Crap. I'd forgotten about Nancy. Mentally making a note to call Nancy after the meeting was now at the top of my to-do list. "Clark also pointed out that Cheeto has the woowoo, but I'm vetoing the idea. She's a baby. If this gets dangerous, I don't want her anywhere near it."

"Agree," Flip said. "Her daddy don't even know she's special."

Jess raised her hand.

"Take that hand out of the air, girlie," Ann Aramini said with a laugh. "You can talk whenever you got somethin' to say. We're equal-opportunity crazy here."

Jess grinned. "Habits. You were my dang high school counselor, Ann Aramini. Anyway, I'm pretty sure Seth is aware that Cheeto is very different from other kids."

"You think he knows she has magic?" I asked, surprised.

"Not *knows*, per se," she said. "I mean, I've lived with this for four years and didn't know. *Know* is kind of a relative word. A label and a tribe make it a whole lot easier to stomach. But while Seth might not be able to name what's going on with Cheeto, he knows there's something unusual happening. I think that's why he homeschools her. I'm just happy that when the time comes, Cheeto will have a group of women who understand her."

Sally put her plate down, got up with effort and a boost from Flip, then walked over to Jess. She leaned over and kissed the top of my bestie's head. "I'm so sorry, sweetie. I wish we had known. We would have taken such good care of you."

Jess took Sally's bony hands in hers and kissed them. "Better late than never. And thank you."

"Jessica has damn good manners," Ann Aramini pointed out. The woman clearly had a thing about etiquette. "And I agree with the wrangler. We leave Cheeto out of this crap until she's old enough to understand it."

"Wrangler?" Jess asked, confused.

"Me," I said with a wince. "I'm leading our posse on a trial basis. My Granny used to be the Woowoo Wrangler. She also had imaginary buddies."

"That offends me," Stephano called out from the kitchen. "I am not imaginary. I'm sexy."

"My bad," I yelled back.

"Is there more catsup or did the ladies eat all of it?" Stephano asked.

"Aunt Flip, Stephano wants to know if there's more catsup," I said, wanting to get to more important matters.

"Tell him it's in the pantry next to the Grape Nuts," she replied.

"Ohhhhhhh," Albinia squealed. "I *love* Grape Nuts."

273

She raced from the living room to the kitchen with Sasha and Mina on her heels.

I glanced over at Cassandra. She raised a brow as a small smile pulled at her lips. "Do you have blueberries?" she asked archly. "I don't do Grape Nuts without blueberries."

"I do," I told her. "Go have at it."

Holding her head high, she waltzed out of the living room. Clark was the only one who remained with us. I guessed he wasn't a fan of crunchy cereal.

"What were they yackin' about?" Flip asked.

"Grape Nuts," I replied with a laugh. "So, we're short a soldier even with Nancy. And to make matters worse, I don't know who or what we're searching for."

"I didn't find anything last night," Ann Aramini announced. "I prowled the entire dang town. Got chased by a horny raccoon and had to hide from a pack of dogs. My kitty schnoz didn't pick up an iota of danger."

Thick Stella hissed at Ann Aramini. She hissed right back. Thick Stella was wildly impressed and picked her fat ass up off the ground to rub her body against the woman's legs.

"Cats love me," Ann Aramini commented as she reached down to give Thick Stella a scratch.

I held my breath and waited for Ann Aramini to lose a finger. It didn't happen. Now I really wanted to see her shift. Later. We had business to cover. "Did you get to sniff the pecker wrecker?" I asked, knowing it was probably a dead end. But since we had no clues, any clue was good right now.

"The whore wasn't home," she said.

"True that," Joy agreed. "No one was there when I got ripped and rearranged her apartment. That Jinny Jingle's got shitty taste, by the way. Also, I reported her on sixteen citations with the town council. I'll put forty more in on Monday morning. But I gotta say, I think she's too stupid to remember what she ate yesterday. Not sure that piece of trash would remember havin' the woowoo as a child."

"Thought the same thing," Flip said.

When you were grasping at straws, any straw would do. "Maybe we're wrong about the darkness coming." I glanced over at Clark, who simply shrugged. It was getting abundantly clear that none of us knew what was going on. "Alrighty then, moving on."

I wasn't sure what we were moving on to. I was hoping for a little input.

"Keep goin'," Flip encouraged. "You're doin' great!"

"I agree, honey! Just fantastic," Sally said, clapping her hands.

"You got this," Jess said with a grin.

"Actually, I don't," I admitted. "I'm not sure what we should do."

"We wait," Ann Aramini said with a sigh. "Danger has a way of knockin' on your front door when the time is right."

As if on cue, someone knocked loudly on the front door.

Every single woman in the room screamed, including me. I was pretty sure I heard Stephano scream from the kitchen as well. We were going to suck big time as an army.

Glancing over at the gals for backup, I pointed to the door. "Do I answer it?"

"Do you have a peephole?" Joy asked.

"Yes," I replied.

"Then use the dang peephole," she grunted.

"Where's my stun gun?" Flip asked.

"In my car under the driver's seat," I said, regretting that I hadn't brought it inside. It was a point-and-fire weapon, according to Flip. That would be much easier than stabbing someone in the eyeballs with scissors.

Tiptoeing over to the door, I peeked through the hole and let out a very audible sigh of relief. "It's Nancy."

"Son of a bitch," Joy grumbled, smacking herself in the head. "My bad. I invited her because she has the woowoo juju."

I squinted at Joy. "Did you use the term woowoo juju when you invited her?"

She thought about it for a moment. "Don't think so. Why?"

They really did need a wrangler. "*Because* as far as we know, she isn't aware that she has woowoo juju."

"Well, that could have been awkward," Joy said, sitting back down and digging into her mound of catsup.

"Understatement. Everyone watch your mouths," I warned. "Nancy's in menopause. We have to be careful. If she doesn't understand she has the woowoo, we have to be delicate in how we explain it. You feel me?"

"Clementine, you must stop asking people to feel you," Albinia chided, coming up behind me with the others. They were all eating Grape Nuts. "It's not appropriate."

Ignoring her, I opened the door and smiled at a very sweaty Nancy. "Hey! Come on in."

"I'm so thrilled to have been invited somewhere," she

gushed, wiping the sweat from her brow. "And tell Flip her brownies saved my life."

"You can tell her yourself," I said. "She's here."

Nancy barreled into the house and made herself comfortable. Flip got her a plate of mystery casserole and promised to bake her some more pot brownies. Sally set her up with a cup of coffee.

"This is so exciting," Nancy said, looking around the room. "Your house is beautiful, Clementine. I just love it!"

"Thank you," I said with a laugh. Nancy's joy was contagious.

Nancy kept glancing around. She seemed a little perplexed. I wondered if another hot flash was coming on. The coffee might have been a bad idea.

"Would you like a glass of ice water?" I asked, wanting to help her out without stating the obvious.

"That would be awesome," she said gratefully. "Now, I know most of the people here, but who on Earth is that handsome man in the corner with the bottle of catsup in his hands?"

The entire room went silent. Nancy was so busy trying to place the *man in the corner*, she had no clue everyone was gaping at her.

If there was a feather, if could have knocked me down. "I'm sorry. What did you just say?"

"He looks so familiar," she said, shaking her head. "Have I met you?"

Stephano was confused. He pointed to himself to make sure she was talking to him.

"Yes, you!" Nancy said with a giggle. "I feel like we've met."

"I'm Stephano the vampire," he replied, glancing over at me to make sure that was okay.

I shrugged. I was still trying to process what was happening.

"Ohhhhhhhhhhh!" Nancy squealed. "Like Stephano from the Good to the Last Bloody Drop series. You look just like how I imagined him to look! Are you a cover model? Are you doing press with Clementine?"

"Umm... I'm a vampire," Stephano said, wildly unsure what to do.

I was the wrangler. I was in charge. I was also in shock. "You can see him?" I choked out.

Nancy paused, then glanced at Flip and the gals. "Can you people see him?" she asked carefully.

"Nope," Flip said with a grin. "Only Clemmy can see her characters."

"Well, shit," Nancy said, letting her chin fall to her chest in defeat. "Go ahead and ask me to leave. I'm used to it." She stood up, put her plate down and walked forlornly toward the front door.

"Sit your sweaty ass back down," Joy Parsley shouted. "You're not the only freak here."

Nancy's head shot up. "I'm not?"

"Not even close," I told her, leading her back to the chair. "So, you see characters from books?"

"Don't I wish," she said with an eye roll. "Nope. I see dead people. All the damn time. It's gotten so bad, I don't know who's dead and who's alive. My husband won't go out in public with me anymore."

"You help the dead?" Ann Aramini asked, fascinated.

"Help? No," Nancy said with a laugh that verged on a scream. "They don't need help. They just want to talk… and talk … and talk. It's driving me crazy! Ran into a woman at the grocery store last week who wanted to discuss vinyl siding. Yacked with her for about two hours before I realized she was dead. Thank God, I can blame menopause on my mental breakdown. I hate the sweats, but it's a fine excuse when you have a tenuous grip on reality."

It was all I could do not to laugh. "But you see my characters?" I asked.

She glanced around the room, then gasped. "Oh. My. GOD! Is that Cassandra La Pierre? She's more gorgeous in person than in the books."

"Thank you," Cassandra said with a very satisfied smile. "I am."

"And Sasha and Mina!" Nancy ran around my living room like she was five-years-old on Christmas morning. "Oh, my goodness. Clark Dark! You're one of my favorites! And Stephano, I'm so sorry, I should have recognized you immediately. You're quite dashing."

"Yes," he said, bowing to Nancy. "Everyone thinks so."

I heard Mina gag. The vamp was very full of himself.

"And who have we here?" Nancy asked, approaching Albinia. "You must be Lady Albinia Knightley Wynch!"

"Oh my! You've read *Scandalous Sensual Desires of the Wicked Ones on Selby Street*?" Albinia asked, delighted.

"Five times," Nancy said. "Loved it."

I pressed the bridge of my nose and tried to make sense

of the new wrinkle. I couldn't. Making sense of things was no longer in my repertoire. It was also alarming to find out Nancy loved *Scandalous Sensual Desires of the Wicked Ones on Selby Street*. She might be the only one.

"She's got the woowoo juju for sure," Flip said, grinning.

"Seeing dead people has a name?" Nancy asked, looking hopeful.

"Yes, but there's a whole lot more to it," I told her, indicating that she should sit down.

"I'm all ears," she said, sounding so relieved I laughed.

"You sure?"

She nodded and gulped back the glass of ice water Jess brought her. "Positive."

Two hours later...

"Well, I have never!" Nancy yelled, eyes huge with delight. "I thought I was the only batshit crazy lady in town. This is such a relief."

"I feel you," Jess said, patting her on the back.

"My goodness," Albinia muttered. "Do all these women want to *feel* each other? Maybe I should try it."

"Jessica isn't being literal," Nancy explained to Albinia. "It's a saying—a figure of speech. It's hip lingo. It means, I understand."

"So, then Clementine is *not* attracted to me?" Albinia asked, insulted.

There was no winning.

"I think you're beautiful," I assured her. "However, I'm not attracted to you in a sexual way."

"I see," Albinia said, nodding. "I feel you." She giggled and danced in a little circle. "I'm hip!"

"Yep," I said with a laugh. "You are. So, Nancy, you're okay with all of this?"

"Better than okay," she assured me. "Although, I'd really love to see Ann Aramini shift into a house cat."

"Join the club," I said. "When did you start seeing dead people?"

Nancy pulled a washcloth from her purse and mopped her forehead. "It was soon after I stuck a bobby pin in an electrical socket and had the living daylights shocked out of me. Singed the dang hair off the left side of my head and my right eyebrow."

"That's kinda weird," Flip said. "You'd think that if the hair on the left side of your head was burned off, it would be the left eyebrow too."

"Right?" Nancy said. "That part I never understood."

"Might be some kind of physics thing," Joy grunted. "You know, depending on which hole Nancy shoved the bobby pin into, that might determine which side of the head and face goes bald."

I actually considered what Joy had said for a full thirty seconds until I realized it was utterly ridiculous. "When did this happen?" I asked, wondering how many years she'd been seeing the dead.

"Last year," she replied. "Was trying to make a point with my grandkids about why it was dangerous to shove metal into light sockets. It didn't really end well, but those kids are now terrified of sockets."

Nancy often left me speechless. Today, she left everyone speechless.

"Do we get woowoo juju t-shirts or membership cards?"

Nancy asked.

Sally was intrigued. "We've never had anything like that," she said. "It might be lovely."

"Or how about a special handshake," Nancy suggested.

"I vote for the handshake," I said quickly. "Shirts are a bad idea. We don't really want to advertise."

"I can see how that might backfire," Ann Aramini said.

"And then some," Jess muttered.

"This house," Nancy said, looking around and clasping her hands together. "It feels magical."

Flip cackled and slapped her thigh. "You're the first to notice it."

"Am I?" Nancy asked, pleased.

"It's magical?" I asked.

"Darn tootin'," Flip said. "It sits on a ley line that no one knows about. Jumper and I could feel it. It's why we bought the house and why we left it to you. Probably why Nancy can see your characters. I'm curious if she can see 'em off the property like you can."

"Interesting. We can test that out sometime." I sat still to see if I could feel any magic. Nope. But it did feel like home. That was magical enough for me.

"What's the next step in finding this darkness?" Nancy asked, tucking a hefty bag of brownies into her purse that Flip had baked while we'd gotten Nancy up to speed.

"We don't know," I admitted. "We're open to suggestions."

"Let me think on that," Nancy said, checking her watch. "I have to take the grandkiddies to the park. I sure as hell hope there are no dead folks there today. It's just gettin' downright embarrassing that I can't tell the difference between the living and the dead."

"I can see how that would suck," I said, biting back a grin. Nancy was *dead* serious.

"I say we take the rest of the weekend off and reconvene on Monday night," Joy suggested. "I need to mow my lawn, then measure the neighbor's grass to see if I need to report them."

"Joy Parsley," Ann Aramini chided her. "That's an asshole thing to do."

"Your point?" Joy asked with a grin and a raised brow.

Before Joy threatened to report all of us for something, I chimed in. "We can celebrate my divorce. Papers are getting signed Monday afternoon. Hopefully."

Hallelujah," Jess said, giving me a hug.

"Well, hot damn!" Flip yelled. "I'll make weed brownies and we can have a shindig."

"The shindig will be here," I said firmly. There was no way I wanted to party in public with a bunch of old gals who were as high as a kite. "We can all have dinner together. Here."

"We should invite Cheeto and her daddy," Flip said. "That little gal needs us."

Jess shot me a look and waggled her brows. It reminded me I needed to talk to her about what she'd said at Velma's Vittles.

"Maybe just Cheeto," I said. "And if Cheeto is here, you dummies are not getting high. Am I clear?"

"Agreed," Flip said, with a nod. "But I'm not sure Seth's gonna let her come without him. He's a little helicopter-y."

"All we can do is ask," I said. "It should be a girls'-only evening."

I wanted to celebrate, not make an idiot of myself. Seth Walters made me feel wonky. I was done with wonky.

I was Clementine Roberts—romance author, woowoo juju wrangler, soon-to-be-divorced person and all-around nice gal who saw imaginary people.

I'd take it.

It was good to be me.

"SETH HAD A *HUGE* CRUSH ON YOU IN HIGH SCHOOL," JESS SAID as we did the dishes from the brunch.

"Shut up! He did not," I said with an eye roll, even though a silly zing shot through my body.

"One hundred percent did," she shot back with a grin. "Can't believe you didn't know."

"My head was always in the clouds in high school," I reminded her. "Why didn't you tell me?"

Jess wrinkled her nose in thought. "I could swear I did."

I shook my head. I definitely would have remembered that. "Whatever," I said, blowing the news off. "That was a long time ago."

"Yep," Jess agreed, trying to hide a smirk. "Loooong time ago."

"Stop," I said, eyeing her. "Don't do that."

"Do what?" she asked innocently.

"That thing you do," I said, tossing the dishrag at her.

"Not a clue what you're talking about," she lied and tossed it back at me.

She knew exactly what I was talking about. Again, whatever. I wasn't divorced yet. And when I was finally free, I wasn't going to complicate my life with a man. I was going to live just for me for a while. Period.

"Men aren't going to be in the picture for a looong while," I told her. "Even pretty ones who may or may not have had a crush on me in high school. You feel me?"

Jess went from silly to serious on a dime. "I do. And I agree with you," she said, turning off the water and sitting down at the breakfast bar. She pointed to the empty area in the kitchen. "Are you going to get a new kitchen table to celebrate that the teeny weenie is out of your life for good?"

I stared at the spot in my kitchen where the beginning of the end had taken place. "I'm not sure."

We sat in silence for a few minutes. Flip had gone to play poker with Ann Aramini, Sally and Joy over at Sissy's salon. I was pretty sure all of my characters had gone with her. There had been a running Saturday night poker game at Curl Up and Dye for years. I'd joined Granny and Flip about twenty years ago. It was a blast. Maybe I'd join Flip next time she went. I was a single lady now... or soon.

I turned and looked at Jess. "You had to swallow a whole lot yesterday and today. You good?"

"Honestly, I haven't felt this good in years," she said, reaching out and tucking my hair behind my ear. "Knowing that I'm not losing it goes a seriously long way towards feeling sane. Trust me on that."

I grinned. "I do. Believe me, I do. You want to sleep over, watch crappy romance movies and eat popcorn?"

"Hell to the yes," Jess said. "Let's invite Mandy."

"Perfect," I agreed immediately. "But we can't talk freely about the woowoo juju in front of her."

She laughed. "After this afternoon, I'm fine with that. But I still wanna see Ann Aramini shift into a damn house cat."

"Me too."

When that day came it would be crazy memorable—emphasis on the word crazy.

MANDY HAD INDEED SPENT THE NIGHT WITH US ON Saturday, and it was perfect. We'd plotted out a new and horrifying romance novel combining all of my characters from different series. Little did Mandy know, the very people we were talking about sat in the living room and listened with horrified expressions on their faces. Well, all except Stephano. He announced several times that the idea gave him a boner. I was thrilled no one could hear him except for me.

Sunday passed uneventfully for the most part. Aunt Flip made *flower* deliveries, and I'd cleaned and set up for the Monday-night shindig.

It took five tries before I got up the courage to call Seth and ask if Cheeto could come. I was shocked, but he was more than okay with Cheeto spending the evening with me and the ladies on Monday. I'd felt my old schoolgirl nerves return when I'd called, which annoyed the heck out of me. It made me want to headbutt Jess for telling me that my secret high school crush had crushed on me.

It was decades ago. Living in the past was for idiots. I was done with that.

It was time to live in the present as a free woman—no men with small packages and penchants for women young enough to be their daughters allowed. I just needed Darren to sign the papers to set me free.

Monday, here I come.

CHAPTER TWENTY-THREE

THE DAY HAD DAWNED DARK AND CLOUDY. I'D HOPED FOR sunshine, a quick spring shower, then a rainbow, but no such luck. I'd lugged an umbrella along to the law office since the sky was so angry. I didn't want to show up to my divorce proceedings looking like a drowned rat.

I'd arrived at the law office thirty-seven minutes early and wanted to get it all over with as quickly as possible. Nancy sat behind the reception desk sweating profusely. She had unfortunately chatted with a woman at the park on Saturday who'd tried to sell her designer sunglasses on the downlow. When she'd gone for it, the dead gal disappeared into thin air with fifty of Nancy's hard-earned bucks.

Suffice it to say, Nancy was pissed. She was now on a mission to figure out how to discern dead people from living people. She'd come up with a few unsavory plans that included rectal thermometers and raw chicken. I was wildly relieved when Mr. Ted had shown up and invited me into his office. There was only so much irate, perspiring Nancy I could take.

"We sign and then what?" I asked Mr. Ted, feeling nervous and a little sweaty. Dammit, was Nancy contagious?

"The papers will be sent to the courthouse for the judge's decree. That can take up to twenty days. Once the decree is stamped and signed, you're a free woman, Clementine," he explained kindly.

"And what can go wrong?" I asked with a bizarre and uncomfortable sense of foreboding. Maybe it was the sky-high heels I was wearing. They were stupidly difficult to walk in.

Cassandra, Mina and Sasha had insisted on picking my outfit. Albinia had offered up one of her gowns. That was a big no. Although, the thought of showing up in a mint-green, ruffly taffeta disaster of a dress was funny—just not funny enough to actually do it.

Albinia had been wildly insulted that I'd declined her generous offer and pointed out that I'd worn a muumuu on my date with Seth. I put an end to that thinking quickly. While yes, I'd worn a muumuu in public, I had *not* been on a date with Seth. They'd all exchanged obnoxiously knowing glances. The more I argued my case, the more exaggerated their glances grew. They were all dicks and laughed hysterically when I told them so.

In the end, I wore red—a red, raw silk, fitted Chanel dress that I'd purchased when I'd done a press tour a few years back. It hugged me like a glove and I felt freaking great. The black Jimmy Choo stilettos... not so much. I'd tried to negotiate for flats, but Cassandra had threatened me so hideously, I gave in. She could be incredibly mean.

"Highly doubtful anything will go wrong," Mr. Ted said, patting my shoulder. "Darren's lawyer confirmed he agreed to the settlement. Once your husband understood what was at stake—as in very little for him if he pressed for more than you offered—he caved on his demands."

Mr. Ted's words were comforting, but I still felt extremely left of center.

The wonky feeling had consumed me since I'd woken up. Clark Dark had trailed me from the moment I'd gotten out of bed until I walked out the front door. I'd had to ask him three times to let me take a shower and pee by myself. After casing the master bath for ten minutes, he'd finally agreed.

I'd never taken a faster shower in my life. I was terrified they'd all join me.

"And the house?" I asked.

"I went over everything again. We were correct. *Your house* is not on the table, Clementine. It never was. Darren's demand was greedy and had no legal standing. It's not an asset that can be divided. It's basically locked in a life-trust for you. Your grandmother and aunt were very smart with that move. To be quite honest," Mr. Ted said with a tight-lipped smile, "I don't think Darren's own lawyer has enjoyed representing him."

I nodded. That wasn't surprising, but I needed a little more clarification. "So, he didn't push for the house?"

Mr. Ted sighed. "From what was implied, it was his fiancée who wanted the house, not Darren."

Why did the black and decker pecker wrecker want my house so damn bad? It was just a house—

Holy Hell on a Sunday. Thunder rumbled in the sky and lightning cracked. It was the ominous soundtrack to the puzzle pieces clicking together in my head.

It was not *just a house*. It was on a ley line. It was magical.

Crapcrapcrap. The darkness was right in front of my nose and I'd missed it. To be fair, I had no clue what the heck I was looking for, but Jinny Jingle had given me a few dang good clues, and they'd gone right over my head. The weather hooker thought if she owned my house, she could get her magic back.

Maybe she could. I'd been told a person needed an external disaster to get the woowoo, but I didn't know if that applied to someone who had lost it and wanted it back. I needed to talk to my woowooers. Now.

"How long will this take?" I asked as my stomach began to roil.

Mr. Ted glanced up from the paperwork and eyed me strangely. "Do you have another appointment?"

"Umm... yes," I lied. "Can I just sign the papers and book it out of here?"

"I suppose you can," he said, still looking at me with a concerned expression. "You don't have to be here. We can have Darren sign, and I can drive the paperwork to you later today."

"Great!" I yelled, jumping to my feet. "Good plan. I'll make lunch. Are you allergic to anything? Peanuts? Shellfish? Chocolate? Catsup? Meat twinkies?"

Mr. Ted was confused. There was a fine chance he had

no clue what a meat twinkie was. He clearly thought I'd lost it.

Didn't matter. I already knew I was working with half of my marbles. I also knew that I had to *listen to my gut*. The truism had been one of Albinia's messages. And my gut told me that Jinny Jingle was about to do something very bad. My Regency buddy had also told me to get a second opinion. While I was pretty darn sure I didn't need one, I was going to follow the rules. These were rules I had no plans to break. There was a reason for the Goodness Army. Even though we were short a nutbag, I still had woowoo soldiers to go to in a time of need.

"No, no allergies," he replied. "Are you feeling alright? You've gone a little pale."

"I'm fantastic! You're the best," I told Mr. Ted as I turned to sprint out of the office. I wasn't sure my stilettos would let me do that, but I was going to give it the old college try.

One problem. As I was making my getaway, Darren and his lawyer were making their entrance.

The timing sucked—huge sucky suck sucks.

"Clementine," Darren said through clenched teeth, staring down his nose at me.

I squinted at him and wanted to scream. I had to stay. Proving that I wasn't a dishrag was important to me. I wanted the asshat to realize he hadn't broken me.

Ten minutes. I'd stay ten minutes.

"Darren," I replied coolly, sitting back down.

Mr. Ted was now bewildered, but it barely showed. I'd bet if he went to card night at Curl Up and Dye, he'd clean up. His poker face was impressive.

"I have an important conference call shortly," Mr. Ted said flatly. "Let's get right to business."

I loved Mr. Ted.

"I suppose you're happy," Darren snapped, taking a seat across the table from me.

"I am, and I have to thank you."

"For what?" he demanded, pulling on his pornstache. "For leaving me destitute?"

"I'd hardly call the settlement, your cars, a retirement plan, and the country club membership destitute," I replied, staring him down.

He stared right back. There was no glimmer of the man I'd married. He'd disappeared a long time ago, and I'd been too much of a coward to recognize it and do something about it. It took two to tango. It took two to ruin a marriage. We'd both stayed at the party long after it had ended. However, it only took one to cheat, then try to walk away with everything I'd earned while he'd played golf.

I was tempted to ask if Weather Hooker had been the first, but I didn't want to know—didn't need to know. It didn't matter and I didn't care. The thought was so freeing, I laughed.

"Of course, you would think this is funny," Darren hissed, dropping eye contact first. "You're nothing without me. You'll see. You'll come crawling back in no time... and then *I'll* be laughing when I tell you to go to hell."

"Dude," I said, gaping at him. Had he watched a bunch of shitty divorce movies and picked up a few lines? They were as ridiculous as his mustache. "You're engaged. Be happy.

We didn't work. It's okay. It happens. Actually, it should've happened a long time ago."

I watched as the idiot tried to think of a good comeback line. He couldn't. That was part of our problem. We didn't challenge each other. Not to mention, we didn't like each other either.

"Look," I said with a sigh. "We're not going to be friends. Ever. And I wouldn't have said this four months ago when you were balls deep in your fiancée on our kitchen table, but I don't wish you ill. I just wish you gone."

"You can't be serious," Darren said, shocked. "You'll never do better than me."

He didn't get it. He never would. How in the hell had I not known I was married to a narcissistic piece of crap for over two decades? Whatever. I was going out on a semi-high note. Screw him.

"I'm serious," I informed him. "I hope you're happy, and I hope you find a job. It's not attractive to be a moocher. You reeled in a youngin'. I'd suggest a gym membership and possibly a little Botox, along with a penis enlargement."

Mr. Ted choked on his spit and Darren's lawyer's eyes grew huge.

"Kidding!" I said, lying through my teeth with a smile on my lips. "But anyhoo, why don't you sign on the dotted line so Mr. Ted can get to his conference call and I can get on with my new, fabulous, free life."

"Nothing," Darren muttered as he signed the papers like he was trying to carve a hole in Mr. Ted's desk. "You're *nothing* without me. Good luck writing your little books without me to emotionally support you."

I rolled my eyes. "That one is stale and old," I said, signing my part. "You need some new lines and excuses."

"Well," he sputtered, reddening. "You're so old, you need a face-lift."

"Is that the best you got?" I asked, wondering if he and his dumbass gal pal came up with this shit together.

"I find this unnecessary," Darren's lawyer said, staring daggers at his client. "Please sign the rest and we can be done here."

"Should've hired a better lawyer," Darren snipped.

"Done," his lawyer said coldly to Darren, standing up and reaching out to shake my hand. "I wish you the best."

"Thank you," I replied, shaking his hand.

Darren watched the exchange with shocked disgust. "You're fired!" he shouted as he stood up.

"Best news I've heard since taking you on as a client," the man said with a polite nod to Mr. Ted, followed by a glare at Darren. "You'll receive my bill in the mail."

On that mic drop of a note, Darren's lawyer left the room.

"What happened to you?" I asked softly.

Darren shrugged. "I got lucky, and I got out," he said, eyeing me with disdain. "I no longer wanted to be with a pathetic woman. I found a goddess."

Low blow. But I felt the same way he did—not the goddess part. That was deranged. And from the way the black and decker pecker wrecker had talked about Darren at the diner, I didn't think that relationship was long for this world.

Not my problem.

I shook my head. When they go low, I go high. Or at the very least, I give it a shot.

"Be happy, Darren," I said, extending my hand to shake his.

He ignored my outstretched sign of peace, turned and left the room, slamming the door behind him.

Mr. Ted said nothing. What was there to say?

I glanced over at my fatherly lawyer and grinned. "That went well. Dontcha think?"

He laughed. I joined him. It was either laugh or cry. I was done crying. Darren didn't deserve my tears.

"Thank you," I told Mr. Ted, walking around the desk to hug him. "Thank you so much."

"My pleasure," he said, hugging me back. "Would you like my professional opinion about something?"

"Am I paying for it?" I teased.

"No. It's on the house."

"Shoot."

"You're one of the smartest and most delightful young women I have had the pleasure to work with... and you do not need a face-lift," he said. "Darren's gravely mistaken. You could date a horse's ass and do better than him."

I giggled. "Thank you."

"You are most welcome," he replied. "Go on now and get to that appointment. We'll chat soon."

"Right," I said, grabbing my purse and hightailing it out of his office.

I had important woowoo juju shit to do.

CHAPTER TWENTY-FOUR

"Wow, you look beautiful," Seth said as I ran smack into his broad chest in the reception area.

I was afraid my knees might give out from the compliment or the sheer impact of slamming into his rock-hard chest. "Because I normally look like a train wreck?"

Seth's eyes widened. The light caught the blue of the irises as he backpedaled. "Oh my God, I mean... I'm sorry. I meant... I meant I didn't mean... It wasn't exactly... you know, appropriate."

His struggle to find the right words was amusing. "You want to take it back now?" I asked with a laugh.

Seth chuckled and dropped his chin. "No. I stand by my first statement, but the timing might be a little off."

I inhaled deeply and nodded. "It kind of is," I replied, glad that Nancy wasn't sitting at her desk. I didn't want to have to explain anything to anyone. Nancy was a talker.

Seth nodded. "Right. Of course. I figured."

"Right," I repeated, not knowing what to say. The crazy part of me wanted to take it back and ask him out on a date. However, the sane part knew that was a very bad plan. Jumping into something when I still had to figure out who I was on my own had disaster written all over it.

Seth ran his hands through his hair and smiled. I realized I was jealous of his damn hands. I wanted to touch his hair.

"You know," he began casually—too casually. "There's no reason we can't be friends. Everyone needs friends, right?"

I pressed my lips together. I'd been out of the flirting and dating game for so long, I had no clue if friends actually meant friends.

"Define that," I said, knowing that I had to leave, but *really* wanting to stay.

"Friends," he said, looking up the word on his phone. "A person whom one knows and with whom one has a bond of mutual affection, typically exclusive of sexual or family relations." His gaze met mine and his mouth quirked up at the corners before he continued. "Terms subject to change when the time becomes right."

I laughed. This was fun. "That addendum at the end was ballsy," I pointed out.

Seth shrugged. "I'm a ballsy kind of guy."

I stared at him. He stared right back. Could it hurt to be his friend? I adored his little girl, and even though he didn't know it, Cheeto needed me and the other gals. Of course, it could hurt a whole hell of a lot if I let my heart get involved, but a future concern was not a right now problem. I had no plans to fall in love with anyone ever again. It hadn't ended well the first time.

"What the heck? Why not? Yes," I said. "I'll be your friend."

His smile made my heart skip a beat.

"Excellent," he said. "Friends we will be."

"Friends who wear muumuus every other Tuesday," I informed him.

His eyes narrowed playfully. "And every third Thursday… in public. Preferably at the bowling alley."

"You drive a hard bargain," I pointed out.

"I'm good like that," he replied. "Have to get to a meeting. Talk to you later, *friend*." He winked before he turned and walked away.

I rolled my eyes as my pulse kicked up with giddiness. "Friends don't wink at friends," I called after him.

I heard him chuckle as I watched him walk away. To be more specific, I watched his ass as he walked away. I was in so much trouble.

"Leave now," I told myself, moving toward the front door of the office. "Jumping a *friend* and sticking your tongue down his throat is a crappy plan."

"Clementine," Nancy said, entering the reception area in a tizzy. "Have you seen Cheeto? She was with me and then she was gone."

"Cheeto?" My stomach tightened and I felt light-headed. Was Jinny Jingle after Cheeto? Was that why I was so antsy? If the horrible woman had indeed recognized the magic in me, could she see it in the others? Was I concocting shitty plots because I was on edge? Hopefully.

"Yes. Cheeto," Nancy said, looking under her desk. "She likes to play hide-and-seek, but she usually tells me where she's going to hide."

"Cheeto talks to you?" I asked.

"A little bit," Nancy said, looking in the supply closet. "I offered to watch her while Seth took a call."

It didn't surprise me that Cheeto talked to Nancy. Nancy had the woowoo juju. However, it did surprise me that Cheeto would take off. "Does she do this often?"

"Never," Nancy said, sounding frantic. "She normally sticks right to my side."

Warning bells exploded in my head. "Do you think she went outside?" I asked, getting on my hands and knees and checking under the furniture.

"Possibly," Nancy said, wringing her hands in distress. "Can you walk around the building and I'll keep looking in here?"

"Yes," I said, back on my feet in a flash. "Get Seth and tell him."

Nancy nodded and took off. I was out of the door in a hot sec. My heart raced and I thought I might puke. Why would Cheeto run away? Was I nuts to think the weather hooker took her? Seth wouldn't make it if something happened to his daughter. I was certain of that. Hell, I wasn't sure I would make it either. Cheeto had weaseled her way into my heart and set up a permanent place for herself.

"Calm down," I told myself. God, I wished my characters were with me. They would come in handy right now. Clark

Dark could find a needle in a damn haystack. "Cheeto?" I called out.

"Beautiful Clementine!" she answered.

She was standing next to my car in the parking lot, smiling and waving. My relief was visceral. Running in stilettos was not fun and I was pretty sure I looked like I was about to go down, but my adrenaline was pumping and my instincts took over.

"Baby," I said, squatting down and checking her over for injury. "You can't take off like that. Nancy's very worried."

"I'm sorry," she said, touching my hair. "I wanted to go home with you and play with Flip."

My heart sill beat irregularly, but I was so relieved, I laughed. "In the future, before you make big decisions like that, you need to ask a grown-up."

"You're a grown-up," she pointed out with a giggle.

At that moment, the skies opened and the rain began to fall. Quickly opening the car door, I put Cheeto in the driver's seat so she wouldn't get soaked. Popping open my umbrella, I stood next to the open door and searched my purse for my cell phone to call Nancy.

"I'm a grown-up, but you need to check in with the grown-up who is watching after you first."

"Okay," she said, putting her little hands on the steering wheel and pretending to drive.

"You were supposed to get me the damn house!" a shrill voice screamed.

It was a sickeningly familiar voice. The sound cut through the rain like a bolt of lightning.

"Baby. Come on, baby," Darren said. "I tried. You know

I'll give you anything you want. I'll buy you a house. I'm your boopy."

"I wanted *that house*, you useless piece of shit," Jinny Jingle snarled. "We're done."

They were on the other side of the parking lot. The parking lot wasn't large. It could hold about twenty cars and was only half-full right now. However, I couldn't physically see them, which hopefully meant they couldn't see me.

"You don't mean that," Darren whined. "How about we go on over to the jewelry store and I'll buy you something expensive?"

"How about you keep your word?" she demanded. "I told you what I wanted, and you failed."

"Not my fault," he insisted, sounding pathetic.

The conversation was one I didn't want to hear. While a small part of me got some satisfaction out of eavesdropping on their imploding relationship, the reality of it was gross and unsettling. Neither one of them was my problem. Honestly, they deserved each other.

"Here you go, sweetie," I said, grabbing my tablet from my purse and quickly opening Candy Jelly Crush. Cheeto didn't need to hear this crap. I turned up the volume and hoped it would block out the ugly sound of the voices while I called Nancy. "Do you know how to play this game?"

"Yes!" Cheeto said. "It's my favorite." She began to play and seemed oblivious to the outside world.

Cheeto and I had more in common than I'd originally thought.

"I've wasted months on you!" Jinny shouted.

"Try decades," I muttered, digging for my cell phone.

"What are you doing?" Darren shrieked, sounding alarmed.

"What does it look like?" she asked in a tone that sent shivers up my spine.

"Baby, put the tire iron down," Darren said. "Quit playing around. Let's go to the jewelry store."

The sound that came next made me ill. My imagination was creating something that couldn't possibly be happening.

"Oh my God!" Darren cried out as I heard the grotesque noise of something hard connecting with flesh. "What the hell are you doing?"

"What I should've done weeks ago," she hissed. "Bye-bye, Darren."

I felt the bile rise in my throat as the sounds of a physical beating went down. Darren's shouts grew frantic and Jinny's grunts grew crazed. What the hell was happening? Was she hitting him? With a tire iron?

Instincts I wasn't aware I possessed took over. I felt like a character from one of my novels. Grabbing the stun gun from beneath the driver's seat, I kicked off my stilettos.

"Cheeto, I'm going to close the car door so you don't get wet," I said, hoping I sounded calm. "I need you to stay here."

Cheeto nodded without looking up. She was so engrossed in the game she'd barely heard me.

The door clicked shut and I ran like I was running from a murderer. Only, I was running *toward* the murderer... not away.

Darren looked like hell. They were behind his car. The

trunk was open and he'd backed into the spot like he'd always done for as long as I'd known him. He was on the ground and Jinny Jingle stood over him with the tire iron raised over her head. Rain fell from the sky as heavily as the blood poured from Darren's face. It was horrifying.

His eyes were swollen, his nose was definitely broken and there was an open, oozing wound on his forehead. Thick red blood streamed from his slack jaw. Darren grunted in agony as the tire iron connected with his neck. She was trying to kill him.

"Back off," I shouted, holding the gun and aiming it at Jinny. Aunt Flip had said point and shoot. I hoped she was right. "I said, BACK OFF. NOW."

Her head jerked to me. Weather Hooker's eyes grew wide with delight. She was out of her freaking gourd.

"Back away from Darren," I yelled as the rain began to come down in torrents.

"Make me," she snarled, raising the tire iron in preparation to strike him again.

I wasn't even sure he was alive. And if he was, he couldn't take much more.

"Fine," I said calmly, even though my insides were churning. "I will."

Pulling the trigger was easier than I'd thought it would be. Watching Jinny fly backwards into a car with a loud thud was shockingly satisfying. I was sure Clark Dark would be proud.

I, on the other hand, thought I was going to vomit.

Jinny was out like a light. Darren was moaning, which

meant he was alive. My damn purse was in the car. Calling an ambulance was going to be a little difficult.

"Are you okay?" I asked, kneeling down on the ground next to my seriously wounded asshole ex. The question was absurd, but it was the first thing that came out of my mouth. Darren looked at me. His eyes were almost swollen shut. The tire iron, covered in his blood, was on the ground next to him. I'd fantasized about beating him up a few times, but the reality of seeing him in this state made me sick to my stomach.

"I think I might have made a mistake," he choked out with effort. "Let's not get divorced. What do you say we give it another shot?"

If he wasn't possibly dying right now, I would have punched him in the head. "Umm… that would be a hard no," I said, wondering if I should try and move him to a sitting position so he didn't choke on the blood gushing from his mouth.

I needed help, but I was afraid to leave him.

"Finally," Jinny grunted with satisfaction, getting to her feet with effort. "Fucking finally!"

The shock of her voice and the fact that she could stand up was terrifying. Thankfully, the stun gun was still in my hand and the tire iron was out of her reach. Standing up on shaking legs, I aimed the gun at her. This time, I was prepared to stun the living hell out of her.

"What is wrong with you?" I shouted. "You almost killed him."

"He's still alive?" she asked, disappointed.

"No thanks to you," I snapped. "Attempted murder isn't a good look. You're in a lot of trouble."

"That's where you're dead wrong," Jinny shot back with a smile so ugly, I winced. "You just handed me my *external disaster* on a silver platter."

What was she talking about? Had she been concussed when she slammed into the car?

"Are you confused, Clementine?" she inquired with a sneer.

"Enlighten me," I said.

"With pleasure, *old lady*. When one loses their magic and happens to remember it, they need a bitch who still has the enchanted power to cause the external disaster. It certainly took you long enough," she informed me with a laugh that made my skin crawl. "I screwed your husband. I set up the film crew to catch us. I threatened to take your new boyfriend. I terrorized you. You were a hard nut to crack."

"You're insane," I said.

"Maybe," she replied with a shrug. "But I always get what I want."

I stared at her. She wasn't nearly as stupid as I'd thought. There was now a slight golden glow around her, but it was marred with a grayish-black mist. I hadn't been wrong about the darkness. My vision had been correct—partially. But I also hadn't known the full extent.

This was bad.

Darren moaned and spit up more blood. Jinny Jingle laughed. She was a soulless horror of a human being.

"Watch your back, Clementine," she warned. "I wouldn't want to be you right now. It's going to get ugly."

A crack of lightning and a rumble of thunder punctuated her parting words. With another laugh that would live in my nightmares, Jinny Jingle turned and ran from the parking lot.

"Help me," Darren begged.

"I will," I said as Nancy and Seth came tearing out of the building. "Call an ambulance! Darren is hurt."

"Did you find Cheeto?" Seth asked, glancing around wildly for his daughter.

"She's safe," I said quickly. "She's in my car. She wanted to come to my house and play with Flip."

"Hi, Daddy," Cheeto said, standing in the rain. Her wet blonde hair clung to her face as she stared at Darren with an undecipherable expression on her face.

I hoped she hadn't seen what had just happened. If she had, she was going to need therapy. I was pretty sure I was going to need some therapy too. I also needed to tell Flip and the gals that Jinny had gotten her magic back and was on the loose.

"Cheeto," Seth said gruffly, scooping the little girl into his arms and holding her tight.

"What the hell happened?" Nancy screamed, taking in Darren's state and pulling her cell phone from her pocket.

"Jinny Jingle beat him to a pulp with a tire iron," I said. "Call the cops and tell them to send an ambulance. Now."

"On it," Nancy said, shaking like a leaf. "The station is right around the corner. They'll get here fast."

That was good. Small towns had their advantages.

Kneeling down in a puddle of blood and rain next to the man who had been my husband for most of my life, I gently put my hand on his arm. "It's going to be okay, Darren," I promised. "The ambulance is coming."

"Give me the house," he whispered.

"I'm sorry, what?" I asked, sure I'd heard him wrong.

"Give me the house," he repeated, even softer.

"Have you lost your mind?" I asked, shocked to the core.

His lover had almost just beaten him to death and he was still trying to get her what she wanted. My fury rose, but outwardly, I stayed calm.

"You have thirty seconds to make a decision," Darren warned as a cop car with lights flashing pulled into the parking lot.

"You are not getting the house," I ground out. "Give it up."

Darren smiled through all the blood. It was not a pretty picture.

"What happened here?" a cop I didn't recognize asked, standing over me.

"Darren Bell was beaten with a tire iron by Jinny Jingle," I said, still thrown by what Darren had just asked for. "She ran that way." I pointed in the direction Jinny had escaped.

"No," Darren said, trying to sit up. "She's lying."

My head jerked to him and my eyes narrowed dangerously.

"Clementine Roberts tried to kill me. She's devastated that I divorced her. She begged me to take her back. I said no and she tried to kill me. I want to press charges," he said, glaring at me with sadistic victory in his eyes.

My blood ran cold at his chilling accusation. I had half a mind to pick up the tire iron and finish him off.

"That's a lie," I ground out, standing up and backing away from the vile man I'd wasted years of my life on. "I did no such thing."

"Beautiful Clementine is telling the truth," Cheeto said. "I saw it."

My heart lodged in my throat. As thankful as I was that there was a witness, I was horrified it was Cheeto.

Darren's laugh was deranged as it gurgled in his throat mixed with all the blood. "She's a child," he choked out. "And everyone knows she's not right in the head. The word of a brain-damaged child is proof of nothing. I'm pressing charges against my ex-wife for attempted murder."

It took everything I had not to dive for the tire iron and kill him dead. He'd crossed the line of decency for the last time. Cheeto was off limits.

"I didn't do this," I said as the rain picked up even more.

"Put the stun gun down, ma'am, and raise your hands over your head," the cop said.

"I didn't try to kill Darren," I repeated as Seth moved immediately to my side and I followed the officer's direction. "I didn't. I used the stun gun to stop Jinny Jingle from killing him."

The cop nodded. "Step away from the woman," he advised Seth as he put his hand on his weapon.

How in the hell was this happening?

Seth slowly moved away, but his eyes held mine. "I believe you," he said softly.

I was so relieved, I almost dropped to the ground like a sack of potatoes. The EMTs pulled up, immediately put Darren on a stretcher and into the ambulance. I despised

Darren, but sent up a quick prayer that the bastard didn't die. I'd be screwed if he did.

"We're going to have to take you into the station for questioning," the cop said.

Nancy was texting like a madwoman on her phone. I hoped to hell and back she was alerting the ladies. I might need bail money shortly.

"I'm her lawyer," Seth told the cop. "She won't be talking to anyone until I'm with her at the station."

The cop nodded curtly.

One of the best days of my life was fast turning into the worst. I'd thought the viral video was horrible… this beat it hands down.

Seth leaned into the back of the cruiser after I was placed inside. "I believe you," he said again. "My dad and I will meet you at the station. Do not speak to anyone until we're with you."

I nodded, terrified. "I didn't do it."

"We know," Cheeto said softly. "I will save you. I'm not brain-damaged. I'm just different."

Seth closed his eyes for a brief moment, then smiled at his daughter. "Different is good, munchkin."

"I know, Daddy. Clementine's different too."

Seth gazed at me with an intensity that made me feel raw and exposed.

"I can see that," he told Cheeto. "Like I said, different is good. It's beautiful."

My breath caught in my throat. I wondered how much he actually *saw*. "Thank you for believing me and helping me," I whispered.

"You're my friend, Clementine," he said. "That's what friends do for each other. We'll work this out. I promise."

Seth's words warmed me and brought a small amount of comfort as the officer of the law ushered him aside.

"I'm going to have to ask you to move," the cop said to Seth, putting the tire iron into a plastic evidence bag.

"Not a word," Seth reminded me as he backed away. "We'll be there soon."

I nodded and tried not to cry. He was probably regretting wanting to be my *friend*. However, I was thanking my lucky stars. As Albinia had warned me, *a friend in need is a friend indeed.*

"WELL, THIS IS CERTAINLY A MESS," CASSANDRA MUTTERED.

"A definite twist I didn't see coming," Clark agreed.

They had appeared in the back of the cruiser the moment the cop closed the door. I'd never been so happy to see imaginary people in my life.

"Am I screwed?" I asked, as the cop walked around the car to get in and drive me to the station.

"Remains to be seen," Cassandra said. "The plot has gotten quite messy. It's sad you're not a demon. You could have incinerated both of them to ash and the rain would have washed the worthless pieces of dreck away."

"Not helping," I muttered.

Clark said nothing. That didn't bode well.

"I didn't do it," I told them. "I despise Darren, but I would never try to kill him."

"Affirmative," Clark said. "We shall just have to prove it."

"Will it be easy?" I asked. My head pounded and my mouth felt like sandpaper.

"Nothing worthwhile is every easy," Clark said cryptically, much to my sinking disappointment.

I was seriously hoping for a succinct yes.

"Are you ready for the adventure to begin?" Cassandra inquired.

"Do I have a choice?" I asked.

She laughed. "No. You most certainly do not."

I closed my eyes and let my head fall back on the cracked leather seat. I was sitting in a place where criminals had sat. I wasn't a criminal. I was a forty-two-year-old romance author in a soaking-wet, ruined Chanel dress. Being charged with attempted murder was not going to help my career or my mental health. My ex-husband was a lying asshole with a greedy black heart and revenge on his mind. Jinny Jingle had woowoo juju mixed with darkness, thanks to me. That alone could be disastrous. Cheeto had witnessed something no child should ever see. Flip and the woowoo gals were going to flip. I was flipping. Jess and Mandy were going to freak. The plot to my life was hellish and rewriting it wouldn't help. I wasn't in charge of the storyline.

"Fine," I said, opening my eyes and watching the rivulets of rain run down the windows of the cruiser. "I'm ready." I wasn't sure if I believed my words, but if I said them enough, they would come true. They had to. "There's always sunshine after the rain. Let the adventure begin."

The end... for now.

MORE IN MY SO-CALLED MYSTICAL MIDLIFE SERIES

ORDER BOOK TWO NOW!

No one in their right freaking mind ever said midlife was magical.
Apparently it is.
Or at least mine is...

Once upon a time there was a paranormal romance author who caught her husband in a *compromising* position. One divorce later, she's free and ready to start her new life at forty-two.

Right?
Wrong.

Divorced idiot ex: Check
Saved idiot ex from getting murdered by his new nasty gal pal: Check
Idiot ex accused me of trying to kill him: Umm check
Still seeing my fictional characters: Check
Teeny tiny crush on my lawyer: Check check
Town under siege by dark forces: Of course
Crazy enough to try and stop it: You bet

With the darkness on the horizon, I need to clear my name and get to work. Forming a Goodness Army is on the top of the list. Shockingly, my army consists of my wacky tabacky smoking aunt, my high school counselor who can shift into a house cat, the town gossip who turns invisible after downing five beers and a few fabulous others with nefarious talents. And of course, a cast of fictional characters...

who I created and definitely have an opinion on how I should proceed.

What could possibly go wrong?

I'm going on pure gut instinct at this point, and I can't wait to see how the plot turns out.

I may be wrong. I may be *write*. Either way, I'll just keep turning the pages until I find my happily ever after.

ROBYN'S BOOK LIST

(IN CORRECT READING ORDER)

HOT DAMNED SERIES
Fashionably Dead
Fashionably Dead Down Under
Hell on Heels
Fashionably Dead in Diapers
A Fashionably Dead Christmas
Fashionably Hotter Than Hell
Fashionably Dead and Wed
Fashionably Fanged
Fashionably Flawed
A Fashionably Dead Diary
Fashionably Forever After
Fashionably Fabulous
A Fashionable Fiasco
Fashionably Fooled
Fashionably Dead and Loving It

GOOD TO THE LAST DEATH SERIES
It's a Wonderful Midlife Crisis
Whose Midlife Crisis Is It Anyway?
A Most Excellent Midlife Crisis
My Midlife Crisis, My Rules
You Light Up My Midlife Crisis

SHIFT HAPPENS SERIES
Ready to Were
Some Were in Time
No Were To Run
Were Me Out
Were We Belong

MAGIC AND MAYHEM SERIES
Switching Hour
Witch Glitch
A Witch in Time
Magically Delicious
A Tale of Two Witches
Three's A Charm
Switching Witches
You're Broom or Mine?
The Bad Boys of Assjacket

SEA SHENANIGANS SERIES
Tallulah's Temptation
Ariel's Antics
Misty's Mayhem
Petunia's Pandemonium

Jingle Me Balls

A WYLDE PARANORMAL SERIES
Beauty Loves the Beast

HANDCUFFS AND HAPPILY EVER AFTERS SERIES
How Hard Can it Be?
Size Matters
Cop a Feel

If after reading all the above you are still wanting more adventure and zany fun, read *Pirate Dave and His Randy Adventures*, the romance novel budding novelist Rena helped wicked Evangeline write in *How Hard Can It Be?*

Warning: Pirate Dave Contains Romance Satire, Spoofing, and Pirates with Two Pork Swords.

NOTE FROM THE AUTHOR

If you enjoyed reading *The Write Hook,* please consider leaving a positive review or rating on the site where you purchased it. Reader reviews help my books continue to be valued by resellers and help new readers make decisions about reading them.

You are the reason I write these stories and I sincerely appreciate each of you!

Many thanks for your support,
~ Robyn Peterman

Want to hear about my new releases?
Visit robynpeterman.com and join my mailing list!

ABOUT ROBYN PETERMAN

Robyn Peterman writes because the people inside her head won't leave her alone until she gives them life on paper. Her addictions include laughing really hard with friends, shoes (the expensive kind), Target, Coke (the drink not the drug LOL) with extra ice in a Yeti cup, bejeweled reading glasses, her kids, her super-hot hubby and collecting stray animals.

A former professional actress with Broadway, film and T.V. credits, she now lives in the South with her family and too many animals to count.

Writing gives her peace and makes her whole, plus having a job where she can work in sweatpants works really well for her.

Made in the USA
Coppell, TX
13 September 2021

62287084R00194